*"Dee—"*

"You said all I had to do was say yes," she told him, wreathing her arms around his neck. "Don't tell me you've changed your mind already?"

"I wouldn't exactly say that." Chase settled his hands on her hips and turned, lifting her onto the kitchen counter.

She caressed his thick, wavy hair and guided his mouth toward hers. "What *would* you say?" she asked him.

"I'd say, what took you so long?"

Before she could respond, his mouth slanted over hers in a searing, toe-curling kiss.

"I want to feast on you," he murmured against her skin.

"Hmm. Sounds…intense."

"Do you like it…intense?"

"I like it hot," she said, her voice a breathless whisper.

His fingers worked the buttons of her blouse. "Just hot?" His hands traced a slow trail along her skin, over her rib cage and upward to cup her breasts.

"The hotter, the better."

Blaze™

Dear Reader,

Harlequin Blaze is a supersexy new series. If you like love
stories with a strong sexual edge then this is the line for you!
The books are fun and flirtatious, the heroes are hot and
outrageous. Blaze is a series for the woman who wants *more*
in her reading pleasure....

This month bestselling Harlequin Presents author Miranda Lee
delivers #9 *Just a Little Sex...* about one night of passion
that turns into much more! Rising star Jamie Denton says you
need to break the rules in #10 *Sleeping With the Enemy,*
a story with sizzling sexual tension and erotic love scenes.
Talented Isabel Sharpe takes us to #11 *The Wild Side,* a
fun, lusty tale about a good girl who decides bad might be
better. Popular Janelle Denison rounds out the month with
#12 *Heat Waves,* another SEXY CITY NIGHTS story set
in fiery Chicago—where the heat definitely escalates after
dark....

Look for four Blaze books every month at your favorite
bookstore. And check us out online at eHarlequin.com and
tryblaze.com.

Enjoy!

Birgit Davis-Todd
Senior Editor & Editorial Coordinator
Harlequin Blaze

# SLEEPING WITH
# THE ENEMY

*Jamie Denton*

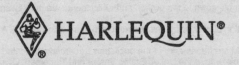

TORONTO • NEW YORK • LONDON
AMSTERDAM • PARIS • SYDNEY • HAMBURG
STOCKHOLM • ATHENS • TOKYO • MILAN • MADRID
PRAGUE • WARSAW • BUDAPEST • AUCKLAND

For Birgit Davis-Todd and Ethan Ellenberg

Thank you for accompanying me and guiding me through every step of this incredible journey.

As always,
Jamie

ISBN 0-373-79014-7

SLEEPING WITH THE ENEMY

Copyright © 2001 by Jamie Ann Denton.

Visit us at www.eHarlequin.com

Printed In U.S.A.

# A NOTE FROM THE AUTHOR...

When I received the call from my editor asking me to become a part of the new Harlequin Blaze line, it was like a dream come true. Writing for Temptation has been, and still is, one of the highlights of my career, but here was an opportunity to be able to expand upon the sexy books I love to write and create a character who doesn't exactly fit into the norm. The result of this exciting new endeavor is deep cover FBI agent Chase Bracken.

Chase is a loner, a trait that makes him the perfect man for the worst assignment the FBI has to offer—to bring in a fellow deep cover agent gone bad. But his only link to solving the case is the agent's sister, Destiny "Dee" Romine. Dee has her own secrets, but Chase always gets his man...or woman, even if it means *Sleeping With the Enemy*.

I hope you enjoy Chase and Dee's romance. Be sure to look for the sexy sequel, *Seduced By the Enemy*, coming in 2002 from Harlequin Blaze. You wouldn't want to miss Jared Romine and Justice Department attorney Peyton Douglas's rocky road to romance as they're forced to work together to clear Jared's name, provided they can work through their past.

I love to hear from readers! You can send me e-mail at jamie@jamiedenton.net or write me at P.O. Box 224, Mohall, North Dakota 58761.

Until next time,

*Jamie Denton*

# 1

THEY KNEW SHE WAS HIS ONLY weakness. They knew, and they hovered like vultures, waiting.

Dee clutched the single, bloodred rose to her chest, breathing in the intoxicating perfume while struggling against the instincts screaming inside her to stand up and search the crowd gathered beneath the sun-drenched southern California sky. She couldn't. Not without risking his life. Not without letting the bastards know he was there. For her.

He should have known better than to come here. She could just imagine her brother's determination, but the University of California at Los Angeles wasn't some Podunk medical school. The governor would be addressing the graduates momentarily and security was tight, the campus literally crawling with federal agents and secret service men. Yet, somehow, someway, Jared Romine had taken a great risk to let his little sister know he was proud of her.

The valedictorian took the stage for his address to UCLA's graduating class. The speech could have easily been hers, if she hadn't intentionally thrown a couple of classes so as not to draw too much attention to herself for Jared's sake. The Feds would've had a field day, she thought with an uncharacteristic flare of rebellion. And her brother would have loved the irony—rogue agent Jared Romine's little sister, valedictorian.

She let out a slow even breath and looked in all the obscure places she possibly could without craning her neck or drawing attention to herself. Her brother wouldn't be sitting in the crowd with the other family and friends of the graduates from one of the country's top medical schools. No, Jared could be posing as anyone from building security to a janitor sweeping the walk, to the guy testing the sound equipment prior to commencement and no one, not even his fellow agents would know he'd been within their grasp until it was too late.

She was used to the silence from her brother. When he'd decided to join the FBI, he'd done so knowing his work in Naval Intelligence could very well place him in deep-cover assignments where contact with family and friends was as dangerous for the family as it was for the undercover agent. Other than one brief visit before she started med school, they hadn't seen each other since parting ways in Washington all those years ago. Silence from her brother for three months at a time was still a bit unusual, albeit not completely unheard of, which was the only reason she hadn't been alarmed by Jared's lengthy absence. She'd figured him on an undercover assignment, until she returned from classes three months ago to find two agents waiting for her outside her dorm room.

She expected them to tell her Jared had been killed.

What they'd told her had been far worse.

Jared Romine was on the FBI's most wanted list…as an agent-gone-bad, accused of murder. Of murdering one of his own and a top senatorial aid. The government claimed their evidence was rock-solid. Even though they wanted Jared and not her, until they had him in custody, they watched, they invaded her privacy and they waited.

Jared's whereabouts were a mystery to her. From the

work he did, she suspected he had numerous contacts, not all of them above the law. No doubt he was hiding out until it was safe for him to come forward and tell his side of the story. All she could do in the meantime was hope and pray he was safe. From the day her parents died, Jared had taken care of her and protected her. Now it was her opportunity to return the favor.

Her gaze landed on a rather spry elderly gentleman hanging out near the edge of the staging area. Dee's heart fluttered behind her ribs, praying it was Jared dressed in a disguise of some sort. Her breath stilled as she willed the man to turn around, only to be let out in a disappointed huff when he did.

She secretly hoped the Feds would get tired of the chase, or that Jared had slipped into and assumed a new identity, starting a new life for himself. As much as she missed him, she'd rather have him safe and alive than...

The Feds wouldn't let up, though. In the three months they'd been following and watching her, she learned just how relentless they could be. They picked her life apart, and the life of her brother who remained elusive to the government wanting to prosecute him. She was Jared's only weakness. If it hadn't been for the blank postcards that showed up occasionally, or the one extremely brief phone call where a scratchy, unfamiliar voice whispered he'd been framed and he had no choice but to go underground, the Feds might have left her alone. If it hadn't been for the late-night calls with no one on the other end of the line every few weeks, they might have backed off. But Jared continued to take those small, meaningful risks just to let her know he was alive.

When their parents died, Jared had promised her she could depend on him. He'd done the best he knew how, and she loved him for it. Considering the example their parents had set, Jared's care and support had been a vast improvement.

The day they'd gone their separate ways, Dee to Los Angeles to attend college on a partial academic scholarship and he to Quantico to work for the FBI, he'd given her a bus ticket and two hundred dollars. "To destiny," he'd said, then handed her a single bloodred rose, told her he loved her...and drove away without looking back.

Because of the constant back-to-back deep-cover assignments, other than a weekend visit three years ago, she hadn't seen her brother. Now under such dangerous conditions, he was close. She could feel it and wanted nothing more than to at least catch a glimpse of him. They'd be allowed nothing else. A hug would be as impossible as five minutes alone. All she'd have to carry her through, possibly even for the rest of her life, would be a quick smile or a surreptitious wink. Despite the danger, she needed that, needed just one small token other than the rose handed to her by a stranger to hold in her cherished memories of her brother.

The ceremony continued, and still Dee could find no sign of Jared. Frustration nudged her when she spotted two federal agents posted on either side of the stage where the graduates passed once their names were called to receive their diplomas. She walked slowly toward the stage, waiting as the dean called the graduates, shook their hands and congratulated them before handing them the piece of paper that declared them physicians.

Standing, she was able to scan the crowd. She desperately wanted that new imprint for her memory. But she knew the risks. Anything other than the rose with no note attached could cost her brother his freedom, maybe even his life.

The dean called her name, shook her hand and congratulated her before handing over her diploma. She clutched the document to her chest, along with the rose, and smiled brightly for the benefit of the agent waiting at the other end of the stage as she made her way down the steps. Moving slowly toward the rows of chairs to reclaim her seat until the end of the ceremony, she finally saw him.

Her brother stood toward the back of the crowd, dressed in a dark blue suit, with the bored, but alert look of a secret service agent, complete with an electronic communications device tucked in a nondescript manner behind his ear. He looked much older than his twenty-nine years, his face more lined than she expected and his rich sable hair lightly touched by gray at the temples. Despite his aging features, his body was still as fit as she remembered and his green eyes more watchful but just as mischievous. She glanced hastily around, hoping she wasn't being watched, but when she looked back at her brother, the barely perceptible shake of his head told her otherwise.

For his sake, she had no choice but to return to her seat. All she wanted to do was run into Jared's arms and weep for the injustice keeping them apart, and the future they might never be able to share. She knew in her heart by the time the ceremony ended the secret service agent would be gone as if he never existed.

Just as Jared Romine no longer existed.

Dee would stoically return to her small, furnished dormitory room following the graduation ceremony and ready herself for her job at the San Vicente Medical Center where she'd interned in the emergency room six days a week. Instead of the grand celebration most of her classmates would no doubt partake, surrounded by family and friends, her solo celebration would consist of a double shift in the E.R.

She'd shed not a single tear for the brother she might never see again. Lessons taught to a young girl were hard learned and not easily forgotten. And no one would know Special Agent Jared Romine's only weakness would go on as if her heart did not lay tattered beneath her breast.

*Two Years Later*

CHASE BRACKEN DRUMMED HIS pen on the yellow legal pad, staring absently at the pile of banker's boxes containing months of work that were stacked neatly against the wall of his Manhattan apartment. The list of men who had worked on the Romine case was long and distinguished. None, however, had managed to apprehend the elusive rogue agent.

Nor had they been able to gain an ounce of information from his only living relative.

Chase planned to rectify that little problem.

He tossed the pen on the table and tipped the chair back on two legs. Using the balls of his feet for balance, he rocked gently back and forth and folded his hands behind his head, a habit he'd developed despite his foster mother's lectures that one day he'd fall and break something, more than likely his neck.

Jared Romine was the unresolved thorn in the backside of the Bureau. A degree in rocket science was hardly a necessity for Chase to understand why he'd been given the worst assignment the Bureau had to offer. Bend-the-Rules Bracken had screwed up, big time, and his pain-in-the-backside superior officer was determined the Romine case would have Chase turning in his shield. Or worse, his boss would try to pull him out of the field and make him ride a desk until retirement. And that was just a little too long for Chase Bracken to be cooped up inside an office.

He'd find a way to redeem himself in Pelham's eyes. He'd been on the superior's hit list before and he usually managed to find a way off by solving the next case with as little muss and fuss as possible. The less covering up the Bureau had to deal with, the better Pelham liked it. Except after the fiasco of his last case, Chase wasn't so sure of his continued upward mobility within the Federal Bureau of Investigation.

He had to admit he'd really made a mess of things this time, and the chance of him bringing in Romine was slim, making his likelihood of redemption in Pelham's eyes even more scarce. But Chase had just enough arrogance to acknowledge he could be the agent to finally capture the rogue agent.

He let out a sigh and dropped the chair back on all fours. Arrogance was one thing, stupidity was quite another. Not to mention the small fragment of insecurity he'd never been able to completely conquer.

Years of combined on-the-job experience by some of the best men the Bureau had to offer hadn't been able to capture the agent-gone-bad. What made him think he stood a chance at succeeding where others had failed?

His own damned ego, that's what, he thought, shoving himself away from the table and heading into the kitchen. He poked his head in the fridge and winced at the barren shelves before snagging the last remaining imported beer. Leo Mitchell, his foster father, had always been fond of warning him that the bigger the man, the bigger target the man makes. Chase was a target of his own making, he decided, and bound to suffer the consequences of his own arrogance.

He swore mildly, then shoved the door closed with his hip. An unopened birthday card from his folks lay on the counter next to the registration renewal form for his Ford Expedition, both of which required his attention.

Chase picked up the colorful envelope, opened the card from his foster mother and read the handwritten note. A grin tugged his lips at the humor behind the birthday sentiment lamenting his thirtieth birthday. It'd be just like his mom to mark the day with humor instead of one of those sappy cards that made hormonal women cry and grown men shift uncomfortably. He was once again reminded of how lucky he'd been when Leo and Susan Mitchell came into his life. Yet, despite his good fortune of being raised in a loving, caring home, Chase had spent most of his life trying to prove something to someone. According to the Bureau shrink, the chip on his shoulder existed because his entrance into the world was highlighted by an addiction to his birth mother's drug of choice. Consciously he understood he *was* good enough. The problem was good enough wasn't always sufficient. For Chase, he always had to be better.

He dropped the card back on the counter and returned to the small dining area, twisting off the beer cap on his way. The Romine case was nothing short of a guaranteed failure. He knew he had only one option, to pull off what agents for the past thirty months could not—apprehend Special Agent Jared Romine, wanted for the murder of a fellow agent and the top aid to Senator Martin Phipps.

With a sigh of disgust, he dropped into the chair beside the oak table. As much as he would have liked to, he really couldn't argue with Pelham. Not this time. He'd created a reputation for himself, and now he had to live with the consequences. It was common knowledge Chase Bracken didn't play well with others. He took risks, calculated risks in his opinion, but still risks the Bureau had warned him about time and again. After his last assignment, Pelham had called him a cowboy. Funny how the superior officer seemed to conveniently forget Chase had the highest success rate in the New York office. At least until the Gleason case.

Psych had cleared him. So had I.A. Chase didn't see a problem. In fact, in his opinion so long as he got the job done, there shouldn't *be* a problem. Was it his fault things weren't wrapped up all nice and tidy? He wasn't the one who shot at innocent bystanders, even if Pelham did blame him for firing first at the perp in a less than perfect scenario. Usually by the time Chase wrapped up a case, there were fewer criminals roaming the street and the Gleason case was no exception. Because additional body bags had been involved this time didn't mean he was getting careless or losing his edge…just that he was doing his job.

Psych and Internal Affairs had agreed with him, and that was all the confirmation he needed to continue onward under the status quo. Bend-the-Rules Bracken would still get the job done…his way.

He set his beer aside and flipped the lid off one of the boxes, pulling out the most recent file with the name Destiny Romine, M.D., printed across the tab. According to the surveillance reports, the good lady doctor was the only link to her brother.

From the first initial contact, no one had ever been able to trip her up. If she knew her brother's location, she wasn't talking.

A slow grin eased across Chase's mouth. He always knew how to make them talk.

He opened the first file and spread the surveillance photographs over the table. Something deep in his gut twisted at the forlorn expression captured in Dr. Romine's eyes in several of the FBI photographs. Still, even the hint of sadness surrounding her failed to detract from her natural beauty. Her driver's license photo said she was a green-eyed, five-foot-seven brunette. The Bureau photographs depicted a rich cascade of sable hair that hung halfway down her slender back. The photographer managed to capture Dr. Romine right at a moment when she appeared to be staring directly into the camera. Her eyes, an intriguing shade of green mixed with pale gold, momentarily held him spellbound.

He shoved the glossy color photograph of the subject back into the file. For the next forty-eight hours, Destiny Romine, M.D., was the least of his problems. He had a series of meetings scheduled with various Bureau officials regarding his new assignment. There was one way to catch Romine, and Chase was positive that meant getting close to Baby Sister. And in order to do that, he needed to come up with a damned convincing cover.

He opened the file and looked at the photo again. She didn't look like the sister of a murdering FBI agent. She *did* look like a woman with secrets.

Secrets that Bend-the-Rules Bracken had every intention of learning, using whatever means at his disposal.

*Three Weeks Later*

DEE RELUCTANTLY FORCED herself out from under the downy softness of the comforter she hadn't bothered to remove from her double bed before climbing between the silky, cool sheets. She'd barely managed to keep her eyes open long enough to shower before dropping into a dead sleep.

It had better be good, she thought, tossing back the comforter as the doorbell chimed a second time.

She slipped into her robe. It couldn't be an emergency, or else her phone would have been ringing instead of her doorbell. Especially following the difficult breach delivery of Cole Harbor, South Carolina's newest resident. She'd placed the baby boy into the exhausted arms of his parents only three hours ago and if some complication had arose, Lucille, the clinic's nurse, would have called her. The birth had been long and difficult, and Dee had very nearly had to perform an emergency cesarean section right there in cranky old Doc Claymore's clinic. However, by using a few techniques shouted at her by her crabby nemesis, she'd managed to turn the baby enough to perform a vaginal birth.

The bell rang again by the time she reached the living room of her small triplex apartment. "I'm coming," she grumbled, managing to avoid the rented sofa and cocktail table without jamming her bare foot as she so often did.

She had no idea who could be standing on her doorstep so blasted early on a Monday morning, but she suspected it was nothing life threatening. Since Doc Claymore's semiretirement, she was the only physician on-call for the quaint seaside town nestled between Georgetown and Charleston on the Carolina coast. The ringing doorbell rather than a frantic phone call from George, Cole Harbor's answer to law enforcement, or Ed the ambulance driver, meant a fishhook was more than likely the reason for her interrupted, and desperately needed, slumber.

She tied the sash on her pale blue cotton robe. Cole Harbor was probably one of the safest places she'd ever lived, but that didn't stop her from latching her door or having a peephole installed. Crime wasn't her concern. No, it was the *alleged* good guys that had her worried.

She peered through the lens in the center of the door to determine the identification of the visitor. She wasn't sure what or whom she thought she'd find on the other side of her door, but the last thing she expected was the gorgeous sight awaiting her.

Even through the distortion of the peephole, she had no trouble classifying the man standing on her doorstep as more handsome than sin. Tall and powerfully built, he had wavy hair blacker than midnight that was a fraction too long for a label like clean-cut. The soft sea breeze teased the rebel strands brushing the collar of a navy polo shirt he wore tucked into a pair of blue jeans. Jeans she was positive would be faded to a well-worn white in all the right, interesting places. She couldn't tell the color of his eyes, and before she could stop herself from being silly, she had the fleeting hope they were blue. She'd always had a weak spot for dark hair and blue eyes, especially when they came in a package as athletically fit and so well put together as the gloriously handsome stranger ringing her bell.

The last vestiges of sleep were nudged aside by the return of her customary common sense. The gorgeous male specimen was probably her new upstairs neighbor. She'd recalled seeing a moving van two days ago, but although she'd been too busy at the clinic all day Friday, she recalled hearing Netta and a couple of the younger, single Cole Harbor residents speculating on the social, and marital, availability of the Cougars' new football coach.

Still, she hesitated and did another quick once-over as he turned around, his back to the door. He didn't have that spit-and-polished FBI look, she decided. At least not through the fish-eye lens of the peephole he didn't. In the flesh could be a different story.

She ran her hands through her hair in a vain attempt to smooth the tangles, then opened the door. The peephole didn't do him justice. As up close and personal as the safety chain allowed, she couldn't help noticing his blue jeans were exactly as she'd imagined them, hugging a masculine posterior she found way too intriguing to be written off as her professional medical opinion.

"Can I help you?" she asked, managing to keep her tone cool and remote. The last thing she needed was for him to suspect she considered him a mouthwatering example of masculine perfection.

He turned around and locked the clearest, most startling gaze she'd ever seen on her. Maybe it was the exhaustion, but she could swear this man, a total stranger, with the sexiest pair of lilac eyes she'd ever had the pleasure of gazing into, could see clear down to her soul.

Dangerous, she thought the second he flashed her a breathtaking grin. Way too dangerous, especially for a woman with something to hide.

# 2

AT FIRST GLANCE, SHE WAS exactly what Chase expected.
Dr. Destiny Romine had the look of an upper-middle-
class professional from an upper-middle-class family, the
only surviving daughter of a brilliant neurosurgeon and
world-renowned psychologist, both dead before their
time. She did not look like the Bureau's last hope to bring
down a murdering agent. Even dressed in a thin cotton
robe and peering at him through the small gap in the door
allowed by the safety latch, there was something about
her that exuded elegance.

And not just elegance, class, he thought, unable to take
his eyes off her. Sex appeal. Lots of it, too.

"Can I help you?" she asked again, pulling his
thoughts away from a very interesting and far too dangerous path for a guy in his position.

Despite the slightest hint of irritation, her voice was
even more silky-smooth than he'd imagined.

"Sorry to bother you so early," he said, taking advantage of the chance for a closer second look. The FBI
photos hadn't come close to capturing an earthy beauty
that belied her privileged upbringing. Nor had the photographer managed to seize the exact way her green eyes
flared with color in the early morning sunlight or how
tiny flecks of gold highlighted her irises. "I was hoping
I could use your phone."

She flicked that intriguing gaze over him, as if he was

nothing more interesting to her than a lab specimen. He wondered what she'd think if she knew she was simply a means to an end for him.

"My phone?"

"Mine's out," he lied easily. The first of many, he suspected. "It was supposed to be hooked up last week before I moved in, but it looks like it didn't happen." How many more lies would he tell to this woman until she finally gave him what he wanted?

Chase knew the answer…*as many as necessary.*

Her gaze slipped away, darted around the area, then zeroed in on him again. "And you are?" she asked, her sable eyebrows lifting quizzically.

He extended his hand, but she continued to stare at him through the small opened space between the door and the jamb. What he could see of her expression gave absolutely nothing away. She didn't so much as budge the safety catch, either.

He shrugged and dropped his hand. "Your new neighbor," he said, hooking his thumb upward to the apartment over hers. "I'm the new defensive back coach for the Cougars."

His second quasi lie. He *was* the Cougars' new coach, and no one, not even the administration at Cole Harbor High knew his true identity, or his reason for being in town.

Small towns put a lot of stock in gossip. He was counting on Cole Harbor fitting the stereotype of down-home southern hospitality, even if it was part of the Atlantic coastal region where the people tended to be slightly more cautious than their inland counterparts.

A wry twist transformed her mouth into the semblance of a brief grin a half second before she closed the door.

Relief shot through him at the rattle of the chain sliding off the security rail.

First rule of undercover work, sell your cover.

And she'd just bought his.

"Come on in." She swung the door wide and stepped back to let him into her unit. "You're Coach Bracken."

He nodded. "Call me Chase," he said, stepping into her apartment. "And you are...?"

He let his voice trail off, while his eyes took in everything, mentally cataloging the layout of her unit, which was similar to his own but smaller. Dr. Romine's apartment hosted only a single bedroom while his larger upstairs unit held two bedrooms and a minuscule dining area in the kitchen visible from his living room. From the look of things, the good lady doctor took her meals at the breakfast bar that separated the kitchen and small living area. Thanks to the building plans tucked inside his closet, he knew the remaining unoccupied unit next door to Dr. Romine's was identical, only reversed.

Her gaze slid to the red digits on the VCR's clock—it was a few minutes past ten—then back to him. "Dee. And shouldn't you be at football practice at this hour? I thought it was Hell Week." She remained near the door, her hands disappearing into the side pockets of her robe.

Cursory interior surveillance achieved. He turned and gave her a smile. "Next week," he supplied. "The Cougars are just starting to condition in gear this afternoon."

Upon entering her living room, he'd immediately surveyed most of her uninspired kitchen, her equally sterile bathroom and a portion of her bedroom with only a rumpled double bed visible. He didn't have to look again to recall that the tangled sheets of the bed had been the only sign that a living, breathing person resided in the downstairs apartment. From what he'd seen already, not so much as a decorative throw rug covered the hardwood floors. Serviceable off-white miniblinds, rather than frilly, feminine lace curtains covered the windows; the blinds blocked out the hazy morning sun. There weren't any boxes stacked along the walls to indicate she was moving.

She'd lived here a long time. Where were all the normal trappings a person carried with them from place to place, the ridiculous souvenirs people collected and displayed? There wasn't so much as a cheap framed print from the local five-and-dime hanging over the institutional-looking sofa. The walls were as bare and vacant as the unit next door.

The reports indicated Destiny Romine had resided in Cole Harbor a little over two years after finishing her residency in L.A. She'd played it smart and had taken the government up on their offer to forgive a large portion of her student loans in exchange for practicing medicine in the small seaside town for two and a half years. According to the bank statements he'd reviewed, she also worked two weekend shifts a month at the Berkeley County Hospital for extra cash. He also knew that at the age of fifteen she'd been left virtually penniless when her parents died and that her then eighteen-year-old brother, Jared, had raised her. It was that bond, the one forged between Dee and her brother when they'd had no one but each other to depend on following the unexpected death of their parents, that practically guaranteed Chase would be the agent to stamp a big red Closed on the Bureau's most frustrating, not to mention embarrassing, case.

One thing he could say for Destiny Romine: she was a survivor. He admired survivors as much as he admired intelligence, even in the criminals he busted. She was a smooth one though, and she'd talk. They always talked when Bend-the-Rules Bracken finished with them.

"There's a wall phone in the kitchen," she said. "By the window."

"Thanks." He headed into the kitchen, his sneakers silent on the bare wood floor. A faded half-moon rug with colorful berries lay in front of the sink, the only personal touch in the place.

He waited for her to follow him, but instead he heard the distinct click of a door. Unable to believe his luck, he peered around the corner. The bathroom door was shut, probably to afford him the illusion of privacy.

He dialed the 800 number to the Bureau, waited for the automated response, then quickly punched in his voice mail number. Water ran in the background as he waited to hear his own voice instruct him to leave a message. He didn't have much time. Fishing in his pocket, he pulled out a pocketknife, then used it to pry the face off of the telephone receiver.

The water stopped.

Chase muttered a curse, then started talking to his voice mail, asking the make-believe telephone company to please do whatever necessary to initiate service today. Yes, he could be reached at the high school after one o'clock.

He paused, and counted to ten.

Silence.

He felt like an idiot, but continued the one-sided dialogue anyway.

In the watch pocket of his blue jeans, he eased out two credit-card-thin silver discs, and wedged them inside the guts of the receiver. He slid the white plastic, protective covering back on the phone, then snapped it in place.

"Thank you," he said into the mouthpiece, as the door to the bathroom swung open. "I'd really appreciate it."

He turned, pressed the button to disconnect the call and mentally counted to ten before sliding his thumb over the six button, followed by two hits to the number one to erase the Bureau number from the redial memory. It wouldn't do for Dr. Romine to become suspicious. The last thing he needed was for her to end up with the Bureau's automated recording instead of the phone company he'd been pretending to call.

"Should be taken care of now," he said, hanging up the telephone just as Dee walked into the kitchen.

"They're usually pretty good about service," she said, giving him the hint that occasionally the small regional phone company wasn't as prompt as she'd sometimes like. "Someone probably just forgot to flip a switch somewhere."

She'd brushed her hair, he noticed, and pulled the long silky strands into a ponytail, which swung over her shoulder when she bent to pull a teakettle from a low cabinet. Chase couldn't help himself. He was a man. A man alone with a beautiful woman. When she bent over to look under the cabinet for the teakettle, his gaze landed right on her backside. A very curvy backside, too, he thought.

She moved to the sink to fill the kettle with water, then set it to boil on the stove. He reluctantly dragged his attention away from the curves beneath her robe and flashed her a grin when she looked his way.

"Sorry I can't be more neighborly and offer you a cup of tea." She lowered the flame under the kettle. "I really have to get to the clinic soon."

"No problem." He'd gotten luckier than he'd hoped by being able to place the dual transmitters in her telephone. He still couldn't quite believe a woman who'd learned to be suspicious of just about everyone she came in contact with would leave him alone for any length of time in her apartment. "I better get going. More unpacking to do."

The space between the stove and the sink was incredibly narrow. Whether she just didn't think about the cramped space or she was playing some game of territorial one-upmanship he wasn't privy to, he couldn't say. All he knew was that she didn't move and he'd have to touch her in order to pass. With no other choice but to squeeze between her and the speckled counter, his hand automatically landed on her hip as he attempted to ease his way around her.

Nothing could have prepared him for the electrical charge of sexual awareness that shot from the tips of his fingers straight to his groin. His fingers weren't the only body parts that flexed, either. Telling himself she was the final piece of the puzzle to the whereabouts of her brother didn't help. Pulling his hand back and putting some much needed physical distance between them was equally useless.

His body acknowledged hers with a fierce surge of good old-fashioned lust. He hoped like hell it'd just been a long time since he'd been with a woman. The instantaneous desire collided with his staunch denial there was nothing else to his physical reaction to Dee. She was a means to an end. The very nature of his job, his reason for even being in her apartment at ten in the morning on a late-summer day, forbade any emotional involvement with her whatsoever.

That didn't stop the blood from pumping hard and fast through his veins.

"You work at the clinic?" he asked, putting more distance between them while attempting to redirect his thoughts.

She frowned. Had she felt it, too? he wondered.

"Yes," she said, the note of awareness in her voice striking him right in the midsection with a ball of heat that burned, then shot lower and simmered.

*Damn.*

He edged out of the small kitchen into the living-room area. "So are you the one I call if I need an appointment to see the doc?" He already knew everything there was to know about her. Everything, he thought, except the way his body reacted to the nearness of hers. *That* had been a complete surprise.

"Are you asking me if I'm the receptionist?" she asked, settling her hands on the counter. Her hip, the one he swore he could still feel the imprint of against his fingers, tilted slightly to the side.

"I guess I was."

A brief smile canted her mouth. "No. I'm not the receptionist."

"Nurse?"

Her smile deepened. "Wrong again."

He frowned, then lifted his eyebrows as if surprised. "You're the town doctor?"

"And would you believe it? I went to school and everything," she countered. An interesting light flashed in her gold-green eyes that matched the sass in her voice.

He grinned. "Sorry. I didn't mean—"

She closed her eyes briefly, then shook her head. "It's not your fault. I'm just a little tired this morning."

She folded her arms in front of her. "I don't mean to be rude, but you're going to have to excuse me. I really need to get ready for work."

"How about you let me buy you lunch?" he asked

quickly. Whether his invitation stemmed from his need to solve the case or something more interesting he had no intention of pursuing, he couldn't say. He opted for case related. "It's the least I could do since I woke you up to use your phone."

She let out a puff of breath and padded across the bare floor to the door. "That's not necessary," she said, swinging it open in a silent, but pointed, invitation for him to get out.

"I insist," he pushed, walking toward her. "I feel bad about waking you."

She looked away as he passed in front of her. He stepped onto the front porch and turned around, his hopes climbing a notch at the regret in her eyes.

"I'm sorry," she told him. "I have to work."

"You get a lunch break, don't you?"

"Yes, but I'm really busy today. But thank you anyway." She let the door swing closed. The rattle of the safety chain told him she wouldn't be changing her mind anytime soon.

He let out a frustrated stream of breath. The morning hadn't been a complete waste. He'd managed to get the transmitters placed in her telephone. All incoming or outgoing calls from that telephone would be recorded. While any information he learned would be inadmissible, he couldn't risk a leak, which was a real possibility if he attempted the legal route by obtaining a court ordered tap. She didn't own a cellular telephone, but she did have a beeper. He also hadn't been able to determine whether or not she had another extension in her bedroom.

He reined in the baser thoughts that readily flowed through his mind when he considered the means by which to gain entrance to Dr. Romine's bedroom.

Shoving his hand through his hair, he stepped off her

porch into the bright morning sunlight and headed across the small concrete courtyard bordered with overgrown, neglected foliage to the stairs leading up to his apartment. He'd stretched the boundaries of the law before to suit his own ends and he wasn't above doing so now. When it came to tracking down those on the FBI's most wanted list, he wouldn't hesitate to stretch the rules to the point of breaking. Every now and then, he'd even managed a few stress cracks, but never had he ever completely ignored the laws he'd sworn to uphold. That didn't mean he didn't enjoy a challenge, and the Romine case definitely qualified.

Except Chase Bend-the-Rules Bracken had a problem. A problem that consisted of his body's reaction to his only lead in the case he had to solve, or he'd be donating his dark blue suits to the Goodwill.

With a sigh of self-disgust, he walked into his apartment and headed straight for the locked spare bedroom. He flipped on the light and crossed the room, ignoring the high-powered scope set up near the window. Without bothering to sit, he leaned over and punched a series of keys on the computer keyboard. In the recorder next to him, surveillance tapes whirred to life then paused until triggered by the subject's telephone. The red lights on the recording devices glowed.

He was ready, in the preliminary sense. If Jared Romine contacted his sister by telephone, Chase would know about it. His gut told him the rogue agent wouldn't be so careless; it wasn't Romine's style considering he'd been underground for almost three years without so much as a hint to his whereabouts. The Bureau knew that somehow Romine maintained contact with his sister. Chase needed to determine exactly how the murdering agent did it. Then and only then would he be able to track the suspect down.

He arrogantly figured within two weeks he'd know everything he needed to finally apprehend Jared Romine.

A slow smile spread across his face. He wouldn't uncover the information by using any of the high-tech surveillance equipment lining the walls of the spare bedroom. He'd learn it the old-fashioned way, by interrogating the suspect's sister, in ways Chase was positive would never be found in any reference manual.

LONG HOURS WEREN'T NEW to Dee. Nor were shifts that extended long beyond her scheduled twelve hours. She learned to survive the grueling pace by napping whenever possible and drinking as much strong black coffee as her stomach lining could tolerate.

After the weekend she'd spent at the county hospital, followed by the fourteen-hour labor and delivery of Erma Dalton's sixth child, she should be exhausted, but serving her internship in a busy Los Angeles emergency room two years ago had conditioned her for the endless hours young physicians often handled in the beginning of their careers.

Every other weekend she served as an E.R. resident at the Berkeley County Hospital, but this past weekend had been particularly rough as she'd had to pull a double shift to cover for a colleague away on holiday. After that, she only had a four-hour break before starting her own second shift of the weekend. Sneaking what little sleep she could manage during the occasional lull, she'd made it through the roughest forty-eight hours she could remember since her early intern days. Her plans to sleep until noon, however, had been effectively derailed by her new upstairs neighbor.

Her very handsome and sexy new upstairs neighbor, with wavy black hair, eyes such an interesting shade of blue they looked almost lilac. Add in the sweet musky scent that clung to his skin, and her dormant feminine instincts had awakened from slumber.

Just what she didn't need. Or want.

At first she'd tried to write off her physical reaction to the newcomer as nothing more than sheer exhaustion. So what if she'd experienced an accompanying thrum of anticipation when she'd first looked into his intense gaze. She'd had an extraordinarily busy weekend and probably only slept seven out of the last sixty hours. As dog-tired as she'd been, was it so unusual for her to feel a rush of longing when a tall, gorgeous stranger asked to borrow her phone?

For her, yes. He made her uneasy, in a man/woman, sexual desires running in high gear sort of way. As far as explanations went, she couldn't find one worthy enough to rationalize the way her heart had ricocheted around in her chest when he'd laid his hand on her hip as he squeezed past her in the kitchen, or the way her thighs had tingled when he'd brushed against her.

No doubt about it. Coach Bracken made her hot.

Too bad a cool shower, followed up with a steaming cup of herbal tea and a crispy toasted bagel slathered with her favorite strawberry cream cheese, did nothing to alleviate the sneaking suspicion that sexual deprivation, *not* lack of sleep, was her problem.

At five minutes before noon, she pulled into the rear of the clinic and parked beneath the voluminous shade of an ancient elm. After locking her used Honda Civic, she followed the concrete path along the side of the building to the front door. There wouldn't be any patients waiting for her, with the exception of Erma Dalton, whom she hoped to send home soon, which would give her time to get caught up on paperwork.

She climbed the wooden steps of the old Victorian where the Cole Harbor clinic was housed. The bottom floor had been converted to a medical office over sixty years before by the first Doc Claymore, with the living quarters taking up the two top floors. Three generations later, the clinic still existed, but the gruff old buzzard Dee put up with was the last of his line.

She pushed open the door and breathed in the sterile scent of disinfectant mingled with the more tantalizing aroma of the mulberry scented candle burning in the reception area. Netta, the clinic's receptionist, was just pulling her oversize canvas bag from the bottom drawer of the filing cabinet.

"Good afternoon, Netta. Any messages?"

Netta, who dressed like a twenty-two-year-old, although Dee and Lucille both swore she couldn't be a day under thirty-five, dropped her bag on the desk. She gave the short hem of the black knit skirt hugging her ample bottom a tug, followed by a dramatic put-upon sigh. The receptionist's job was to take messages and schedule appointments. In Dee's opinion, they were lucky to get that much from the five-foot-two bottle blonde, and had learned early on anything more taxing than answering the phone was asking for trouble. If it was up to Dee, Netta Engels would be history and she'd hire a real front-end person capable of taking the administrative load off the shoulders of Lucille, the registered nurse who'd worked for Doc Claymore the last twenty-five years. The decision wasn't Dee's, however, and for reasons that defied common sense, cantankerous old Claymore liked Netta.

As did ninety-eight percent of the male population of Cole Harbor, Dee thought with disgust, certain Netta's talents went far beyond the kind best put to use in an office.

Two more months, Dee told herself. Provided she came to a decision about where she wanted to practice medicine once her contractual obligation with the government ended. One thing she knew for certain, no matter which offer she accepted, it'd be in a very large metropolitan area where she'd just be another face in a very large crowd. She had managed to narrow her choices down and was seriously entertaining offers from Presbyterian Hospital in New York, Boston's Massachusetts General and a rather lucrative offer from a private, smaller bed facility in Miami, which would include a gradual partnership buy-in with stock options. Since living on the Atlantic Coast, she decided she preferred the eastern coastal regions to those on the Pacific, and was even beginning to like the idea of a white Christmas, a feature which would effectively eliminate Miami from her list. So, she wasn't sure she was quite ready to narrow her choices just yet.

Netta thrust a small stack of pink messages in front of her, then sashayed around the counter in an overpowering cloud of perfume. "I have a lunch date," she said, her big brown eyes filled with impatience. She slipped out the door before Dee managed to flip through all the notes.

Nothing out of the ordinary, she decided, except no call from the lab at County with pathology results from the Dalton delivery.

Dee made a mental note to call for the results as the bell over the door rang again. She looked up from the messages in her hand. Her heart stuttered beneath her breast, then resumed at a pace worthy of a few concerned bleeps from a heart monitor. Everyone in Cole Harbor knew the clinic was closed from noon until two.

Everyone, that is, except its newest resident...the incredibly sexy Chase Bracken.

# 3

NOT IN A MILLION YEARS would Chase ever place surgical scrubs under the heading *Erotic Attire*. That is until he'd had the distinct pleasure of seeing firsthand how the burgundy cotton played hide-and-seek with his neighbor's curves. Since he had more than a hint of just how curvy she was under the boxy top and drawstring cotton pants, he considered himself a minor authority on the subject.

She set the pink scraps of paper she'd been reading when he'd walked through the door facedown on the desk. "The clinic doesn't open until two," she said. Her delicately arched eyebrows pulled together over a distrustful gaze filled with just enough curiosity to keep him encouraged.

His own curiosity was also piqued, and it had little to do with the case. Thoughts of what those enticing curves would feel like beneath his fingertips, without the cotton barrier, had occupied his mind the past two hours. Fantasies, rather than focusing on his purpose for even being near her, occupied his mind.

Fantasies better left unexplored.

Fantasies that had his body in an aching state of awareness.

He flashed her a grin and held up a white paper sack. "I figured I owed you one. Just wanted to drop by and say thanks for being neighborly, neighbor."

Distrustful, curious or just plain cautious, he couldn't

care less because interest resided at the top of the list. He didn't miss the way her fingers tightened around the back of the secretarial chair as if she had to force herself to concentrate on something solid instead of...what? Him? The way his body had felt brushing along hers as he'd slipped behind her this morning? The way his fingers had pressed into her hip? The way his thighs had grazed her bottom?

She had plenty of reasons to be cautious of him, but instinct told him her apprehension had more to do with the sexual awareness arcing between them than any suspicion about what he was really doing in Cole Harbor. Still, he had to get close to her, and the best way to do that was to set every single one of her suspicions aside, one by one until nothing lay between them except naked trust.

"I really don't have—"

"It's okay," he said, rounding the corner of the low partition standing between them. "I'm not staying. Where's your office?"

She let go of the chair and shifted to face him. Clasping her hands behind her back, she drew the cotton fabric tight over her breasts. "You're not staying?"

"'Fraid not, Doc." It took every ounce of willpower to keep his gaze focused on hers when he really wanted to look his fill elsewhere. "I'd like to stick around and share lunch, but I need to be heading over to the high school for a faculty meeting."

"I didn't mean you weren't welcome, it's just that—"

"You're busy," he finished for her. "I know. I just wanted to say thanks for helping me out of a jam this morning."

And had she ever, he thought. Especially since he was

pretty sure she hadn't a clue how much trouble it was to obtain a *legal* wire tap.

She made a sound that might have been a laugh, but he couldn't be sure. She tilted her head slightly to the side, causing her unbound sable hair to skim over her right shoulder and tease the gentle slope of her breast. "Why are you doing this?"

"Like I said, you did me a big favor this morning." He held up the bag and wiggled it back and forth. The heavy aroma of fried burger and French fried potatoes wafted between them. "Office?"

A tentative smile curved her mouth before she reached up and gingerly took the bag from his hand, as if trying not to make physical contact. She almost reminded him of the stray dog he'd found one summer as a kid. The poor animal had been teased and tormented by the neighborhood bully and as a result, had grown fearful of a human's touch. He'd worked for months trying to get the dog to trust him, and by the end of summer, he'd finally managed to win him over. For twelve years Hobo, as Chase's foster mother had named the mutt, had taken up residence on the Mitchells' back porch and had been Chase's staunchest protector.

He hoped he'd be able to win over the pretty doctor just as thoroughly.

"I don't have an office," she admitted, then opened the bag and inhaled deeply.

She looked up at him and offered him a smile brighter than anything he'd seen in a very long time. Too long, but he rapidly quashed that stray thought. Unable to stop himself, a satisfied grin tugged his lips in response to the pure pleasure lighting her intriguing eyes.

"Really? You're the town doc, and you don't have an office?" *Boy, wait until Pelham gets a load of this daily report,* Chase thought smugly. He'd have Pelham and the rest of the superior bastards scratching their heads in wonder with the progress he was making after only two hours of initial contact with the subject. They'd think twice about stuffing him behind a desk for the duration.

"It's a long story," she said. She set the bag on the blotter protecting the wood grain surface of the desk. A wry grin eased across her sweet-looking mouth. "I wouldn't want to bore you with the details." He'd read the files. There wasn't a single detail about her he didn't know.

No matter how much he wanted to stay and test the getting-to-know-you waters, he figured he'd better continue to play it smart and put some distance between them. He wanted to build trust, not spook her by coming on too strong.

"Enjoy your lunch," he said. "And thanks again." He cut across the reception area to the front door. There really was a faculty meeting scheduled for the coaching staff and he was already at risk of being late. Not quite the kind of first impression he wanted to make, even though he had a good feeling about the kind of impression he was making on the *formerly* illusive Dr. Destiny Romine.

He paused at the door, his hand on the knob and looked over his shoulder at her. "Oh, and for the record, Doc," he said, not bothering to contain the cocky grin, "I'm certain there isn't anything about you that would bore me."

DEE CRUMPLED THE LAST of the lightly wax-coated paper and tossed it in the white bag. As much as she hated admitting it, her new neighbor's thoughtful gesture was very much appreciated. How he knew she adored grilled onions on her cheeseburger was as much a mystery as to why, after years of practically ignoring the opposite sex, did *he* have to be the one to reawaken her dormant feminine senses.

Her *insistent* feminine senses, she thought.

From the number of charts stacked up on the corner of Netta's immaculate desk, Dee had a slew of patients to see before the end of the day. A welcome distraction, she decided, from the more intriguing thoughts of her sexy new neighbor that had been battering her senses since she'd found him on her doorstep this morning. His parting shot hadn't done a thing to help curb the more base thoughts demanding attention, either.

She shoved him from her mind. She had work to do and suspected Lucille was keeping watch over Erma Dalton and the newborn until Dee released them. She certainly didn't want to perform an exam with something so offensive as onions on her breath.

After quickly perusing the charts and list of patients with scheduled appointments, she made her way into the staff's private bathroom to brush her teeth then slipped into her white lab coat. Before she could head upstairs to see about discharging mother and child, the telephone rang. The stack of messages Netta had left her hadn't included one from the County lab. She'd feel much more comfortable about discharging Erma and the baby *after* getting word that the path report was indeed clear.

She snagged the ringing telephone before the call rolled over to the answering service. "Cole Harbor Clinic." She grabbed her pen and searched the surface of Netta's desk for a scrap of paper.

Silence.

"Hello?" Dee frowned and slipped the pen into the pocket of her lab coat. "Is someone there?" she asked.

Nothing…until the distinct sound of a horn shattered the silence. She'd recalled a similar sound, but it only teased the fringes of her memory bank. *A foghorn?* she wondered, seconds before her heart slammed painfully into her ribs.

She pressed her hand over her exposed ear, shutting out the steady hum of the office machinery, listening as closely and carefully as possible for anything she might recognize—a sound, a voice, another blare of the foghorn. All she heard was the painful thud of her own heart and her blood racing through her veins as her endorphin levels skyrocketed.

Frantically she calculated the weeks since she'd last heard from her brother.

The foghorn sounded again, breaking the silence.

"Hello? Is someone there?" she asked again, unable to squelch the desperation from filtering into her voice.

She *knew* it was Jared. Her pounding heart told her it was her brother.

She spun around to search the days on the big ninety-day calendar hanging on the far wall. It'd been late June, a little over eight weeks since the phone call with no one on the other end had woken her in the dead of night.

"Jared? Oh my God. Are you all right? Let me help—"

The line went dead. Dee let out a string of curses that would have had an entire ship of sailors blushing crimson if they'd heard her. She hung up the phone with a snap and balled her hands into fists. God, she wanted to scream from the frustration of it all.

She made a mental note to mark the day on the small calendar she kept in the drawer of her nightstand. A small red check mark next to the date as a reminder of the last time her brother had let her know he was still alive.

And still running for his life.

"YOU WANT ME TO TEACH *WHAT?*"

Chase glared when the defensive line coach, Charlie Harrison, snickered. "Senior sex," Harrison blurted, then slapped his hand on the conference table and guffawed with the rest of the Cougar coaching staff.

Chase carefully set his pen on the table next to the yellow pad he'd been doodling on for the past hour. "No way," he said, leaning back in the hard plastic chair, shifting his attention to the principal, Aaron Johnson. "Criminal justice and phys ed are all I'm qualified to teach. No way am I taking on a bunch of hormonal teenagers and talking about sex for forty-five minutes every day."

The principal shot the coaches a look bordering on full-blown irritation. They'd been in the meeting for nearly an hour going over additional assignments. Chase being the new guy had definitely drawn the shortest, dirtiest straw. He knew a raw deal when he saw one and he'd just been dished up one hell of a stinker.

"We prefer Senior Health Issues, Mr. Bracken," Principal Johnson said. His thick southern accent dripped with impatience that equaled the contempt for the coaching staff in his murky brown eyes. "Budget cutbacks have forced our faculty to double up their classload. It's unfortunate that it extends to the coaching staff as well, but unless you want to see the football program completely shut down, then might I suggest you—"

"Bone up on sex," Charlie Harrison interrupted.

"It won't be so bad, Chase," Walter Tompkins, the Cougars' head coach told him, unsuccessfully hiding his grin at Charlie's bad pun. "If it's the only way we can afford to maintain our extracurricular programs without shortchanging the students, then we'll just have to deal with it.''

"We all have to do it, Chase,'' the offensive line coach, Sean Crawford added. "Consider yourself lucky. At least you didn't get stuck with Home Ec.''

"Family and Consumer Studies, Mr. Crawford,'' Johnson corrected.

"Yeah. Whatever.'' Crawford rolled his eyes. "Look, Cole Harbor lives, eats and breathes football. They'd string up old Johnson here, along with the rest of the school board, in a hillbilly heartbeat if they dared cut the football program.''

"Damn straight,'' added Coach Tompkins in his own thick southern drawl. He shot a threatening glance in the principal's direction. "And I'd supply the rope.''

Johnson nervously shifted his attention to the schedule in front of him and wisely remained silent.

Chase glanced down at the class description then back at Johnson. "What do I know about Senior Health Issues?'' he argued, not willing to give in to Johnson's demands so readily. He knew two things and he knew them well—criminal justice and sports, primarily football. Even though he held a degree in criminal justice and a chipped hipbone from a bad hit to back up both claims, he still didn't want to think about the strings the Bureau had pulled to land him this current undercover gig. No one, not even Johnson, knew Chase's true identity or that teaching and coaching were the last items that should be listed on his *curriculum vitae*.

He couldn't care less about the sexual habits of a bunch of oversexed teenagers. What he wanted to know was where in the hell Jared Romine was hiding.

His gut told him Dee Romine had the answer to that burning question, while his record-setting rise in testosterone levels told him the chances of him playing it out hard and fast to get that answer was good. Too good, he thought shifting uncomfortably in his chair. He knew without a doubt he'd definitely enjoy bending more than a few rules if it had the pretty lady doctor talking nice to him.

"You might want to contact Dr. Romine from the clinic," Johnson continued, as if completely oblivious to Chase's objections. "She's come to speak to classes in the past about things like safe sex, condom application and other methods of birth control. All under proper parental consent of course."

"Who?" he asked carefully, not certain he'd heard the principal correctly.

"Dr. Romine," Johnson reiterated, then cleared his throat before looking at Chase, carefully avoiding the constant glare from the head coach. "Dr. Romine was extremely instrumental in the development of the curriculum two years ago. Mrs. Billings taught the class prior to her retirement and you'll be our replacement."

A grin tugged Chase's lips. God, could this assignment get any easier? What could be more interesting than talking sex with Dee? Nothing, in his opinion, so long as she ended up telling him what he wanted to know about her brother.

He picked up the pen and wrote Dee's name on the yellow pad, underlining it twice. Maybe teaching a course in Senior Health Issues wouldn't be such a bad idea after all...especially if it gave him an excuse to get in closer contact with his prey.

Crawford elbowed Harrison in the ribs. "Uh-oh," Crawford said, his voice laced with humor. "Looks like Bracken's met the delectable Dr. Romine."

Chase set the pen aside. "I've had the pleasure," he

answered carefully. Something in his chest tightened. Certainly not jealously for a lady he hardly knew. So why then did he have the sudden urge to give ol' Charlie a poke in his large bulbous nose?

A wide grin split Charlie Harrison's weathered face. Chase ground his teeth.

"You asked her out yet?" Harrison asked.

"What makes you think I'm interested?"

"Ain't a man with a pulse in Cole Harbor who hasn't been interested," Harrison countered.

Forget the poke. A black eye would make him feel a whole lot better.

"Or shot down," Crawford added.

That bit of knowledge gave Chase a surge of pleasure he didn't dare examine too closely.

"Oh, yeah?" he mused unwisely, giving in to his overgrown ego.

Harrison chuckled while Crawford tossed him a knowing look.

It wasn't the thrill of the chase, he told himself firmly. His interest in her was strictly professional.

Mostly.

CHASE WAS NO CLOSER TO DEE Romine the following Saturday than he'd been the day he'd arrived in Cole Harbor. He wouldn't exactly say she went out of her way to avoid him, but he couldn't help wondering if the sparks of sexual attraction between them had only been a conscious awareness of nothing more intriguing than the firing between synapse and neurotransmitter inside his own gray matter.

The accompanying state of semiarousal that occurred whenever he thought of her denied that hopeful musing.

With a grunt of disgust, he closed the file he'd been

staring at for over an hour with a snap and tossed it carelessly on top of the open box containing more of the Romine case. He'd checked and rechecked the detailed schematic of her whereabouts and habits over the last twelve months until he knew them by heart. Since she'd worked the previous weekend at Berkeley County Hospital, she should've had the weekend off, but as Chase had learned from the bug he'd planted in her telephone, Friday morning she'd received a call from the hospital asking if she could work a couple of additional shifts over the weekend. She hadn't hesitated and Chase wished she'd been asked to work the graveyard shift. That was something he could've used to his advantage. There was no way he could risk sneaking into her apartment during the light of day. The chances of someone spotting him were too great.

Twenty minutes later he knew if he didn't get out and *do* something he'd go stir-crazy. He thought about heading off toward town, but this late on a Saturday afternoon, the few businesses that were open on the weekend had either already shut down or were preparing to close up shop. His options ranged from the D.Q. and the high-school crowd, the Surf & Turf Diner and the geriatric generation, or one of three local taverns. The latter appealed to him even less than his first two options. During his college days when drinking and carousing were practically a part of the curriculum, more often than not he'd assumed the role of designated driver. He had a hang-up about drugs and alcohol, but kept his opinions to himself lest he be forced into an explanation. Certain information was better kept buried in the past where it belonged, especially when he had no desire to admit to anyone his less than stellar beginnings.

He was bored, restless and blamed both emotions on

the brunette downstairs who'd cost him six whole days of prime surveillance time by doing nothing more exciting than traveling to the clinic each morning and returning before sundown each evening. Her lights were consistently out before midnight and he hadn't heard so much as a television in the background during the four unremarkable telephone calls she'd received since he'd set the tap.

The restlessness sprang from other, more personal emotions and the fact he could not stop thinking about Dee in a way that bothered him. As in hot and *bothered*. He let out a stream of breath. Had he really been too long without a woman? Must be, he thought, otherwise he'd be able to ignore the fantasies occupying his mind. A little physical exertion would be just the ticket to clear his head so he could start focusing on the job, and not the way her skin would feel when flushed with desire.

He found a few tools for the yard in a small shed at the rear of the triplex, along with an old push mower in serious need of oiling and blade sharpening.

Despite the heavy humidity pushing the heat index higher than normal for the area, for the next four hours Chase trimmed and box-shaped the hedge, then cleared the weeds from the fountain. Armed with a half-empty spray can of lubricant and a sharpening stone he'd found after searching a battered red toolbox in the corner of the shed, he sat on the wooden steps outside Dee's unit beneath the shade provided by the overhang on her side of the wide front porch and started tearing down the mower.

"Mind if I ask what you're doing?"

Chase looked up, surprised to find Dee looking at him, curiosity banked in her eyes. In accordance with the climbing heat index and stifling humidity, she wore a pair of khaki walking shorts with a plain white top tucked into the narrow waistband. With one white sneaker propped on the bottom step and her hand wrapped around the wooden railing, she looked as if she'd been ready to bound up the stairs until she saw him.

Using the shirt he'd pulled off over an hour ago, he wiped the sweat from his forehead. "I thought the place could use a little work."

"Mrs. England has a gardener, you know."

"Then she should fire him because he does a lousy job."

She shrugged, then hesitated long enough to have him wondering if she was debating whether or not she could trust him not to touch her if she passed by him.

As if every nerve in his body wasn't poised for action, he gave the mower blade his attention once again. The sun had begun its descent over the western horizon, yet the air was still heavy with humidity, causing moisture to cling to just about every surface of his body. The moist heat would have been completely unbearable if not for the light sea breeze that occasionally teased his skin and gently stirred the fronds of the palmetto trees overhead.

She must've decided it was safe, because after a few ticks of the second hand on his wristwatch, she climbed the stairs to her apartment. The jangle of keys was followed by the click of the door and the faint whoosh of cool air from the central air conditioning that brushed against his skin.

The screened door snapped shut about the same time her front door closed. *Well, now what?* he wondered. He had been waiting for her to return, so now what did he do? The equipment was set to record if she received or made a telephone call. Maybe he could even come up with a plausible excuse to gain entrance into her apartment again. The "my phone is out" trick wouldn't fly a second time, but he could always pull the lame borrow an egg or cup of sugar routine if he got desperate enough. There was the Senior Health class, but it wouldn't make sense for him to contact her so soon about speaking to the class when school wouldn't be in session for another two weeks.

Before he could conceive a viable plan, her door opened. "Are you drinking enough water to replenish what you're losing?" she asked abruptly, keeping the screened door between them.

He detected a note of irritation in her voice, but finished his stroke along the mower blade before looking over his shoulder at her. Definitely irritation. Her sable eyebrows slanted into a frown. He couldn't see her eyes clearly, but he easily imagined the gold highlights sparkling due to her annoyance. Annoyance he'd bet his badge was unwanted.

The question as to the cause of her aggravation held all sorts of interesting possibilities, and had him curious as hell. Because she didn't want to care if he was running the risk of dehydration? Or did her attitude stem from some other, more base instinct? The same base instincts he'd been unable to stop thinking about since they'd touched that morning in her compact kitchen.

"I'm fine, Doc," he said, forcing himself to return to sharpening the mower blade and not try to see for himself if those gold highlights were indeed sparkling. He flicked his finger over the sharpened blade. *Not bad.* Satisfied, he started working the opposite side.

"By the way you're sweating, I'd say you're dangerously close to dehydration, unless you're taking in plenty of water."

A smile kicked into a grin when he glanced over his shoulder at her again. She'd been watching him. And paying attention. "Is that strictly your professional opinion?"

He couldn't be sure, but he could've sworn her eyes narrowed slightly.

"It's an observation," she said, the husky nuances of her voice conjuring plenty of images, but not a single one of them professional.

"So you've been observing, huh?"

Her mouth opened, then snapped shut. Damn, but he wished he could see her eyes clearly.

"It's not what you're thinking, it's… Just drink plenty of water. And that *is* my professional opinion." The sound of her door closing was followed by the slide of the safety chain.

He shrugged and went back to the mower blade. Not exactly the kind of conversation he'd envisioned, nor would it even remotely classify as a success as far as getting closer to her.

He slid the stone along the dulled blade. Considering his lack of progress all week, he supposed today's encounter ranked right up there with mediocre success.

She noticed him. She noticed him and it bothered her. If that was the case, then Chase knew it'd only be a matter of time before he located the right combination to unlock the secrets that would lead him right to Jared Romine.

He heard the gentle glide of metal against metal again, followed by the jingle of the safety chain.

He looked up expectantly as her door opened one more time. She pushed open the screen door and stepped onto the covered porch. "Have you eaten?" The slight irritation he'd detected earlier hadn't dissipated. The gold highlighting her green eyes intensified, almost flaring to life.

God, she had the most intriguing gaze. He couldn't help wondering what they'd do when banked in passion.

He shrugged and shot for a casual attitude he was far from feeling. He was close, he could feel it, and he had to play it cool so he didn't blow it. "Not since lunch, why?"

She slid her hands into the front pockets of her khaki walking shorts and frowned. "I have some halibut defrosted. It's too much for just one person and it'd end up going to waste..."

"You inviting me to dinner, Doc?"

She let out a puff of breath. "I guess I am."

He grinned, and set the blade and sharpening stone on the step beside him. "Then you got yourself a date," he said rising.

"Uh, this isn't, isn't a date."

Chase just grinned. He didn't care what she was calling it. He'd just gotten closer, and that's all that mattered. Almost all that mattered, he amended.

# 4

"IT'S NOT A TYPICALLY southern dish, but it's healthy," Dee said, hating that her voice trembled. She added a covered casserole dish filled with rice pilaf to the breakfast bar next to the salad and glazed carrots, and hoped he didn't notice how her hands shook nervously.

He set the pan with the grilled halibut by the stove. "Then it should suit my Yankee taste buds," he said, a teasing grin slanting his mouth in a way that had her heart thumping a few beats too fast.

He took the seat she indicated and poured them each a glass of wine. She added the halibut to their plates before climbing onto the bar stool kitty-corner from him. She'd changed the place settings a half-dozen times while he'd been grilling the fish on the little portable grill the previous tenant had left behind. Finally she'd aimed for the safest seating arrangement, one that would give her the most distance physically. There was enough awareness sizzling between them to send her into sensory overload. Sitting directly beside him where their thighs could brush, their knees lightly touch, or their feet tangle would be like flicking a lit match onto a bale of dried straw.

She cleared her throat, then offered him the plain glass bowl filled with glazed carrots. "So where are you from, Yankee?" He took the dish from her, his thick tanned fingers brushing against hers. She should've expected it, but the tingles rippling through her and landing right in the tips of her breasts still surprised, and annoyed her. *Why now?* Why did her well-trained and dormant hormones have to choose this time, this place, *this man* to become unruly and zing to life? Why, when she would be leaving the adorably quaint southern coastal town for a new life, did she finally find herself responding to the opposite sex?

Her feminine senses went haywire when he was around. They didn't even fully function when he wasn't around, either, and that was a very big problem. Especially when she took into consideration how she'd allowed herself to become distracted by his very kissable-looking mouth, imagining his kisses twice as intoxicating as his eyes when he looked at her *that* way. Like the way that said he knew every nuance, every curve, every aspect of her body as intimately as his own.

Impossible, but she couldn't stop the wayward thoughts any more than she could stop the sun from shining.

There were times, she concluded, reaching for the dish of pilaf, when life just wasn't fair.

"Ohio originally," he said, drawing her attention back to his uniquely handsome face. His slightly crooked nose had been broken at least once in his life. But his eyes. Oh, a girl could really get lost in such an interesting shade of blue. That deep lilac color combined with the way he looked at her were just way too sexy. Factor in those long, dark lashes a tube of the highest quality mascara could never hope to duplicate on any woman, and her previously controlled hormones were history.

His mouth wasn't so bad, either, she thought, absently cutting her fish with the edge of her fork. His lips, with the lower slightly fuller, could only be called sensual.

Definitely sensual, she thought as she stared, watching them move as he spoke.

"Doc?"

His voice was sharp enough to snap her right back into reality. She forced her gaze from his lips back to his eyes. "Did you say something?" Well, of course he said something. His lips *had* been moving and she'd been staring at them like a love-struck schoolgirl for crying out loud.

He grinned while she struggled to regain her usual cool, calm composure. "I'm sorry, you were saying?"

"I asked where you were from," he said.

She pushed her fork through her rice. She'd learned to mix the truth with the lies, but she'd always told the same story. She no longer had a family. At least none she could openly discuss. As far as anyone knew, she was Dee Romine, the *only* living surviving child of the late David and Ellen Romine. Her decision on exactly what to say when asked by anyone was based in fact, for the most part. Never the superstitious type, she still wouldn't dare to tweak fate's nose by saying that her brother had died as well, afraid if she did, she might be predisposing Jared's fate. The lies weren't something she cared for, so she simply never mentioned her brother.

"Washington state," she said after a moment.

He reached for his wineglass. "That's a long way from family."

"I don't have family." The practiced lie slipped easily from her lips. Too easily. "What about you?" she asked, bringing the conversation back to him. "The Carolina coastline isn't exactly a good stretch of the legs from Ohio, you know."

He lifted the wineglass to his lips and drank slowly. "My folks are both retired," he finally said, almost as if he was deciding how much to tell her, which was silly. She just had a guilty conscience is all.

He took another sip of wine before setting his glass aside. "My old man taught history and government at the local high school, and mom was the Home Ec teacher."

"Is that why you went into teaching? Following in your parents' footsteps?"

"Something like that I guess. Speaking of teaching, Johnson said I should contact you."

She stopped with her fork poised in midair. "Principal Johnson? Contact me? Why?"

He pushed his near empty plate aside and rested his tanned forearms on the counter. "He's punishing the coaching staff, and I got caught in the middle of the battle between him and the head coach," he said with a wry grin. "I guess it could be worse, but I doubt it. I've been assigned one of those half-semester senior-seminar classes."

"Let me guess. He's taking it out on the coaches because he'd rather put money into academia than the sports programs right?"

"That about sums it up."

"It's been a long-standing battle around these parts," she told him. "Don't take it personally." She polished off the last of her halibut before asking, "But what does it have to do with me?"

He let out a sigh and reached again for his wineglass. "Senior Sex."

He had to be kidding. She'd assisted Ellen Billings with the curriculum when the older woman had been assigned the class two years ago. Dee had gone to speak to the students about the varying types of birth control available, stressing abstinence was *the* most acceptable form. Teens being teens, no matter what she told them, she knew peer pressure would often lead to sexual experimentation regardless of the dangers to their emotional and physical health. At least after her presentation the students were more than prepared, and had gone away with more than just a basic understanding of the concept of safe sex.

She set her fork on the plate. "You're joking, right?" she asked, hopeful that he was in fact teasing her. The thought of showing the senior class the appropriate method of applying a condom, in front of the one man who'd managed to awaken her libido wasn't exactly the most appealing.

"No joke, Doc," he said, his voice tinged with humor. "So would you be willing to show the class how to put a condom on a banana?"

She reached for her glass, pausing before taking a long and much needed drink. "I use a cucumber actually," she quipped. "It's easier for the students. Contrasting colors and all that."

He chuckled, the sound a low, sexy rumble. "Isn't that just a little ambitious?"

"You were a teenage boy once. Wouldn't you rather the girls saw you as a cucumber than a banana?"

His spontaneous burst of laughter brought a smile to her lips. It was no use, she suddenly realized. Fighting the sexual awareness buzzing between them was an effort in futility. Unless of course she was willing to pack up and move tomorrow to either Boston or New York, which she wasn't. Besides, she knew he felt it as well. It was there, in his smile, in the sound of his laughter, but mostly in his eyes, a deeper shade of violet now and twice as intense when he looked at her.

"I didn't realize cucumbers were more…anatomically correct."

Her responding laughter was a tad too close to a nervous twitter. She set her glass aside. "Why are we having this conversation?"

He shrugged. "You started it, Doc."

No, she didn't. *He* did. "Let's change the subject," she suggested.

"Interesting."

"What's interesting?"

"That you'd want to change the subject. I had the impression you wouldn't mind discussing…anatomy."

She stood and started clearing the bar with trembling fingers. "You take a lot for granted, Coach." What did he expect her to do? Roll over on her back and yell, *Take me now, stud?*

"Chase."

She turned to find him standing less than two feet away from her. That made her even more nervous since he blocked her only hope for an exit. "You take a lot for granted, *Chase.*"

He reached for her, but she pulled away before he could touch her, leaning back until the edge of the counter bit into her lower back.

"Do I?" he asked.

Her tactical temporary escape failed. Definitely not a smart move, because he inched closer, then leaned toward her. He planted his hands firmly on the edge of the counter, bracketing her within his strong tanned arms and the muscled wall of his chest. They weren't even touching, but the charge between them was still powerfully electric.

By some miracle, she remembered to breathe, and all she got for her trouble was an intoxicating mix of freshly showered man and a hint of musk that teased her senses. "I'm not looking to get involved," she told him, then wet her suddenly drier than dust lips with her tongue. "I was only being, uh, I was being neighborly."

"Then why so nervous, Doc?" he asked, his voice low and husky.

"Why are you so close?"

He lifted one eyebrow and shrugged his wide shoulders. "I dunno. It'd be kinda hard to kiss you from across the room."

"Kiss me?" The words tangled up in her vocal cords and came out sounding like a husky whisper filled with invitation.

"I thought you'd never ask," he said, in that same sexy rumble that had her insides quivering with sweet anticipation.

Before she could tell him he was wasting his time, that she didn't *have* the time to get involved, his tongue brushed lightly across her lips.

Before she could think of the words to protest what was going to be the most promising moment of sexual awakening, he swept inside and tasted her deeply.

Before she could even summon her lost common sense and stop his gentle assault on her mouth, she tangled her tongue with his.

Moaning softly, she straightened. Her breasts barely brushed against his chest, but the contact had enough spark for hard peaks to form and rasp enticingly against her sensible cotton sports bra. Unable to resist the honeyed temptation of his mouth moving so provocatively, so seductively over hers, she wreathed her arms around his neck and just enjoyed the thrill racing through her veins.

Before she became completely swept away by the toe-curling kiss, he lifted his head and firmly set her away from him. The grin he gave her was filled with enough arrogance to let her know he hadn't missed one iota of her body's response.

"Thanks for the meal, Doc," he said, then turned and walked away.

Her breath came in short pants as she watched him cross the living room to the front door. How could he just walk away after igniting sparks like that? She might have responded like a feline who'd snuck out the back door and made it into the alley, but he hadn't exactly been unaffected, either.

"Where are you going?" she asked against her better judgment.

He swung the door open, then stopped in the threshold to look over his shoulder at her. "You've got an early day tomorrow. I'll take you to dinner after your shift."

He stepped through the door without answering her question, or waiting for a response to his invitation that hovered close to an arrogant demand. He was gone. Just like *that*, she thought with a snap of her fingers. He tipped her world upside down then left her, alone and feeling achingly frustrated. *From a kiss!*

There was more. A whole lot more and it all zeroed in on her growing sexual attraction to the new guy in town.

HE'D VERY NEARLY BLOWN IT. God, he couldn't believe he could be so careless. Not with an investigation as important as the Romine case. And especially not with a case as important to his continued employment with the Bureau.

He stood on the forty-yard line with Crawford and Harrison, each with their feet braced for impact, their backs to the sun and each holding a blocking dummy gripped tightly in their hands. A red Cougars ball cap helped to shield Chase's eyes from the brightness of the evening sun, but nothing could alleviate the thick humidity, except maybe a good summer storm. Between the heat, humidity and thoughts of Dee, his concentration on the Cougars' practice was no more effective than what he'd had on the investigation Saturday evening.

Dee hadn't mentioned her schedule to him once throughout the time they'd spent together four nights ago, and he'd gone off feeling damned cocky just because she'd responded to him. He'd been lucky he hadn't blown the whole operation. But he'd covered. He decided some distance would be in his favor so he tacked a note to her door the next afternoon, telling her something had come up and he'd have to give her a rain check on that meal he'd promised. Then after making certain all the surveillance equipment was in top working order, he'd taken off to a neighboring town to a motel for the night. It'd been a risky choice, but he didn't think he had any other option. Obviously his instincts had paid off, because he hadn't seen nor heard from Dee in the past four days. By the time they did meet up again, he suspected she'd probably have forgotten the incident. At least he hoped so.

He muttered a curse as he took a rough hit from Jimmy Sanders, a defensive lineman tipping the scales at two-twenty. "Watch it, Sanders," he complained. "You put that head down again, I'm gonna put my cleat on your backside."

Sanders spit out his mouthpiece. "Sorry, Coach."

Chase braced himself for the hit by the next player. After the way Dee had been sending him more signals than a faulty traffic light, he wasn't sure what he was supposed to feel, or do for that matter. What was he supposed to do when she kissed him like she wanted him? Wanted him as badly as he wanted her. He was a good agent, even if he wasn't above taking risks, but he doubted even the director could keep his hands, or his mouth, off someone as delightfully sensual as Dee.

She'd gotten to him. There was no other explanation, no other excuse. She'd gotten to him good and driven him practically insane with her pretty mouth and witty conversation. Every ounce of his strength had been forcefully summoned in order for him to walk away from her when all he'd wanted to do was take that kiss one step further, and another, then another until they were both too sated and exhausted to move. He couldn't remember the last time he'd been affected so intensely by a sweet, dewy mouth capable of drawing out secrets he'd never shared with another living soul. What was a guy supposed to do when a perfectly matched pair of breasts were pressing against his chest or slim hips were cradled within his own so unconsciously and so naturally?

"Sanders, get your head up," he yelled at Jimmy, who was charging straight for Crawford.

The defensive lineman hit the pad, head down. Chase swore and dropped his blocking dummy. Snagging Sanders by the face mask, he pulled the player toward him. He managed to shout a few oaths common on the football field, then threatened Sanders with a seat on the junior varsity bench for the season.

The kid started to say something, but Chase didn't hear him. From out of nowhere, he took a direct hit. And that was the last thing he remembered before his world went dark.

"THIS IS RIDICULOUS. I'm fine."

Dee offered Chase her best tolerant expression, the one

she reserved for difficult patients, particularly the male population being as they were the ones more apt to complain about obeying doctor's orders. Especially orders from a female doctor. Regardless of how great he kissed, Chase was a credit to his gender in the doctor/patient relationship area.

She slipped the otoscope back into the holder, before making a notation on the chart. "You were tackled, hit the ground and rendered unconscious." She glanced up from the chart and graced him with a smile. "Be a good boy and let me do my job, Chase."

He narrowed his gaze and glared at her from his seat on the edge of the exam table. "I'm fine." The firmness of his voice held a determination that didn't sway her in the least.

He probably *was* going to be perfectly fine, but she wasn't about to take any chances. She never did when it came to her patients, and right now, Chase Bracken was *her* patient. "A CT scan will tell me if you're fine or not. It's just a precaution," she added in the face of his deepening scowl.

"Whatever happened to the customer always being right?" he complained.

"You're not a customer, you're *my* patient. And if you haven't noticed, the reason I get to wear the white coat is because I'm the doctor."

He let out a stream of breath filled with frustration. "This is bull, you know."

She opened a drawer and retrieved the small hammer used to check reflexes. "I know it is, because you should know better," she scolded, wheeling her backless chair closer to the table. A quick tap just below the right knee showed a good reflex. "You're an athletic coach and trained in sports medicine. Chances are that you have a concussion, which I'm sure you already suspect as well. Considering you were unconsciousness for a few minutes, I'm going to play it safe, so just stop arguing with me."

She tapped his other knee with the plessor, satisfied with the reaction. "You of all people should know the dangers involved."

"I don't need a lecture," he groused.

She begged to differ, but kept her opinion to herself. "How many fingers am I holding up?"

He rolled his eyes, then winced. "Two," he said, sounding a little more cooperative as he slumped forward and massaged his left temple.

His irritability could easily be attributed to one monster of a headache, or a symptom of a concussion. She suspected a combination of the two since he'd been down-and-out for a good three or four minutes according to the coaches who brought him into the clinic. Dee wasn't pleased about their actions, either, because they, too, knew the dangers of moving an injured person. Regardless of her own irritation with the irresponsibility of Crawford and Harrison, in her medical books, Chase's symptoms spelled Grade 3 classic concussion.

She made a note in the chart. "When was your last tetanus shot?"

He straightened. "Shot? Why do I need a shot?"

Dee sighed. So much for *me big strong man, show no fear*. Mention a needle and they all became little boys again. "You don't," she said, and smiled. "But I do need the information for your medical history."

"Last year."

"What was it for?"

He looked away suddenly. "I stepped on a nail."

His tone held more than a fraction of annoyance at her

question. She was curious, but considering his increasingly foul mood and the pain from the headache he'd be suffering for a good twelve hours or more, she decided to lighten up and to not push him. At least for the time being.

"You shouldn't be so testy. I'm only trying to help you."

He let out a rough breath, then scrubbed his hand down his face, the stubble from his beard rasping against his fingers. "Patronizing little thing, aren't you?"

"Whatever works," she said and stood. Using her foot, she pushed the chair back under the counter before slipping into the corridor for a wheelchair. She stifled a grin at the horrific expression on his face when she brought the chair into the exam room.

He shook his head. "Uh-uh. No way, Doc."

"Don't think you're gonna walk over to the radiology clinic, Chase. You can either go quietly with me, or I'll be forced to call in reinforcements."

His gaze shot from her to the chair and back again. "What reinforcements?"

She gave him her sweetest, and most intentionally patronizing smile. "Lucille. You'll like her. She has a special way of handling uncooperative patients. If you don't believe me, just ask Principal Johnson next time you see him."

"Aw, come on, Dee. A wheelchair?"

"Me or Lucille." She glanced at her wristwatch and gave the chair two quick jerky rolls forward and backward. "Time's a wastin', Coach."

Chase issued a few, low murmured complaints, but allowed her to assist him off the table and into the chair. Aside from the initial flash of alarm that had sparked inside her when she'd seen Coaches Harrison and Crawford hauling him into the clinic, she'd maintained her cool. She'd instantly regained control of her emotions and had taken charge. With Dr. Claymore keeping Lucille busy seeing to the two other patients in the clinic, Dee had taken his vitals and performed the initial examination herself, her hands steady. So why the moment he slipped his arm over her shoulder to help support his weight as he eased into the wheelchair did her senses go haywire and pulse skyrocket?

One answer rose above the rest. She had a case of the hots for the new guy in town that no amount of professionalism could squelch.

Adjusting the footrests played hell with her cardiovascular system. She crouched low, flipped the footrests down, then wrapped her fingers around his partially bared calf. Like most of the coaching staff, he wore red twill gym shorts, a white polo shirt with a miniature red cougar embroidered on the front and white calf-length athletic socks with twin red stripes separated by a thin gold line at the top. Crouched as she was in front of him, she couldn't help the perfect view she had of the erection springing to life beneath the red twill.

Mesmerized, she reached for his other leg, her malfunctioning mind cataloging scents, textures, the essence of pure male. And more than a mild curiosity about what making love to Chase would be like. Fantastic. Intense. Heavenly.

"Dee." The soft, husky undertone in his voice drew her attention, first to his mouth, then to his eyes erupting with desire. A desire she understood all too well, and regardless of the uselessness of getting involved, it was a powerful enough force to have her seriously contemplating further exploration.

Carefully she lifted his foot onto the rest, uncertain

what to do next. Smooth her hands up his firmly toned and deeply tanned thighs? Or taste his mouth for another breath-stealing kiss? Or maybe she could...

A high-pitched squeal from an infant receiving a vaccination followed by the soothing, hushed tones of its mother, shattered the silence, along with the moment. Dee reentered reality with the force of a space capsule returning to the earth's atmosphere and crashing into the Atlantic.

Chase's hands gripped the padded arm of the wheelchair. "What was that?"

She stood, but regaining her composure was a struggle. "Reinforcements." The light tone she aimed for fell flat thanks to the tremor in her voice.

She stepped behind the chair and pushed, wishing she could push away the disturbing electrical force between them just as easily. Unfortunately she was too much of a realist to believe such a thing was even remotely possible.

# 5

CHASE SUFFERED THE humiliation of having Dee cart him out the back door of the clinic. Barely. By the time she wheeled him back across the paved walkway and up the handicap access ramp of the clinic offices, his mood hadn't improved by any stretch of the imagination.

Served his arrogant hide right, he silently groused, sitting alone in the exam room while Dee tended to other patients. He dodged bullets for a living. Just his luck, he'd been taken down by a pubescent teenager who'd done what no other had ever fully managed, although many had tried. He'd been knocked on his ass, out cold and left with a bump on his head he'd bet was no less the size of a honeydew melon.

His head hurt too much to figure out how to put a positive spin on his current situation, but he was sure if the intense pounding lessened by any degree, he'd figure a way to make it work in his favor and put his flagging investigation back on track. He'd been in Cole Harbor for less than two weeks and all he'd managed to do was make initial contact, tap her phone and put a lip lock on the subject. Despite how rotten he'd been feeling, his body had responded like a buck during rutting season the moment she'd laid her cool, smooth hands on his body.

No wonder he was in such a piss-ass mood. He didn't know which hurt worse, the pounding of his head or the semierection still straining against his gym shorts. If she touched him or looked at him again like she wanted to devour him with her lips, her tongue, her body, he'd end up embarrassing them both.

A soft knock followed by the swinging of the door drew his attention away from his own sorry state. The receptionist, a bleached blonde in serious need of a root job, wiggled her way into the exam room.

"Dr. Romine will be with you in just a minute," she said in a low pitched, and obviously practiced, tone. "Is there anything I can get for you, Coach?"

From the way her hungry brown eyes kept sliding over his body, he could just bet what she'd be willing to offer. "Some aspirin would be nice, ma'am." He was, after all, in the South where hospitality and formality still went hand in hand for the most part.

She sashayed closer, nearly choking him with the over-used, sticky-sweet scent of her cologne. Did she bathe in the stuff?

"Call me Netta," she purred. She inched closer, her breasts thrust forward, reminding him of a sad imitation of Jessica Rabbit. The black scooped-neck top clinging to her slightly plump middle didn't help matters. "Everyone does."

They called her more than that, he thought, watching as Netta threaded her fingers through her teased and tortured bleached hair. He'd been trained to pay attention to whatever was going on around him, which explained why getting flattened by a kid rubbed him in such a bad way. But he'd heard his fellow coaches' conversations and not so flattering innuendoes about Easy Engels, Cole Harbor's answer to the *femme fatale*.

She leaned toward him, a softly murmured, "Ooh," sliding from her painted mouth. "That's a nasty bump."

He pulled away before Netta and her push-up bra had

the chance to smother him. "That aspirin would be a big help," he said, hoping she'd take the hint and leave.

She straightened and pulled in a deep breath in what had to be a move she'd practiced in front of the mirror. Chase leaned as far as he dare over the side of wheelchair without toppling over.

"I'll have to check with Dr. Anal," she said, rolling her eyes in a show of exasperation. "She's pretty fanatical about her patients."

If his head hadn't been throbbing, he would have chuckled at Dee's narrow-eyed gaze as she stood in the doorway glaring at Easy Engels. "Thank you for getting the films, Netta," she said, her voice tight.

Netta and her push-up bra did that practiced deep breath sigh thing again. "No problem, Dr. Romine," Netta replied before moving toward the door.

Dee ignored Netta and the instantaneous flare of unaccustomed jealousy still sparking her temper at the sight of the other woman attempting to share her...her *charms* with Chase. She slapped the films onto the lighted panel with a little more force than necessary and snapped on the light.

"The good news is there's no swelling, however," she said, trailing her pencil along the film, "right here is some extremely minimal bleeding. Nothing too serious, but a cause for caution."

"Bleeding?"

She turned to look at Chase. The alarm darkening his eyes matched that in his voice. "I would like to recommend hospitalization."

He shook his head, which didn't surprise her. She'd expected a fight.

"Just an overnight stay for observation," she attempted to reassure him.

The determination in his eyes let her know she would indeed have a battle on her hands if she pushed the issue with him, something she wasn't sure she should do considering his already agitated state, but he couldn't be alone.

His dark brows pulled into a deep frown. "I'm not going to any hospital," he told her, his deep voice hard.

She leaned her backside against the counter and folded her arms, holding his chart close to her chest. "We have a room available here at the clinic where we can keep patients if necessary—"

"No."

"But our nurse is leaving for Charleston tonight, so—"

"Good. I'm going home."

He attempted to stand, only to sway on his feet. Dee dropped his chart and was by his side in an instant, right along with Netta. The sight of Netta's red claws on Chase's arm irritated the hell out of her.

"Be reasonable," she told him, battling to maintain her white coat persona and regain her stock control. She was *not* going to act like a jealous female. "You shouldn't be alone."

"I wouldn't mind staying with him, Dr. Romine," Netta offered.

Dee just bet she wouldn't mind, but Dee would. A lot. From the way the other woman had been practically crawling all over Chase and damn near thrusting her breasts in his face, he'd never get any rest. No doubt Netta had a plan or two on exactly how she could help Chase recover.

*Not on your life, sister,* she thought irritably.

"That's not necessary, Netta." Dee eased Chase back into the wheelchair. "Mr. Bracken is my neighbor. I can look in on him during the night. I'd feel more comfortable having a *medical* professional be responsible for his care.''

"Are you serious?" he asked.

"Yes, I am. The breakage of that tiny blood vessel isn't all that uncommon, especially when you consider the force with which your head hit the ground. You're already suffering with a headache and are in an agitated state. Since you refuse a hospital stay, you'll need someone to stay with you.''

Netta swept her tarantula eyes over Chase. "I *really* don't mind.''

"Thank you, Netta. That *will* be all," Dee said, her tone sharper than normal. The receptionist took the hint, but Dee still waited until she carted her buxom figure out of the exam room before turning her attention back to Chase.

"Are you sure I can't convince you to let me keep you here at the clinic? It wouldn't be the first time I've stayed the night with a patient. It's all part of the job.''

"I'd be more comfortable at home.''

"Chase, I really don't recommend it. I'd prefer to have you transported to Berkeley County Hospital, but at least here I have emergency equipment handy and—''

"Let the boy go home, girlie.''

Dee briefly closed her eyes at the sound of Doc Claymore's gravelly voice caused by too many years of smoking his favorite cigars. She slipped her hands in the pockets of her lab coat. "Chase, this is Dr. Claymore. Dr. Claymore, Chase Bracken, he's the—''

"I know who he is," Claymore rasped at her. He looked down at Chase, and graced him with a kind smile he reserved only for patients and Netta, causing the lines on his weathered face to deepen. "Cougars looking good this year, Coach?"

"Yes, sir. We have a pretty mean defense coming up from the junior varsity this year."

Claymore chuckled. "Must be. I hear it was Robbie Butler who took you down."

Chase winced. "Not quite the stellar beginning I'd hoped for, that's for sure."

"Dr. Claymore," she interrupted before he continued on with the tangent about the high-school football team. "The patient really would be better off here for the night, if not the hospital."

Claymore's eyebrows pulled together in the frown he saved for her and Lucille, making it look as if a bushy salt-and-pepper caterpillar were perched above his alert brown-eyed gaze. "He'd be better off at home where he can be comfortable in his own bed. Wouldn't you, son?"

"Definitely." Naturally Chase would agree with her cantankerous old nemesis.

"Dr. Claymore, in my professional opinion—"

"Bah on your professional opinion, girlie." Claymore plucked Chase's chart from the counter where she'd dropped it. "The patient will improve if he's able to rest. Who the hell can get any rest with all them dang-burned contraptions a wheezin' and a whirrin' while you're trying to sleep?"

"And nurses poking me with needles all night, too," Chase added.

*What was this? A gender conspiracy?*

"Exactly," Claymore agreed with a stiff nod of his nearly bald head. "Bet your fancy medical school didn't teach you that sometimes home is the best place for a patient to recover, did it?"

*No, in* this *century they teach doctors that hospitals are a good thing for the infirmed.*

Dee bit her lip to keep the sarcastic reply to herself.

"Take him home, put him to bed," he said to her. To Chase he asked, "You got one of them fancy cordless phones, Coach?"

At Chase's nod, Claymore turned his attention to the chart, his caterpillar brows wiggling as he wrote. "Put the phone near him and call him every couple of hours. If he don't answer, go see for yourself to make sure he's still kicking, but chances are he'll be sleeping peacefully."

"But—"

"Those are my orders, girlie. And this is still my clinic." He grinned at Chase and settled a freckled hand on Chase's wide shoulder. "Give them Cougars hell, Coach."

He left, muttering something derogatory about little girl doctors she didn't quite catch, escaping before Dee could issue another argument.

"Nice guy," Chase said, but Dee couldn't tell from the tone of his voice if he was complimenting Claymore or not.

"He has his moments." She pulled the CT films from the viewing screen and slipped them back inside the protective sleeve. "Where do you think you're going?" she asked as Chase slowly pushed himself out of the wheelchair.

"Home," he said, not looking at her. He patted the side pockets of his twill shorts. "After I figure out what happened to my truck keys."

She crossed her arms and gave him a stern look. "No driving. Besides, one of your players took it home for you. Jimmy Sanders, actually."

Chase muttered a curse. "It's his fault I'm in this mess."

"He felt pretty bad about what happened." She knew he'd refuse to use the wheelchair again, so she moved it aside. "So did Robbie Butler. They came to see you while you were in radiology, but I sent them home."

A wry grin twisted his lips. "No wonder my lights got knocked out."

Dee agreed. According to the coaches who brought Chase in, Robbie Butler was a six-foot-four-inch lean-muscled safety that hit like a freight train. After getting a look at the boy in question and factoring in the duration of Chase's unconsciousness, she suspected Sean Crawford's assessment wasn't too much of an exaggeration. "Robbie said the sun was in his eyes and he couldn't see you. He didn't know you weren't holding the blocking pad."

"Then why the hell did he follow through?" Chase rubbed carefully at the back of his neck.

Dee was instantly alert. "Are you having neck pain?"

"No. Two pains in the...backside that'll be running laps from now until the end of the season."

Dee relaxed slightly.

Chase straightened and turned toward the door. "Thanks for everything, Doc. I'm going home now."

She shot around him to block his path. It didn't matter that he could easily pick her up and set her aside if he wanted to. He was still her patient, even if it was Claymore's precious clinic. "Not by yourself you're not," she told him, crossing her arms while giving him her own determined look.

He stopped and braced his hand on the exam table. To steady himself, no doubt.

"You're dizzy, Chase. Sit down before you fall and make matters worse."

"Hey, Claymore said I could go home, and I'm going home." Determination made his eyes hard. "Straight home. I promise. And right to bed with the cordless phone so you can interrupt my beauty rest every two hours."

She stepped away from the door and moved next to him, lightly resting her hand on his forearm. He tensed, the muscle beneath his flesh tightening and moving beneath her fingers.

"I know what Claymore said," she told him, concentrating on his well-being and not the way her fingers flexed in response against the enticing warmth of his skin. "But there's no way I'm letting you go home alone."

"What are you going to do? Send Netta?" he returned sarcastically with an upward lift of his eyebrows.

"No." She pulled her hand from his arm and hoped she wasn't making a mistake. Ever since her parents died, or maybe even longer, she'd lived by the edicts of others, always taking the path of least resistance and keeping a low profile. Until it came to her patients. Then and only then did she do whatever was necessary. When it came to the care of her patients, she didn't hesitate to challenge others for what she thought was best, and had devised her own methods of getting around Claymore. Now, with Chase, it was no different, and as far as her cantankerous old nemesis would know, she'd done as he'd ordered and taken the patient home. With one minor variation.

At least that's what she told herself when she looked into Chase's eyes and saw the same need coursing through her reflected in his gaze.

"You're coming home with me for the night."

"ARE YOU ALWAYS THIS difficult?"

"Only when someone's pestering the hell out of me when I want to go to sleep."

Chase scowled and pushed away the coffee mug filled with half-eaten chicken soup. He didn't understand why she insisted on pouring the stuff down him when he'd told her half a dozen times already hunger was the least of his problems. He had the mother of all headaches and all he wanted to do was sleep it off.

"Eat," she insisted anyway, dipping the spoon in the oversize ceramic mug. "Then after I check your vitals, I'll give you something for the pain and let you sleep for a couple of hours."

As if that was possible, he thought grumpily taking the mug from her. He'd always known he had a stubborn streak a mile wide. Always a quick learner, he'd quickly discovered Dee's was two miles wider than his own. Forcing him into her too-short-for-him double bed and feeding him chicken soup as if he was a toddler breaking a molar was bad enough. But nothing was worse than the light floral scent of her cologne that clung to the silky sheets and played hell with his libido. Headache or no headache, he was in an uncomfortable state of semi-arousal.

It'd taken some fast talking, but he'd managed to convince her he wouldn't fall and break his neck on the stairs if she allowed him to go up to his apartment alone to shower and change. She'd agreed all right, but only granting him ten minutes to grab his gear. The shower, she'd informed him, was his choice. His place or hers, but she'd be there either way in case he had another dizzy spell.

There was no way he was letting the subject into his apartment to be left alone to look around while he showered. The surveillance room might be locked, but a locked door was as tempting as a freshly filled cookie jar to a toddler.

And that's exactly what she was to him, The Subject, he reminded himself, watching her pour a glass of iced water from the pitcher. She still wore those boxy scrubs that hid more than they showed, but he didn't miss the way the pale peach cotton outlined the gentle roundness of her hips or her curvy bottom. She wasn't supposed to be attractive or sensual or have his body responding to a whisper of a touch or the scent of her cologne. She was The Subject, to be studied, followed in hopes of leading him to his ultimate prey. She was *not* the woman who looked at him with need and desire flaring to life in her eyes. She was *not* the woman whose light, feathery touch made a pair of loose-fitting cotton sweats feel as uncomfortable as restrictive denim. And she most definitely was *not* the woman for him.

Even if he was looking, which he wasn't, she could never be the woman for him because once she found out what he was after, she'd hate him. So what if she made him smile? What did it matter that he'd tossed and turned for four days because every time he closed his eyes she haunted his dreams? So what if he wanted to pull her in his arms right now and kiss her senseless, mother of a headache be damned?

He was FBI. A G-man. Busting criminals was his job, and he took that job seriously. Dee Romine was a very dangerous kind of woman, he reminded himself. Dangerous to his mind and body, and dangerous to the assignment. Something he'd never compromise no matter how much he wanted the pretty lady doctor.

DEE SNAPPED AWAKE AT THE first beep of the alarm on her wristwatch. Without turning on the inexpensive brass lamp on the end table, she swung her feet to the floor and arched her back. She might not have made a choice in which job offer she'd be accepting, but she had definitely decided upon no more rental furniture after spending only half the night on the sofa. Brand-new or used she didn't care, she thought, slowly twisting and stretching to work out the kinks, just so long as there were no springs to press into her lower back.

Using the light of the full moon streaming into the living-room window, she padded into the bathroom and closed the door before turning on the light so as not to awaken Chase. She'd been checking on him every three hours and for the most part, she found him sleeping peacefully since she'd practically force-fed him chicken soup. There'd been no fever on each examination, and his pulse and blood pressure had been within normal limits. He'd been a little groggy after midnight, but basically coherent with no signs of confusion. Although optimistic for a full recovery with no adverse effects, her pragmatic nature indicated she remain cautious.

She finished up in the bathroom and washed her hands before heading into her bedroom to check on her patient. As she had prior to the last two examinations, she stopped in the doorway and stared in admiration.

He really was a glorious specimen, she thought. All thick sinew and firm muscle beneath skin that felt like satin to her fingertips. The light from the moon slashed across the hardwood floor and her double bed, illuminating his long tanned body. A man in her bed wasn't exactly unheard of, but she'd been so intent on her career and her concerns for her brother, affairs were too far and few between. She'd never been the one-night-stand type, although two forgettable liaisons during college added to her sorely lacking sexual history. For a brief time she'd believed her involvement with the chief E.R. resident at the medical center in Los Angeles could have been something more serious. However, when she'd applied for the government's program of providing her medical training in exchange for forgiving a large portion of her student loans, her transfer to Cole Harbor had been the end of that relationship.

Since arriving in South Carolina, the occasional dinner and a movie with Lucille comprised her social life. On a few occasions she'd gone to a jazz club in Charleston with a group of doctors from the E.R. at County. Otherwise, she practically lived the life of a nun.

She swept her gaze longingly over Chase. Sometime after she'd last checked his vitals, he'd removed the plain white T-shirt he'd worn to bed, leaving his glorious chest bare. There was no denying Chase bothered her. Not just physically, but emotionally as well. The awakening of her long dormant hormones got all tangled and twisted with feminine emotions and her goals. She didn't exactly believe happily-ever-after was waiting for her with Chase on the horizon, but involvement with him, no matter how much her pulse might skyrocket whenever they were within two feet of each other, could be dangerous. Mutual sexual attraction aside, there was an intensity about him that had her doing a lot of wondering about *what if.*

She didn't operate in *what if* mode. Solid plans, a goal for the future and a map on how to get there was her constant focus. Nor could she forget Jared's safety came first and foremost, provided her brother ever decided to do more than just call and hang up after ten seconds on the phone.

Once Jared was safe, then perhaps…maybe.

*Stop being so silly,* she chastised herself. She was leaving Cole Harbor in two months. Geography alone put an end to her ridiculous daydreaming.

With that reminder firmly resurrected, she quietly removed her medical bag from the top of the chest of drawers and moved to the side of the bed where she turned on the bedside lamp. Buttery soft incandescent light glowed in the room, causing her patient to stir. Mesmerized by the play of muscle as he moved his arm from over his head to drape it across his washboard-lean belly, she couldn't help herself—she stared and absently wondered how long it'd take for her to start drooling like one of Pavlov's dogs.

"Back again?" His deep voice, husky from sleep, stirred a fantasy or two about shared pillows and whispered words.

She lifted her gaze to his, no longer surprised by the desire simmering there. "How are you feeling?" she asked softly.

She understood something was happening between them. Whether or not a label existed allowing her to categorize and file the information away no longer mattered. Suddenly the only thing that made any sense was the heat flaring in Chase's eyes and the way his gaze swept over her, and the truth inside her acknowledging she wanted something more.

He propped the pillow behind him and lifted himself up to rest his back against the brass headboard. She breathed in his unique scent, musk mingled with man, all earthy and very real. And extremely alluring.

He slid his hand through his hair, pushing the dark wavy strands off his forehead. "Better. I think."

She reached into her bag for her stethoscope and blood pressure cuff, slipping it around his upper arm and securing the Velcro closure. "Why don't you let me be the judge.'' After positioning the stethoscope, she pumped air into the cuff, then slowly released the valve. ''A little higher than earlier, but that's not unusual since you've been lying down.''

She reached for his wrist to check his pulse, counting the beats within the required time. ''Slightly elevated,'' she said with a frown. ''Is your headache gone?''

''One of them.''

The whiskey-roughened quality of his voice snagged her attention. Her hand stilled in midwrap of her stethoscope as his meaning dawned and she looked up at him. His eyes were dark, a deep violet-blue, reminding her of the color of a midnight sky immediately after a summer storm rolls through, slashing the countryside with an intensity only Mother Nature could summon.

His hand gripped hers, gentle in touch, yet fierce in purpose. She knew what he was thinking. What he wanted. She'd been thinking and wanting the same thing since the moment she'd spied him through the lens of her front door two weeks ago. Oh, yes. They both wanted the same thing. Only now wasn't the right time. As his physician, his health was her first priority. His blood pressure and pulse were already elevated. As a woman, however, her body echoed identical physiological changes.

The smile she gave him held a wealth of regret. ''Chase, this isn't a good idea.''

His dark brows lifted, but he didn't let go of her hand. Instead his thumb smoothed a lazy pattern over her increasingly sensitive skin. ''Why not?''

The grin canting his lips was full of arrogance, causing her smile to widen slightly. ''Because you've suffered a head injury.''

*Because if I let myself, I'd get lost.*

"Trust me, Dee, I'm feeling pretty damned good right now."

She rolled her eyes. "What you're feeling is arousal."

So was she for that matter.

"Oh, I'm pretty sure that's a given, Doc."

Was he reading her mind, or offering up a wicked reply? It made no difference. Either one applied.

He let go of her fingers, trailing his hand up her arm to the back of her neck, gently easing her toward him.

The stethoscope slid from her fingers and clattered to the hardwood floor as he drew her closer.

*Breathe,* she reminded herself. *Just breathe.*

His hand moved to her throat, his thumb pressing lightly at her own lightning-speed pulse.

"From a medical standpoint," she managed to say around the sudden dryness in her throat, "the rise in blood pressure isn't good."

He tipped his head to the side, his thumb now caressing her jaw. "Hmm," he murmured. "But you feel *very* good."

"Your heart rate and breathing have already altered." She tried in vain to think of Chase as her patient, not the man she wanted to make love to. Her own heart rate was going at warp speed. Breathing took a concentrated effort, and her attention span was at an all-time low. Attention on anything but the man caressing her cheek.

"So have your muscles," she said in a soft whisper. "They're becoming tense."

Warm breath fanned her ear seconds before the featherlight touch of his tongue laved her lobe, causing a little muscle tension of her own.

"And hard," she added, turning her head slightly to give him better access.

"That's not all that's hard," he whispered huskily in her ear.

A shock wave of tingles raced throughout her body at the image of him hot, hard and heavy in her hand. And so ready to carry them to that place where physical pleasure reigned.

"Ease my tension, Doc. Think of it as strictly medicinal."

# 6

DEE COULD FIND ABSOLUTELY nothing medicinal about her own heightened state of arousal. Her nipples beaded, rasping against her light cotton T-shirt. Her breasts felt heavy and achy, needing his touch. Her thighs tingled. Her heart raced. Her panties were moist. Deep need tugged hard at her, demanding satisfaction.

She slipped her hand over his torso and around to his side, thinking to put some distance between them. That plan fell flat when his tongue lightly grazed her jaw before darting to her slightly parted lips.

"Kiss me, Dee."

The whispered invitation was hardly necessary because he dipped his head to press his mouth fully against hers.

Without a second's hesitation, she welcomed him, welcomed his tongue tangling with hers in a deep, hot, wet kiss engineered to increase her need.

Mission accomplished. He made her hotter than she ever thought herself capable of being with nothing more than a simple kiss. Although his kiss was far from simple. Demanding and erotic took top billing in her opinion. And what a sellout!

He pulled her against him, crushing her breasts to his chest, then easing her to her back atop the soft mattress. His body parted from hers and she moaned in protest, wrapping her arms around his neck, pulling him closer until she could feel the long, hard, glorious length of him pressed to her.

His bare chest to her covered breasts. She wanted more.

Her bare thighs to his covered ones, the slightly rough fabric from his lightweight sweat bottoms grazing against her skin. She *needed* more.

Shifting, she moved to cradle his hips between her thighs, then gently rocked her hips.

He groaned, and deepened the kiss. His hand slipped beneath her pale peach T-shirt to skim along her tummy, over her rib cage and finally, to cup her breast in his work-roughened palm. Her back arched as he gently rubbed her sensitized nipple between his fingers. She couldn't remember the last time she wanted like this, needed like this. She was wet with a need so fierce she feared she'd drown if he didn't pull her from the whirlpool of desire, or better yet, push her under where logic and reason washed away in the demanding reach, the desperate search for those erotic pleasurable sensations of ultimate fulfillment.

But, oh, what a way to go!

What was she doing? Chase was her patient, and her patients *always* came first. So what if he was turning her inside out with need and sending her into a tailspin? His health was supposed to be her top priority.

She set her hands firmly on his shoulders and pushed. He lifted his head, his eyes bright with curiosity and a passion so intense she wavered for a split second on her decision to put an end to this before they went too far.

"We can't do this," she told him, her fingers flexing against his warm skin. "It's wrong."

"It feels right to me." His voice was tight, his expression tighter. He didn't look angry, he looked... aroused.

"You're my patient. I could lose my license to practice medicine for something like this."

"Then you're fired," he said, removing her left hand from his shoulder.

"Think of your health," she argued, planting her hand squarely on his chest. "You're suffering from a concussion."

A deep frown creased his forehead. "That's not all I'm suffering from."

She bit back a smile. She understood exactly what he was referring to since equal frustration burned in her belly like a just-fired-and-formed steel ball.

"I'm sorry, Chase, but we can't. I can't because I won't risk your health."

He let out a sigh before he rolled away from her. On his back, he turned his head and asked, "What's the big deal?"

Lying beside him, she looked at him, then promptly pushed herself up to sit on the edge of the bed, hoping to break the illusion of intimacy. Her hands trembled, telling her she was more shaken than she realized, and knew in her heart that the big deal had more to do with her nearly losing control than his current state of recovery. Although the concussion did play a huge factor in her decision to put a stop to things before they passed that all-important stage of no return, it wasn't the *only* factor.

She leaned over to retrieve her stethoscope. "Those physiological changes I mentioned will only increase in intensity."

He propped himself up on his elbows. His firm, hard stomach tightened. The man didn't have an ounce of flab on him anywhere. "Isn't that the point?" he asked wickedly.

She wrapped up the blood pressure cuff and slipped it back inside her medical bag. "That's exactly the point."

"I get the feeling we're making two separate points here, Doc."

She stood, needing distance, and not just physically, either. She'd nearly lost control, and if the conditions were right and he wasn't recovering from an injury, that might not be such a bad thing. Except she didn't lose control. Ever.

"That increase in intensity—"

"Would feel damn good," he interrupted.

"That increase in intensity would elevate your blood pressure in addition to your pulse and heart rates. Your brain wave patterns may change and considering that small blood vessel I showed you—"

He flipped to his side and propped his head in his hand. "Why would they change?" That cocky, killer grin was back in place, making her insides melt just a tiny bit more.

"I think you know why," she told him, snapping her bag closed.

"You're the one with the medical degree," he said. "Why would my brain wave patterns change?"

She set her medical bag on the chest of drawers with a thump. "Orgasm," she said, wishing she'd ignored his question when his grin deepened.

"Orgasm, huh? Just one couldn't be all that bad. For starters."

God, the temptation was killing her. But her life was more complex than the plot of an off-off Broadway production. Her own physical wants and needs *had* to take a rear seat in the balcony section, no matter how splendid it would be fulfilling them with Chase. She had her career. She had the long-awaited and hard-earned job offers from three of the countries most prestigious medical facilities. Shortly, Cole Harbor, South Carolina, would become nothing more than an entry on her résumé.

And then there was Jared. The not knowing from one phone call or postcard to the next whether he was even alive. She didn't believe him guilty, but how could she in good conscience consider becoming involved with anyone? What kind of guy would understand her devotion to a brother accused of murder?

Chase was a temptation, and an enormous distraction she couldn't afford, no matter how provocative.

She folded her arms and faced him. "As intriguing as I might find your offer, it's still not a good idea."

Slowly he rose from the bed. She thought about bolting, but running wasn't her style. Or maybe it was, because that's exactly what she was doing now...running from something that could be wonderful and unique.

He stopped in front of her. Desperately she wanted to turn away before he touched her, before he forced her to look into his eyes and see the questions she'd never be able to answer, lurking in his gaze.

She looked anyway.

There were no questions, only a hefty dose of determination. Determination mingled with simmering desire.

Her pulse leaped.

"I think you find the prospect of making love a lot more than just intriguing. I'd bet my bad...a month's salary you want nothing more than to make love as much as I do right now."

He didn't touch her, and for that she was grateful. As unexpectedly raw as she was feeling, she just might say to hell with everything and leap right into his arms.

"Chase, I can't," she said, shaking her head regretfully. "I'll be leaving soon."

"You're not talking about leaving for the clinic in a few hours, are you?" Despite the gentleness of his voice, a slight frown eased into place.

"No. My contract with the government to practice where they need doctors in exchange for cutting a huge portion of my student loan debt expires soon. I'll be leaving Cole Harbor by the first of November."

"For where?"

"It's not important. I'm leaving and your home is here. Whether I go to New York or Boston isn't the issue. The issue is that in a matter of weeks, I'll be gone, and you'll be here. What's the point?"

He shrugged, the careless gesture belying the determination in his eyes. "The point is, we could enjoy the hell out of each other for as long as you are here."

An odd tingling of disappointment rippled through her. What had she expected? For him to say it didn't matter where she chose to relocate because he'd follow along behind her? More silly, ridiculous notions that played hardball with emotions she didn't want to feel. She couldn't afford to feel. She'd been taught *not* to feel.

She dropped her arms to her sides, shoring up her resolve and recalling lessons learned. "I've never been the one-night-stand type."

"Who's talking one-night stand?"

"What do you suggest we do? Have a hot and heavy affair, then you can help me load a few boxes into the back of a U-Haul trailer?"

She looked away and he let out a rough sigh. "There's nothing wrong with two people taking pleasure from each other, Dee. So long as they're both agreeable."

He placed his index finger beneath her chin forcing her

to look at his face, to see the heat, willing her to feel the desire. "Sweetheart, there's a hell of a lot of pleasure to be had between you and me. All you gotta do is say yes."

*ALL YOU GOTTA DO IS SAY YES.*

The phrase rang in Dee's mind again and again. She splashed cold water on her face. About the only thing the chilly water washed away were the final remnants of sleep, and did zilch as far as eliminating Chase's tempting taunt. A sexy invitation that had her tossing and turning on the uncomfortable sofa for the remainder of the night.

She buried her face in the fluffy hand towel then looked at herself in the bathroom mirror. Dark circles that no amount of makeup could camouflage underscored her eyes.

At dawn when she'd reexamined her patient; he'd thankfully kept his seductive ideas to himself. Considering her reaction to him, she suspected there was little doubt in his mind she was incredibly close to uttering that meaningful little word.

Yes.

Yes!

*Yes!*

By the time she showered and dressed, she heard Chase stirring in the other room. Other than a low-grade fever on her last exam, his vitals had remained within normal limits. She couldn't say the same for her own.

In the kitchen, she made him a very light breakfast. Her meager kitchen supplies didn't include a serving tray, so she set the lightly buttered toast on a dinner plate with a small dessert bowl of freshly sliced strawberries. A mug of weak tea and plate in hand, she headed into the bedroom.

Chase sat on the edge of the bed, gripping the side of the mattress. His head was bent and his shoulders slumped slightly forward.

"Are you feeling all right?" she asked, coming around to his side of the bed. Her heart beat a little faster when he looked up at her and offered her a weak grin.

"One killer of a headache." The pain echoed in his eyes as he rubbed the back of his neck. "I was going to get up, but I got a little dizzy. Is this normal?"

Concerned, she set the light breakfast on the bedside table before snagging her medical bag. "It's not *ab*normal," she said, reaching into her bag for the thin pen-light-type instrument. Placing her hand on his forehead, she gently urged his head back, then flashed the light in and out of his left eye, then followed the procedure again on the right.

"Reaction to light is normal." She crouched in front of him, retrieved her stethoscope and the blood pressure cuff and checked his vitals. Again, all within normal limits.

"Sit up straight, Chase," she told him, then stood to apply the stethoscope to his wide bare chest. She tried hard to ignore the play of muscle and sinew beneath his skin and failed. The beat of his heart, again normal, caused an odd stirring to flow through her at the comfort she felt listening to the strong steady rhythm.

No doubt about it, the man definitely rattled her cage.

She placed the instrument on his back, forcing her mind on his well-being. "Take a deep breath and let it out slowly," she instructed. Resting her knee on the bed, she leaned around him, and gasped.

An angry-looking reddish scar marred the perfection of his back. He stiffened as she slowly pressed her fingers to the puckered flesh, which was dangerously close to his kidney. There was only one thing she knew that would cause a scar like that, and seeing something like this on Chase sent a ripple of fear along her nerve endings. She'd spent enough hours tending far too many gunshot or stabbing victims from street gang confrontations to know a healed gunshot wound when she saw one. "How did you get this?"

"Get what?" he asked, his voice tense.

"This gunshot wound." She traced the tip of her finger over the healed wound. "My God, Chase. Another four to six millimeters and we might not be having this conversation."

"Oh, that." The careless shrug of his wide shoulders defied the tension bunching the hills and valleys of his back. "Nothing more exciting than a hunting accident."

"A recent one?" she asked, but estimated the scar to be somewhere around twelve to eighteen months old at most.

"Last year." An odd note changed the timbre of his voice as he pulled away from her probing fingers.

Despite her curiosity about the incident and Chase's reaction, she let the subject drop and continued her exam.

She put the items back into her medical bag before snapping it closed. "You're still running a slight fever. I'm going to order a minimum of another six hours bed rest then we'll see how you're doing. If you're still running a fever this afternoon, I'm going to have to admit you to the hospital."

He opened his mouth to protest, but she put her hand up to stop him. "No arguments," she told him in her sternest tone.

He reached up to massage his temple. "I don't have the energy to argue with you," he said.

"Well that's a first," she teased gently, then crouched

in front of him again, resting her hand on his knee. "I have to go to the clinic for a couple of hours. My appointment schedule is light today, so I should be home by noon. The phone is in the kitchen and the clinic is number one on speed dial. Call me if you need anything before I get back, or if your fever spikes. You know how to read a thermometer, don't you?"

His gaze swept her face, settling for too many seconds on her mouth before darting back to her eyes. "Yes, I do," he said, a trifle testy. "Don't you have an extension in the bedroom?"

She reopened her bag and searched for the standard mercury thermometer she kept. "'Fraid not. This place is so small I just never saw the need for one. Will you be all right?"

A lopsided grin curved his mouth. "I'll be fine, Dee. Go. Take care of your other patients."

"Only if you're absolutely certain. I can have Netta clear my morning schedule."

He started to shake his head, but winced. "I promise to call if I so much as sneeze, okay?"

From what she knew of Chase, she suspected he'd rather gut it out than admit he needed medical attention, but she did have patients and was already in danger of being late.

"Okay," she relented and eased back to stand.

She felt calm the instant he slipped his hand over her fingers still resting lightly on his knee. A sudden urge to kiss him flared to life and overwhelmed her. Not the bone-melting type, which she suspected any connection of lips between them would shift into with very little effort. No, the need to press her lips to his had more to do with one of those intimate I'll-see-you-later-honey types.

Easily the most dangerous kind.

Before she gave in to the siren call of her body, she pulled her hand from beneath his and stood. She gazed into his eyes, far from disappointed by the answering ignition of instantaneous desire firing the lilac depths, turning them a deep violet-blue.

"I'll be home soon," she said, once he settled back on the bed. Satisfied he'd be fine for a couple of hours, she hurried out of the bedroom before she gave in to the ridiculous notion.

She was going to have to do something about her constant reaction to him, she thought, snagging her keys and purse from the breakfast bar. Except the only singular resolution she managed to summon had her uttering that tiny little word repeatedly…yes.

Yes!

*Yes!*

# 7

CHASE WAITED A GOOD ten minutes after Dee left the apartment before moving off the bed and heading into the bathroom for a hot shower. He hadn't lied to her about the mother of all headaches, but the dizziness he'd claimed this morning had been pure fiction. He knew if she believed him the least bit unsteady, she'd insist he remain right where he was…in her bed and in her apartment. Alone.

The ploy had worked like a charm. He now had what he needed: an opportunity to search her apartment for any clue that could lead him to her brother.

He gave the faucet a hard twist and stepped beneath the spray without waiting for it to heat. Okay, so he had what he wanted. What he couldn't quite figure out was why he felt as low as the bad guys he captured? Bend-the-Rules Bracken didn't suffer from guilt—at least when it came to the job.

And watching Dee *was* a job.

The fact that he'd taken a shower *before* searching her apartment or reporting in to Pelham since he'd been unable to last night, said a lot about his state of mind where she was concerned. He filled out daily and weekly reports of her movements. He kept a log of all incoming and outgoing phone calls. She should be nothing more important to him than a means to an end, dammit, and he'd better start remembering why he was in Cole Harbor—

to locate information that would lead him to the apprehension of the Bureau's biggest embarrassment since the Hoover files went public.

The shower heated quickly and he turned his back to the spray, letting the steamy water sluice over his body to help work out the kinks from yesterday's mishap. While he was at it, he thought, he'd better stop thinking about how good she'd felt in his arms, too. No matter how much he'd been turned on by her, he should also forget all about those delightful fantasies that had robbed him of sleep, and especially about how responsive she'd been to his touch. And if he knew what was good for him, he'd definitely stop thinking about how much he'd wanted to kiss her again this morning, the pounding in his head be damned.

"Time to focus on the job, buddy," he muttered, turning to brace his hands on the blue ceramic tiles. Focus on what's important, such as bringing in Jared Romine.

He dropped his head forward under the water. He knew the contents of his predecessors' reports by heart. Not a single word in any of the miles of paper had warned him he risked being blindsided by Jared's little sister.

He'd known she was intelligent. Not only did she have a medical degree, but he knew it took a lot more than just better than average gray matter to make the grade in one of the country's top medical schools. But was she smart enough to know he wasn't whom he claimed to be, but had been sent to succeed where others had failed?

She would if he got careless again, and this morning he'd been damned careless.

He finished his shower, turned off the faucet and stepped from the stall, cursing himself for being caught off guard when she'd spied the result of an error in judgment. But when he'd felt the tentative touch of her fingertips, his brain had ceased to function. Other than the gentle caress filled with tenderness as she'd traced the wound, all he'd felt was a tightening in his chest that stole his breath and left him momentarily speechless.

He tucked the towel around his waist and dug out his shaving gear from the leather bag he'd carried downstairs last night during his ten-minute reprieve from Warden Romine. "Hunting accident," he muttered, dampening the brush before dipping it into the shaving mug to work up a lather. Even Louie "The Taxman" Lanksy, a "connected" accountant and tax attorney he'd busted for over thirty counts of fraud against the government two years ago could've come up with something a little more creative than a hunting accident.

Hell, Chase thought, covering his jaw with shaving cream. He could've come up with something better himself if his speech capabilities hadn't been rendered inoperative because of a woman's touch.

Ten minutes later, shaved and dressed in a pair of comfortable navy twill shorts and a plain white T-shirt, he still hadn't discovered the answer to the question of why Dee was having such an effect on him.

After checking to make certain the door was locked and drawing the blinds to discourage prying eyes and keep out the heat of the early-morning sun, he walked into the kitchen to call Pelham.

He'd thought it odd Dee only had one telephone in the place, her being a doctor and all, but her argument about the apartment being small had made perfect sense. He doubted she owned a cell phone, or else he suspected the overprotective lady would've left the number for him.

Dialing the Bureau's 800 number, he waited for the recorded message, then punched in the extension for Pelham's office. He'd probably catch hell for not reporting in for two days, but he hadn't been about to take a chance Dee might walk in on him when he'd gone upstairs for his things last night.

Pelham wouldn't answer until after the fourth ring, and only if his secretary didn't pick up first. Chase easily pictured the senior agent, who hadn't been out from behind a desk in nearly ten years, grumbling because he had to answer his own phone. In Chase's opinion, Pelham was a pencil pusher for a reason and, like most of his fellow agents, often speculated on exactly how the officious tight-ass little prick had even made it through Quantico, let alone survive five years in the field without someone putting a bullet in the back of his arrogant head.

Right on cue, Pelham picked up the phone and barked an unwelcome "Yeah" into the receiver.

Chase propped his backside against the counter, keeping his eyes on the front door. "Bracken, here."

"It's about goddamn time you reported," Pelham's voice echoed through the phone lines. "What the hell are you doing out there? You're supposed to be on twenty-four-hour report. That was nearly two days ago. Are you trying to piss me off?"

Chase said nothing because if he opened his mouth, he'd probably tick the guy off anyway.

"You know, if I were you, this is one case where I wouldn't be playing it loose and fast, Bracken. You don't have enough rope this time around."

*Yeah? Well you're not me.* The harsh reply hovered on Chase's lips, but he went against the grain of his personality and kept his mouth shut for a change. Pelham was steamed enough at him and just looking for an excuse to strip him of his career, so he played it smart for one simple reason—he'd be damned if he'd give Pelham the excuse he was looking for now when he'd finally managed to gain some real ground in the case.

In the case, or with Dee?

"I'm making progress," he told his superior. "I've gained access to the subject's residence. I'm here now."

"Well I'll be damned, Bracken," Pelham said without an ounce of admiration. "What did you have to do to accomplish what no other agent has managed to for the last three years? Resort to breaking and entering?"

Chase stifled a ripe curse. "A little accident on the practice field," he admitted reluctantly. "Nothing serious, but enough to have Dr. Romine concerned about me staying alone last night."

"Anything yet that'll lead us to Romine?"

"I plan to spend the morning searching her apartment." Why the idea of doing his job bothered him now, escaped him. Or maybe it was the answer that had him more than a little worried.

"You'd better come up with something solid, Bracken. The assistant director's been on my ass for a week already. She's getting ready to issue the order to pull you out of there, so you'd damn well better find something, and make it fast."

"Wait a minute," Chase snapped irritably. "That wasn't the deal, Pelham. No one said a thing about a time line on this case. Considering I've gotten twice as far as the rest of the yahoos you and the A.D. have sent out since Romine went under, you should be congratulating me."

"Congratulating you?" Pelham laughed. "You're lucky you're still on the payroll after the last stunt you pulled."

"I was cleared," Chase argued.

"Those idiots in I.A. couldn't investigate their way out

of a paper bag with a hole in it and you know it. The only reason you were cleared is because you capped three of the filthy scum. How would it look if the FBI canned the agent who took down the main artery of a group of terrorist bombers ripping apart school yards? Not exactly the kind of headlines the director likes to read with his morning coffee and prune Danish.''

"I did my job," Chase said, struggling to keep his cool. Wasn't the job always the bottom line? Protect and serve the public, and while you're at it, don't forget to bring the bastards down using whatever means necessary to get the job done.

"Your job wasn't good enough," Pelham shot at him in a heated tone. "Not when the body count exceeds the number of wanted suspects."

*Not good enough.*

Chase tried to block the childhood memories from ripping through his mind, but they refused to go back to the place he'd stored them years ago. "I wasn't the only agent on site," he argued. "According to the ballistics report, there's no way to know who fired that shot."

"Says you," Pelham continued, his voice rising.

"Says Internal Affairs."

"If the media hadn't gotten you on tape blowing away the bastard with the bomb strapped to his chest, you'd be issuing parking tickets by now. When are you going to face the truth, Bracken? You're a screwup."

*You're trash, and you'll always be trash.*

Lightning-hot anger seeped through Chase's veins. "The hell I am," he countered coldly. The Feds had been after Max Gleason and his band of terrorists for months when an unexpected lead had placed them at an elementary school. He'd done his job. He'd saved a schoolyard full of kids. Except he'd been called on the carpet by his division pricks because the situation had exploded into open gunfire, killing two teachers and a custodial worker. It didn't matter that he'd been the one to take out Gleason and two of his henchmen. He'd been the agent in charge and around long enough to know the shit always rolled downhill.

*You'll never be accepted here.*

"You made a mess of the last one, and I know even you aren't stupid enough to deny it. The Bureau doesn't like to clean up messes left by their agents. You know how it works. Screw up again, and you're out, I don't give a good goddamn how many friggin' headlines you make. You got that?"

*Not good enough.*

"If there's something in her apartment, Pelham, I'll find it."

"You don't have a choice this time. A week, Bracken. Seven days to bring me a solid lead on Romine's location."

"You know, Pelham," Chase taunted. "If I didn't know you better, I'd say that sounds a lot like a threat."

Pelham swore vividly. "No. It's not a threat. It's a friggin' promise," he shouted before severing the connection.

Chase carefully hung up the phone, his own temper simmering dangerously. Maybe it was a good thing he'd been sent to Cole Harbor, because if he was anywhere near New York right now, he had little doubt Pelham would be picking his skinny ass up off his fancy Persian rug.

CHASE STARTED WITH THE single large drawer of the nightstand where the breakfast Dee had thoughtfully made for him sat waiting stone-cold. Shutting off the old memories wasn't as easy as he'd hoped, so he shoved them aside until later, focusing his attention on the job.

"Screw Pelham," he muttered, slowly pulling the drawer completely out of the nightstand. Lifting it carefully so as to avoid stirring the contents, he checked the underside for any items taped to the bottom. Nothing. The back and sides were clean, as well.

He set the drawer on the bed then searched inside the shell of the nightstand, followed by a thorough check of the exterior. Again, nothing unusual.

So what if they pulled him off the case? They'd only send in another agent to accomplish what they'd deem he failed to do. The idea made his stomach clench in a way that could only be considered jealously, and not the professional kind, either. The idea of another man, an agent he might even know, touching Dee the way he'd touched her, kissing her and experiencing her open response was enough to make him seriously consider strangling Pelham himself.

Turning his attention to the bed, and away from the more dangerous line of his thoughts, he stared at the contents of the drawer, hesitating. Guilt pricked his conscience as he carefully scanned each of the orderly arranged items inside the drawer.

"Subject, buddy," he murmured. "She's The Subject."

He let out a slow breath and continued to peruse the drawer's contents, noting nothing out of the ordinary. A travel-size box of bargain tissues was tucked beside a small crystal bowl holding a ring with a bluish-green stone he was pretty sure held little or no monetary value whatsoever. A couple pairs of plain stud-type earrings he suspected were genuine pearls and emeralds, and a pair of small gold hoop earrings clasped together. A few over-the-counter pharmaceuticals were lined against the inside wall of the drawer along with an unopened bottle of some women's blend multivitamins. Laying beside the pain and cold-symptom relievers, rested a novel with a burning wedding gown on the cover, her place held with a pink tasseled bookmark.

Typical, everyday items that any woman would have in her bedside table. Well, he did classify Dee's lack of jewelry as atypical. In his experience, jewelry, regardless of whether they were the real thing or costume pieces, were more often than not ridiculously plentiful.

He eased the drawer off the bed to slip it back inside the nightstand when he spied something beneath the tissues.

He frowned and set the drawer back on the bed, carefully removing the tissue box and setting it aside. Upon closer inspection, he counted four of those photograph-size calendars his foster mother used to keep track of just about everything from dental appointments to her bridge club meetings, held together by a thick green rubber band. The fact that Dee saved old calendars wasn't all that unusual. A lot of people did for a variety of reasons. His mom kept a square plastic container in the basement filled with them, dating back for a heck of a lot longer than the IRS's recommended period of record keeping.

But it sure was one hell of a coincidence Dee had saved four calendars covering the thirty-five month period her brother had been underground.

He picked up the calendars and eased off the rubber band. Sure enough, the first one dated back to the year Romine had become a fugitive. October, the month he'd first disappeared, hadn't so much as an eraser mark on any of the thirty-one squares. He scanned through November and nearly flipped the page to reveal December when he caught sight of an extremely small red mark next to the twenty-first of the month. He methodically examined the mark, determining the red ink was not a printing imperfection, but a definitely minuscule check mark.

Jared Romine's first contact with his baby sister had been November twenty-first. He knew because of the agent report he'd studied about the botched trace performed by a rookie in communications.

This was no coincidence. He'd bet his badge on it.

Chase had his first real connection that Romine had been in contact with his sister. And from the three remaining calendars still clutched in his hand, he had confirmation that the bastard had been contacting her all along.

He checked the clock. Dee had only been at the clinic for an hour. Worst case scenario, he'd have another hour to continue his search. He sat on the edge of the bed and continued to examine the calendars, filing away mental notes to write later in his report to Pelham.

The contacts occurred every six to ten weeks. One mark, two days past twelve weeks, had a smiley face. The marks varied, from tiny squares to equally minute check marks. Occasionally a page with a contact mark had some sort of initialed code printed at the top directly beneath the month. The codes ranged from *C* to *H,* a couple of *T*s and an *LS.*

He flipped open the most current calendar then glanced at the clock, noting over thirty minutes had passed since the last time he'd checked. The first notation, another small square, was marked on the last day of February. Seven weeks later, a check mark, followed by another in ten weeks with a *C* code noted beneath the month of June.

July, as he suspected, was clear. He flipped to August and swore. Twelve days ago, her brother had made contact with her, as evidenced by a red check mark. Printed neatly below the feminine type set of the August heading were two new letters, *FH.*

He counted back twelve days. The day he'd first made contact with Dee and had bugged her phone.

Impossible. If Romine attempted to reach Dee by telephone, he'd have known about it. Prior to setting up the bug at ten in the morning, her apartment had been absolutely silent. That check mark *had* to be a code for some other form of contact.

He flipped back through the previous calendars. Checks and squares, six to twelve weeks apart. And nothing to tell him the meaning behind those marks.

He opened the first calendar, the one with the initial contact notation. ''A check,'' he said, frowning. A check that coincided with a botched trace.

He continued through the next two calendars. The reports indicated a useless trace and something else he'd momentarily forgotten about...her mail! For weeks agents had been staked out at the postal station examining each piece of mail addressed to Destiny Romine. Provided his malfunctioning brain had returned to its standard operating mode, he recalled an entry in the reports recording a blank postcard.

The date escaped him, but he'd verify that little detail soon enough.

Suddenly the meaning behind the codes sprang to life. The checks applied to telephone contact, while a square indicated contact by mail.

According to Dee's record keeping, Jared Romine had indeed made telephone contact twelve days ago. Which meant he wouldn't be contacting his sister again for another six to twelve weeks. Somehow, he'd missed that call, but he had a bad feeling the contact hadn't been made in Dee's apartment, but at another location. Since she didn't own a cell phone, the only other place she'd been that day had been the clinic.

Somehow he'd find out for certain. In the meantime, he planned to make damn sure he didn't miss another call.

He needed to make a list of Dee's calendar notations, but he couldn't risk being discovered. After making sure they were in the order she'd left them, he returned the calendars to their spot beneath the tissue box, then carefully lifted the drawer to slide it back inside the nightstand.

He wasn't sure what happened first, whether it'd been the rattle of keys in the door, or his smacking the drawer against the nightstand with enough force to tip over the mug of cold tea, but he dumped the contents of the drawer on the hardwood floor a breath of a second before Dee walked through the bedroom door.

# 8

"WHAT ARE YOU DOING?"

The coldness in Dee's voice didn't surprise Chase in the least, nor did the frostiness of her gaze as she looked at him from across the bedroom. Thanks to the long line of agents constantly disrupting and interfering in her life in one form or another, it didn't take a degree in rocket science to understand her lack of trust stemmed more from habit than anything else.

If he'd been the one on the receiving end of all that prying and snooping, all the surveillance and tailing, he'd probably be equally suspicious, so he really couldn't blame her. The fact that she'd left him alone in her apartment while she'd gone to the clinic was so far out of the norm for her, but she was a physician who obviously cared more for her patient's welfare than her own comfort level. Bastard that he was, he'd repaid her by using what little trust she'd granted to his advantage.

He'd only been doing his job, but that didn't explain the guilt ripping apart his gut. For the first time since joining the Bureau, he wasn't so sure he loved his job.

He offered her what he hoped was a sheepish grin he was far from feeling. "I had a little accident," he said, scooping up the tissue box. He pulled several from the box and laid them over the spilled tea before it dripped off the nightstand and onto the hardwood flooring or the peach comforter on the bed.

"Obviously," she said with little warmth.

"I, uh, knocked over the mug and was looking for something to wipe up the mess. The drawer was a lot shorter than I expected," he lied as he stooped to pick up the contents he'd dumped. "I didn't think you'd appreciate me using your sheets."

He heard her sigh and cross the room as he reached under the bed for a runaway bottle of antacids. Bottle in hand, he straightened, relieved beyond reason that the chill he'd detected upon her untimely arrival had dissipated.

"I'm really sorry about this," he said, and for the first time since opening his mouth, he spoke the truth.

He *was* sorry. Sorry he'd been the one assigned to gain information from her, because if she was anyone but Jared Romine's little sister, Dee could easily get under his skin. Hell, she'd already taken up permanent residence in his mind, and not all of it had to do with the case.

"Did you have another dizzy spell?" she asked, taking the bottle from him and setting it on the bed. She efficiently mopped up the last of the tea, cleaned out the inside of the drawer and had it back inside the nightstand before he had a chance to retrieve more of the spilled items.

His fingers brushed against the edge of the bound calendars. For the span of a heartbeat, his hand stilled as he weighed his options.

He let out a sigh. "No, just clumsy is all," he said, then scooped up the calendars and handed them to her.

Within what seemed like an instant, she had everything returned to its proper place and tidied up without a shred of evidence of the mess he'd made.

She balanced the mug on the plate and turned back to

face him. "You showered," she said, skimming her gaze along his body. Appreciation darkened her eyes to a deep shade of green.

The answering call of awakening desire slowly uncoiled in his belly and headed in a southerly direction. "I thought it'd help get rid of my headache." Not exactly a lie this time. The heat from the water had helped to ease some of the muscle soreness and tension he'd been feeling, and by extension, the pounding in his head had waned to the occasional dull throb.

A frown tugged her thinly arched sable eyebrows. "Are you sure you weren't dizzy again?"

He grinned. He liked it that she was concerned, and he'd bet his badge it wasn't one hundred percent medically related, either. "Absolutely sure."

"Pain?" she asked, heading toward the door.

He followed her into the living room, then pulled out a bar stool to sit at the counter. "Practically gone. Hey, aren't you home a little early?" Any earlier and she'd have busted him cold.

She scraped the uneaten food into the garbage can. "Netta actually did something for a change and pulled off a minor miracle to free me up a couple of hours early."

She turned back to face him. The last vestiges of distrust erased from her eyes as a slow smile eased across her very kissable mouth.

He folded his arms across his chest and leaned against the woven rattan back of the stool. "A little anxious to get home, don't you think, Doc?" he teased.

The look she gave him was full of spunk, igniting a fire in her eyes that had him consciously reigning in a pretty erotic fantasy about how her eyes would look filled with passion.

"I had an idea," she said, "but only if you're feeling up to it."

His grin widened and she laughed. Now that was a sound he could get used to hearing. A lot.

Those intriguing eyes of hers rolled skyward. "It's *not* what you're thinking."

He shot her a look of feigned innocence he'd never be fully qualified to impersonate on a regular basis. "What am I thinking?"

"Just never mind."

He chuckled and leaned forward, resting his forearms on the counter. "So what's this idea?"

She propped her hip against the counter. "Since your doctor has ordered you off work until Monday," she said with a grin, "and since you do seem to be feeling better, I thought maybe you'd like to take a drive up the coast to Myrtle Beach for a couple of hours. Nothing too strenuous, just a drive, maybe some lunch..."

"See some local color? A few sights?"

She nodded. "But only if you're up to it."

The prospect of spending the day with Dee held more temptation than even he could resist. He shrugged as casually as possible. "Beats the pants off of sitting in my apartment for three days with only the remote control for company. But I'm driving."

She shook her head. "Not a chance, pal. Doctor's orders."

"I won't tell if you don't."

"Very funny. Sorry, Chase. No driving for at least another two days."

"I like the idea of getting out of here for a while, but there's no way I'm getting back inside that tin can you call a car. After last night, my knees still hurt from being crushed against the glove compartment. We'll take my truck.''

Her grin faded and her hands landed on her hips. "It's unsafe for you to drive. You could have—"

"You can drive, Dee," he said patiently, quickly putting an end to what he'd learned by now would be another one of her well-meaning, albeit unnecessary, lectures. "But we're taking my truck. Okay?"

She regarded him for a few seconds, then finally nodded in agreement. "Let me change," she said, then disappeared into the bedroom.

He tried to tell himself he'd agreed to her suggestion in hopes of gaining a little more of her trust. Who knew where it could lead them if she relaxed a little and let her guard down. Maybe she'd even start talking about herself for a change instead of gently steering his questions away from her and back to himself as she'd done the night she'd fed him dinner.

A slow grin spread across his face. If Dee opened up to him, the possibilities were endless. Possibilities that had nada to do with the boxes of files upstairs in his apartment, and something a lot more interesting. And satisfying.

CHASE NEARLY GROANED. Loudly. The sight of Dee's very feminine backside as she bent over to peer into the glass case filled with antique spray perfume bottles was almost more than he could bear. On the other hand, dragging his gaze higher to safer territory just didn't have quite the same appeal.

If relaxation was on her agenda, he'd yet to find it. Not that they'd done anything to exert energy, but watching her all afternoon was almost more than his increasing libido could handle. Not that he was complaining, he thought, taking a step back to better observe the delightful image in front of him. With every shop they browsed through, he learned a little more about Dee. The more he learned, the more he liked.

Not a word of it would make it into his next report to Pelham, either. Pelham didn't need to know Dee had a thing for classic perfume bottles, or that the feel of a soft, fluffy teddy bear made her smile so bright his heart twisted behind his ribs.

No justifiable reason existed, in his opinion, as to why he should enlighten his superior that when they'd entered a candy shop specializing in saltwater taffy, how absolutely adorable Dee had looked when she'd stepped through the door and had taken a deep breath. She'd laughed, telling him while she couldn't afford the calories, there certainly was no harm in cataloging the rich, sweet aroma of freshly pulled taffy.

She let out a sigh and straightened. "Too rich for my blood," she said before strolling over to a display of Coca-Cola memorabilia.

"How rich is too rich?" he asked, coming up beside her and breathing in her intoxicating floral scent. According to the case files, her parents had left their children with a mountain of debt the estate barely covered. Once the probate had been settled, Jared and Dee had been left with maybe enough cash to cover only the most basic of living expenses for six months to a year. A fact he found all too intriguing considering her father had been a world-renowned neurosurgeon and her mother one of those theoretical rather than practicing psychologists. A papered doctor who played on the lecture circuit to promote her latest psychobabble book. All that money had gone somewhere, but where had been everybody's guess.

She picked up an oval metal tray with an image of a

flapper holding a frosted glass of soda, flipped it over to get a look at the price, then set it back on the display. "A couple of hundred dollars too rich," she said, moving to a table with lace handkerchiefs. "The best place to find old perfume bottles is at garage sales and estate auctions. Sometimes you can really come upon a treasure for next to nothing."

An old, painted wood hutch filled with teapots caught his attention and he walked toward them. His mom, an avid collector, would probably love one of the delicate bone-china ones displayed. "And here I thought all you doctors were megarich."

Dee laughed and joined him near the china teapots. "You've been watching too much television, Coach. We're not all John Carters you know. Some of us actually have to work for a living."

He didn't have a clue to whom she was referring, so he just shrugged. Careful not to disturb the others, he lifted a bone-china pot from the top shelf. "What do you think?"

"Very pretty," she said, her voice tinged with laughter. "The yellow rosebuds are a nice touch. Collector?"

"No," he said, admiring the way her eyes danced with humor. God, he liked her like this, full of humor and sass with a smile so sweet he ached just looking at her. Thoughts about kissing that mouth were even more painful. "But my mom is and her birthday's next month."

Her gaze softened as she looked up at him. "Chase, that's so sweet."

Thinking about the way his insides twisted when she looked at him with that soft, dreamy expression was dangerous. More than dangerous. Downright suicidal. He'd never had trouble keeping his mind on the job. Never once when he'd gone undercover had he questioned his motives for doing so. His methods occasionally left a little to be desired, but he got results and the Bureau liked results. Until now, he'd never actually considered that for once, the Bureau could be dead wrong.

Unfortunately not about Jared Romine. The evidence against the agent was more than circumstantial. They had a weapon and two bodies, even if they didn't have a solid motive. Her brother contacted her periodically. Chase had known that going in, but had finally seen the proof himself just that morning. But his gut was telling him Dee Romine wasn't any more certain of her brother's whereabouts than the hordes of archeologists and religious fanatics attempting to locate Noah's Arc.

"Yeah, well," he said, carrying the teapot toward the register, "Mom's a pretty neat lady and she likes them."

Dee moved away to admire more trinkets while he asked the clerk to wrap the birthday gift for shipping. He pulled his wallet from his hip pocket, handed the clerk his credit card, then leaned against the counter to watch Dee.

So if she couldn't tell him where her brother was hiding, he wondered, how exactly was he supposed to find out for himself? He could count the hours he'd been in her company, and already she was getting to him in ways that had him doubting his reason for even being in South Carolina.

Maybe she couldn't tell him *where* her brother was hiding, but no one knew Jared like his little sister. She knew his history, his habits, his deep down and personal likes and dislikes. There were thousands of minute details that never made it into the employment records, and the Bureau performed one of the most thorough and toughest background checks of the government agencies. Some small particular about the man they'd been hunting had been overlooked. Of that one fact, Chase was dead certain.

She walked toward him, stopping to scan a shelf filled with collectible teddy bear figurines. He let out a slow stream of breath. He didn't have much time. A week was all they were allowing him. A week to get answers that could best be garnered if Dee trusted him as she hadn't allowed herself to trust another human being since the first agents flashed their IDs at her. The problem, however, was not only how to get her to trust him, but how to get her to trust him in such a short span of time.

One answer rose above the rest, and he hated himself for it. Emotional intimacy. The special bond between a man and woman that dictated complete and total honesty in a relationship. The type of intimacy gained through closeness.

A smile brighter than the midafternoon sun lit her face when she plucked a teddy bear figurine from the shelf. Intimacy, he thought again as she held up a bear dressed in medical scrubs, holding a black bag in his paw and a stethoscope looped around his neck.

*Intimacy,* he silently repeated as he returned her smile. Like the kind they were already beginning to establish.

He'd bent the rules before, but never had the idea left him feeling cold and empty inside. He could do it again, even if it meant sharing more of himself than he'd like.

The idea had his chest tightening enough to make him draw a few slow deep breaths. The imaginary weights balanced on his solar plexus and cutting off his oxygen supply had nothing to do with his own dark secrets he might reveal to her if it meant accomplishing his ultimate goal. The clenching pain he felt was caused by something much more distasteful—the very real possibility that Destiny Romine might never trust another human being again by the time he was through.

"LET ME GUESS. You became a doctor because of some predisposed childhood dream to save the world one patient at a time."

Dee traced the rim of her iced tea glass with the tip of her index finger. "Not exactly," she told Chase. "Although I think the predisposition part of it is probably right."

He leaned back and rested his arm over the back of the red vinyl booth of the trendy '50s-style drive-in, complete with roller-skating carhops serving the few customers willing to brave the excess humidity pushing the heat index near the triple digits.

Because of the rising heat and humidity, after a couple hours of browsing through the various antique stores, specialty boutiques and gift shops around Myrtle Beach, she'd declared an end to Chase's activities for the day and they'd started back toward Cole Harbor. He'd spied the diner from the highway and suggested they stop for a late lunch. A deluxe cheeseburger and her second glass of iced tea later, Dee had to admit he'd made an excellent proposition. One she could readily accept, too, although his other more interesting and sexy offer hadn't been more than a thought away all afternoon.

"Meaning?" he prompted over Fats Domino's piano playing, which was a couple of decibels too loud on the jukebox.

"Meaning the medical gene was a gift from my father," she admitted.

"Following in Daddy's footsteps, eh?" he teased, tossing back the same words she'd given him when she'd learned his foster parents had both been teachers.

She grinned, liking the way his eyes swept over her face as if he was memorizing each feature for later retrieval. A wee bit arrogant on her part, but she liked the idea anyway.

"Not exactly," she said. "The Romines really do carry a medical gene, though. David Romine was my father."

Chase shrugged and gave her a blank look, which surprised her to some small degree. Her father was well-known in the medical profession, but her mother had gained popularity with several self-help books and as a regular on just about any television or radio talk show where the guests aired their dirty linen in public.

Dee traced her finger down a line of condensation on the glass. "Dear old Dad was one of the top ten neurosurgeons in the country. As for my mother, ever read any of those self-help books on the market?"

"Can't say that I have," he said, then looked away before reaching for his soda.

"She authored around a half dozen of them."

"She's a writer?"

She reached for an abandoned French fry on his plate and dragged it through a remnant of ketchup. "In a manner of speaking. Today as our guest, we have psychologist, Dr. Ellen Douglas-Romine," she said, using the ketchup-tipped fry like a microphone. "Her bestselling book, *Only You Can Make It Happen,* is surpassed in popularity only by her most revealing look into the inner child, *How To Leave Your Baggage Behind.*" She popped the French fry into her mouth and grinned.

He chuckled at her silly Jerry Springer imitation as she'd intended. "That's your mother?"

"Was my mother," she said, sobering. "Both of my parents were killed when I was...younger." Better to remain somewhat evasive than admit she'd been a minor at the time of her parents' untimely death. A fact that would lead to obvious additional questions. Ones she couldn't answer.

"I'm sorry."

"It was a long time ago," she said quietly. She looked away, out the window as a carhop whizzed by on roller skates, a bright-green plastic tray balanced above her head.

A very long time ago, she thought with a stab of something she could only call bitterness. She still felt it, even after all this time. The truth shook her on a deeper level than she'd believed possible after nearly twelve years. It wasn't just that her parents had died, which had been traumatic enough. The resentment she still harbored had more to do with their selfishness.

Neither of them had the foresight to see to it that she and Jared would be taken care of if something ever happened to them. Poor investments, expensive vacation getaways, entertaining, trips to Europe and a partnership agreement that left her father's share of his successful medical practice in the hands of the surviving partners, without so much as a provision for his family's care in the event of his death. The circumstances of her mother's residuals were no better. In the beginning, they'd receive the occasional royalty payment from Ellen's publisher, after her publicist, agent and other industry professionals responsible for launching her mother's career were paid. What little funds remained had helped to supplement Jared's income, but by the time she'd gone off to college, those had dried up, as well.

"What made you decide on family practice?" he asked, pulling her away from old wasteful thoughts.

*Because I wanted to be nothing like my parents,* she

thought honestly, shifting her attention back to Chase. Because medicine, *real* medicine, and saving lives held more importance to her than fame and notoriety.

"The family practice thing is just until I finish my current contract," she said. "Actually my specialty's emergency medicine."

His brows lifted as he looked at her. "Really?"

"Why are you so surprised?" she asked, then took a sip of her tea. "I thought you knew I worked in the E.R. at County. Which I never mentioned to you, by the way."

"You know how small towns are, but I just assumed your work there was part of that contract you mentioned. As your patient," he said, giving her a look conveying his opinion on *that* subject, "I've been on the receiving end of your medical care. You just don't strike me as the type."

It was her turn to lift her eyebrows in surprise. "And what type is that?"

He leaned forward, resting his forearms on the white-speckled tabletop. "Isn't emergency medicine...I don't know? A little anonymous?"

"You mean because my folks were such big shots in the medical community?"

He shook his head. "No," he clarified, pushing his soda glass away. "What I mean is you could treat any number of patients for weeks and never see the same face twice. How do you get to know the patient that way?"

"You don't. Not really. Depending on what's happening in the E.R. at any given moment, it can really be a treat 'em and street 'em mentality. I've even done it myself a few times, but it's been out of necessity."

"That's a little cold, isn't it?"

"Don't get me wrong," she added, signaling for the waitress to bring the check. "You do treat the patient, not just the disease, although some doctors do tend to forget that trauma victims aren't just a procedure waiting to be performed. But, in their defense, when you've got a school bus full of high-school kids on their way home from a basketball game plowed by a drunk driver going the wrong way on the freeway, or a shoot-out between rival street gangs and there are only four doctors on the graveyard shift with a dozen or more patients between them, taking the time to get personal with a patient could cost someone else their life.

"No matter how much a life-and-death situation might jump-start the endorphins and fire up the adrenaline, the bottom line for me is always to save that life. Plus, with the variety of illnesses and traumas coming through on a daily basis, there's always something new to be learned. That's part of what makes the field so interesting and satisfying."

The waitress dropped off their check then hurried away before Dee could thank her. "What is it about teaching that makes your job so interesting?" she asked, making a reach for the check but losing it to Chase.

He flashed her a grin. "My treat, Doc. It's the least I can do after you played baby-sitter all night long."

She returned his smile, noticing he'd once again side-stepped a direct question. Maybe they were made for each other after all. They had the personal question evasion dance down to a science. "It's all part of the job."

The color of his eyes darkened as he looked at her with that intent gaze. "I say some of that ground we covered last night couldn't be found in your job description." The timbre of his voice became low and husky, and she'd wager intentionally intimate to serve as a reminder of how she'd responded when he'd whispered seductively in her ear.

She reached for her tea to moisten the sudden dryness in her throat. Not certain how to answer, or if she should even acknowledge his truthful statement, she drank deeply. Too bad her body had already decided its course as heat unfurled in her tummy and began to spread seductively through her veins.

She set her glass back on the table. "Chase, I don't—"

"Let's get out of here." He slid out of the booth before she could reiterate how getting involved would lead them down a path to nowhere.

Not exactly nowhere, she amended silently as she exited the booth. Based on her body's instant reaction to something as innocuous as the seductive tone of his voice, regardless of how brief the affair might be, she knew clear to her soul making love to Chase would be nothing short of fabulously erotic and incredibly satisfying.

It could all be hers for the taking. If only she'd say *yes!*

ter could tell. It had very nearly shattered her subconscious resolve.

"What she lost, a patient, the moment in the E.R. wasn't there to just...let somebody focus was all-important present. Instinctively...in so sick it was that very moment, Chase reminded her she had to practice medicine without tossing the daily risk to another lifetime...she could return to the business

9

BY THE TIME DEE PULLED HER car into the carport Sunday morning following two grueling back-to-back shifts at the hospital, she was drained, physically as well as emotionally. She still hadn't said yes to Chase, but only because she hadn't been home to see him since they returned from Myrtle Beach. During the one brief lull in the E.R. late Saturday night, she'd called him, letting him know she wouldn't be home until morning in case he needed her. She also wanted to reassure herself he was doing all right considering his injury, and *not* because she'd desperately needed to hear his deep, strong voice.

She killed the ignition and rested her forehead on the steering wheel, wishing she could be one of those doctors who shut down their emotions just as easily. Everything she'd told Chase Friday afternoon about her decision to specialize in emergency medicine had been true, with one small exception. No matter how hard she tried, she just couldn't turn her emotions off completely when it came to her patients. She did care, and for that reason, family practice wasn't for her, at least not on a long-term basis. Her first six months in Cole Harbor told her as much when an elderly patient came to her complaining of dizziness. She ran him through the gamut of tests only to learn an inoperable brain tumor was responsible. Other than give the patient medications to help him be as comfortable as possible during his last days, there was nothing she could do. It had very nearly had her rethinking her career choice.

When she lost a patient, she mourned. In the E.R., there wasn't time to get attached because there was always another patient waiting to be healed or saved. It was that very anonymity Chase mentioned that allowed her to practice medicine without running the daily risk of finding herself emotionally attached to the numerous trauma victims that came through the E.R.

Some days, however, there would be one that broke past her barriers no matter how hard she tried to keep her emotions under control. And when she failed, she hurt.

Like she was hurting now.

She let out a deep sigh and pulled her keys from the ignition before snagging the gym bag she used as an overnight bag for her duty weekends from the seat beside her. The only early-morning sounds were from the birds perched along the power lines and in the trees surrounding the front of the triplex. She wasn't exactly sure what she'd expected to find, but felt a stab of disappointment just the same when she followed the path past the hibiscus, already buzzing with bees, to the wooden steps up to her side of the empty front porch.

She unlocked her apartment, walked inside and dropped her gym bag by the door. Two steps into the living room, she stilled. Something was...different.

Frowning, she glanced around the cramped space, but nothing appeared out of place. She took a deep breath, and inhaled a heavenly aroma. "Blueberries?"

She followed the scent through the living room and into what her landlady referred to as the efficiency kitchen, but in Dee's opinion was nothing less than sales-pitch jargon for minuscule. Heat brushed her skin. She pulled open the oven door to find a muffin tin resting on the center rack with six freshly baked blueberry muffins.

"What the...?"

Her oven had one of those automatic timers, but she'd only used it once since cooking for herself just wasn't much fun. Besides, she had *not* mixed a batch of blueberry muffins before she left for the hospital yesterday morning.

Her frown deepening, she grabbed a pot holder off the counter to pull the muffins from the oven. She turned to set the tin on the wooden trivet she kept near the sink and stopped, nearly tripping over her broom with a yellow sticky-note attached to the wooden handle.

Knock three times, Doc!

Okay, there was something here that she just wasn't getting. Chase was being cute, but darned if she had an inkling about what. Knock where? On the broom?

"Well that makes no sense," she muttered, putting down the muffin tin.

The automatic coffeemaker came to life, the rich aroma mingling with the mouthwatering blueberry muffins. Chase obviously went to a whole lot of trouble, but she couldn't help wondering how he'd gotten into her apartment to pull off his adorably thoughtful surprise. She wasn't sure how she felt about him gaining access to her apartment without her knowledge, either.

She was still standing in the kitchen with the broom in her hand trying to solve the puzzle when she heard a soft thumping directly above her head.

She frowned, waited and heard it again a few seconds later. Three distinct thumps this time. It had been over twenty years since she and Jared had taught themselves

Morse Code, or at least their rendition of the universal signals, from a secret-agent spy kit her brother had gotten by saving UPC symbols from his favorite comic books, but she didn't think Chase was issuing a distress signal.

There it was again. Three more thumps above her. If it hadn't been for the note, she might have guessed he was in some sort of trouble, except the meaning was suddenly crystal clear. He wanted her to knock on the ceiling. For what purpose, she could only guess.

Dee bit her lip. What would she be letting herself in for if she followed the instructions on the sticky note? She feared that wanting Chase and actually having him would be two separate issues. Physical need she understood, and not just from a physiological standpoint, either. Emotions would come into play, and that was the part of getting involved with him that made her nervous. Emotional self-sufficiency might have been the constant focus of her parents' teachings to her and Jared growing up, but her reaction to Chase went beyond just physical.

Three more clear thumps sounded above her head.

She might not be dependent on another person for her own happiness, but she had a bad feeling knocking on the ceiling three times wasn't supposed to be an invitation to join her strictly for blueberry muffins and coffee.

The thought frightened as well as exhilarated her.

She tossed the broom upward and refastened her grip midway down the handle. Nothing in her life had to change. Chase's touch might set her soul on fire, his kisses might have her insides clamoring with need, but fires and clamoring need didn't mean for a second that her life had to change one iota. She would still accept the offer from New York or Boston and relocate in two months.

"Nothing will change," she said loud enough to hopefully convince herself. She shifted the broom to her other hand, her fingers brushing against the wire-bound straw.

They were consenting adults, she thought, pulling in a deep breath and letting it out slowly. If she and Chase wanted to engage in a mutually gratifying sexual relationship, then that was their business.

She braced her free hand on the counter for support and lifted the broom high above her head, tapping it once on the ceiling.

No strings.

*Y.*

When she didn't hear an answering thump, she hefted the broom handle toward the ceiling a second time and tapped.

And no ties.

*E.*

But most important, under no circumstances whatsoever, were emotional entanglements allowed. "Period," she said firmly, giving into temptation with one last, definitive knock on the ceiling.

*S!*

"I HAVE ONE QUESTION. How'd you get into my apartment?"

Chase sat down on the sofa and propped his foot over his knee. So far, all that appeared to be on his agenda was coffee, muffins and the fresh-sliced cantaloupe he'd brought downstairs with him.

"Mrs. England," he admitted, setting the ceramic mug on the end table. "I took advantage of her hospitality gene."

With her upper back against the arm of the sofa and bare feet resting on the cushion between them, she *almost* felt relaxed. Sleepy even, as the tension of the night ebbed to some small degree.

She looked at him over the rim of her mug. "You mean you lied to her." The accusation lost its impact due to the humor in her voice she'd been unable to suppress.

"I did not lie to her," Chase defended, his own deep, sultry voice laced with laughter. "My intentions were pure."

"Oh, you had intentions all right," she countered, leaning to the side to rest her empty mug on the coffee table. "And I seriously doubt *pure* is an apt definition."

A wicked grin curved his mouth. "Doubting my sincerity?"

She pulled the nubby teal throw pillow from the back of the sofa and hugged it close to her chest. "I'm doubting a lot of things, to be perfectly honest." The gentle flirtatiousness she'd been feeling since she'd knocked three times on the ceiling evaporated. She was too analytical to ignore the signs she'd been reading since Chase had come into her life. Bright, flashy neon warning ones, too.

Until this very second, the atmosphere between them had been light and teasing. Maybe it was time to finally address the awareness between them like the two consenting adults they were, instead of behaving like nervous college freshmen about to embark upon their first real affair.

Chase must've sensed the change, as well, because he slipped his hand around her ankle, and slowly placed her feet on his lap. The denim of his jeans rasped against her calves, the sensation nearly as electric as his thumbs gently pressing into the balls of her feet.

"What is there to doubt?" he asked, continuing with

the foot massage to end all foot massages. "This is real, Dee."

Real? She wondered about that for a minute, closing her eyes as Chase's fingers pressed and rubbed, slowly erasing the tension from her body. Not *real* in the happily-ever-after sense. Could sizzling awareness even be considered real? "I've had about enough reality to last me a lifetime," she said quietly. "I don't think I can afford any more. At least not right now."

"What are you saying? You want to play games?"

She opened her eyes and looked at him. A lock of wavy dark hair fell over his forehead as he looked down, focused on the foot massage.

"No, Chase," she said, drawing his attention. "I'm not the fun-and-games type. But I meant what I said the other night. About getting involved."

His hands stilled, but he kept her feet firmly on his lap. "I know you're leaving soon," he told her, keeping his voice low. "Who knows what's going to happen tomorrow. But isn't *this* moment, the right here and now, what we should be concentrating on?"

"Live for the moment, take it as it comes?" And don't think about tomorrow for a change? For too many years she'd been worrying about the future. She wasn't sure she could do what he was suggesting. The concept was beyond her.

Or was it?

She wanted Chase. There was no denying the truth. So what *was* wrong with living for the moment for a change? Since she was sixteen years old she'd lived for the future. Would she be completely selfish if she stopped worrying about what would or would not happen tomorrow for once in her life?

Whether it was the temptation to live, even if for a

short time, carefree and for the moment she couldn't be sure. One thing she had absolutely no doubt about was that her resistance to Chase was slipping. Fast.

Hadn't she had enough losing battles for one day? Did she really have the strength to fight another?

She reached behind her to pull her hair from the silky band holding the length away from her face. Rubbing her scalp with the tip of her fingers, she shook her hair loose. "So where do we go from here?" she asked him, uncertain exactly how to proceed with this carefree business.

He lifted her right foot and pressed the flat of his palm against her heel, gently urging her to stretch the worn and tired muscles in her legs. A low murmured "Hmm" was about all she could muster.

"From here," he said, repeating the process with her left foot. "You relax. You're tense and you look exhausted."

She dropped her head against the arm of the sofa. "Rough night," she said, closing her eyes.

"Busy?"

"Not really, just…long. I lost a patient this morning." The admission caused her eyes to burn with unshed tears.

"That's gotta be rough," he said, his deep voice infused with sympathy. "But you've been at it long enough to know that sometimes, no matter how good you are, you just can't save them all. Sometimes you're gonna lose, sweetheart."

She opened her eyes and looked at him through the moisture clouding her gaze. Compassion softened the angles of his chiseled features. Since she'd started practicing medicine, she'd been on her own and never once had there been anyone to share in the joys and heartaches of the job. Oh, sure, the nursing staff was always kind-hearted, but when was the last time a doctor literally cried on an R.N.'s shoulder because she couldn't save a patient? On the job, she stayed tough and held it together. Home alone, she struggled to keep her emotions locked away, telling herself in order to survive she had no other choice but to practice the emotional self-sufficiency code of her parents.

Today all she wanted to do was weep like a child and have Chase hold her, whisper nonsensical words of comfort and tell her everything would be okay.

"I hate when the bastard wins," she managed to say around the lump in her throat.

He returned her foot to his lap. Slowly he eased his hand over her calf and continued to massage. "What bastard?" he asked, a slight frown creasing his forehead.

She swiped at the tears with the back of her hand. "Death. We did everything we could to save her, but she just didn't have the strength to survive."

He said nothing, just continued to ease the tension in her legs, waiting for her to continue.

"I've lost patients before. It happens no matter how good you are or how hard you try to save a life. But not like this. I've seen things that would give you nightmares, but never anything so damned self-destructive and cruel. Even when I worked in L.A., where just about anything can happen, I hadn't seen anything quite this bad before."

He extended his hand toward her. "Come here."

She didn't consider hesitating for more than a second. Taking his hand, she let him guide her toward him. He shifted so his back was pressed against the other arm of the sofa, then eased her around so she was practically lying in his lap.

The foot massage was enough to short-circuit her

senses. Placed as she was with her bottom bracketed between his strong thighs and her back resting against the firm wall of his chest, she was dangerously close to a complete and total meltdown.

"Tell me about it, sweetheart." His chest rumbled with the words against her back. Surprising even herself, she found comfort in the intimacy.

"I lost a pregnant woman this morning," she said quietly.

He wrapped his arms around her, holding her against him. She slipped her hands over his resting on her tummy, enjoying the slightly rougher texture of his skin.

"And the baby?" he asked.

She took advantage of her position and reclined completely against him, liking the feel of his body pressed against hers, and his warm masculine scent. With her head resting against his shoulder, she greedily accepted the comfort he offered, trying desperately not to examine too closely how safe she felt in his arms.

"In neonatal ICU," she told him, "hooked up to just about every machine medical science has developed. I don't know if he'll make it or not."

"I'm no doctor," he said, "but even though we can create babies in a petri dish nowadays, I suspect things can still go wrong with a pregnancy, can't it?"

"Unfortunately, yes. There are any number of problems and dangers, but many that threaten pregnant mothers and even infant mortality can be detected early so preventive measures can be taken. But it wasn't the pregnancy that went bad in this case. It was the mother, and the SOB who beat her so badly it'll probably take dental records to identify her."

She didn't have to close her eyes to see the needle tracks on the young mother's arms, deep and riddled with infection. The broken bones that made what had at one time, maybe even a lifetime ago, been a pretty face, almost completely unrecognizable. Deep cuts and horrific bruises, some newly dark purple and reddish, others a faded tapestry of misshapen yellow-and-green, marring pasty skin. And the small perfectly round scars she suspected were cigarette burns. Human waste at its worst.

"I'm not naive. You can't be and survive for very long in emergency medicine, but I still get angry at the waste. When I deliver an innocent child addicted to crack or heroine, it hurts. I'm not supposed to let it, but it does."

His arms tightened around her and Dee closed her eyes against the tears blurring her vision once again. "I can't turn off the pain, Chase."

His lips brushed against her temple. "Pain is what lets us know we're still alive, sweetheart. You don't want to shut it out completely."

"I did this morning," she admitted. "I so wanted to be numb, but we had to perform an emergency C-section when the mother coded out. When I pulled that baby from his mother's womb, I was so angry. If he survives the next forty-eight hours, he just might make it, but I can't help wondering what kind of quality of life he's going to have. He's got so much against him already and he's only a few hours old."

"You might be surprised by the resiliency of a child."

There was an odd note in his voice she couldn't decipher, but it was enough of a change in tone to have her tipping her head back to look at him. His eyes had gone cold and hard, and his mouth was set in a grim line.

She shook her head slightly. "I don't know, Chase. He wasn't to term so his lungs aren't fully developed. Fetal alcohol syndrome is only the beginning of his problems along with an addiction to crack and who knows what else. Malnutrition, jaundice, and I wouldn't be surprised if he has AIDS. And to top it all off, so far as anyone knows, the poor little guy hasn't got a soul in the world to love him.''

He tucked her tighter against him before lips brushed her temple again. "Maybe he'll get lucky," he said. "Like I did.''

# *10*

CHASE SMOOTHED HIS CHEEK against Dee's rich, sleek sable hair, breathing in her light floral fragrance. Two days ago, he'd determined the way to get closer to the subject was to create the illusion of intimacy. Right this very second, holding Dee in his arms, she was anything but a subject whose personal habits were nothing more important to him than a dissection for further study and discovery. Worse yet, he no longer had a clue which version he'd managed to create—the illusionary kind, or the kind that smacked of cold, brutal reality.

His head told him the intimacy was manufactured, no more based in reality than the Tooth Fairy or Santa Claus. Nothing but make-believe, a part of the cover, a part of the plan to unearth information necessary to solve the case.

His heart was busy rallying the troops for a completely different scenario.

"Like you," she echoed. "How exactly?"

Like an over-the-road truck driver suffering white-line fever caused from long hours and too many miles behind the wheel, the roadway representing Chase's conscience, not to mention his dedication to get the job done, began to blur and fade.

"Like me," he repeated, tightening his hold on her. Not because he expected her to bolt, but because the emotions gathering like a fifty-ton weight perfectly positioned on his solar plexus had more to do with the countdown toward the emotional rocket launch he was about to experience. One he suspected could have him hurtling straight back to earth in a ball of flames if he wasn't careful.

"I'm not sure I understand what you're getting at here, Chase," she said, strengthening her own grasp over his hands. "Were you…?"

He nodded, rubbing his cheek against her sleek hair again. "My folks, the teachers? They're my foster parents. They took me in when I was around six years old. I haven't seen my mother since I was fourteen."

"But what does that have to do with the little guy in neonatal ICU? How is he like you?"

He pulled in a deep breath and let it out slowly. In order to weave that damned illusion, he'd have to open up and let Dee into the place he kept safely locked away from trespassers. Stupid was not a character definition applied to her, and although he was a damned good deep-cover operative, he knew clear down to the bottom of his soul if he really wanted the information that would lead him to her brother, he had no other choice but to let Dee inside. If he shut down now and kept her at arm's length emotionally, he'd be defeating his own purpose.

*Quid Pro Quo.*

"Chase?" The concern lacing her sweet voice ripped through his chest and wrapped around his heart, squeezing hard enough to threaten his oxygen supply.

*Quid Pro Quo.* Something for something. The darkest part of himself, for her deepest secret. The part of himself he'd struggled with for most of his life to keep hidden behind the locked door of his past, for the part of herself she'd learned to guard against strangers. The place filled with too many insecurities to name and overflowing to the point he'd finally come to accept he'd never completely escape, for the place she stored memories, habits and idiosyncrasies of a wanted man.

A part of his soul, for a lead to finally solve the Romine case.

*Quid Pro Quo.*

Something for something.

Everything for possibly nothing.

He shut his eyes, but quickly snapped them open again. Because he was unwilling to look into the past? Or because he feared being unable to shut it out again once he turned the demons loose? The truth eluded him, but left him with a bad feeling the answer would be crystal clear momentarily.

"Because," he said, "I started out not too much different than the baby you delivered today."

She tried to move, but he strengthened his hold again, keeping her close to his body. Telling himself he didn't want to shatter the illusion was a lie and he knew it. But it was a whole lot better than admitting that he might actually need someone.

After a moment, she settled back against him and stayed silent, as if sensing he needed a moment or two to gather his thoughts and put them in order before ripping open his soul and laying it in front of her.

"I don't know who my father was, and I doubt Sara knew, either," he said matter-of-factly. "Selling herself for a fix wasn't all that unusual, and she wasn't exactly particular so long as she got what she wanted."

Dee's slender fingers slid around his, lacing them intimately together. "What was she addicted to?" she asked.

"Heroin. Maybe something else at the time, too. How much did they really know thirty-two years ago?" he asked, not expecting an answer. "But I came along about six weeks premature sharing my mother's addiction to her drug of choice."

Her fingers tightened around his. "Oh my God, Chase."

He shrugged. "It was a long time ago." But not long enough that he hadn't been able to completely erase the emotional scars and insecurities about never being good enough.

"How do you know all this?" Dee asked. "Did your foster parents tell you?"

He let out another slow breath. "No. You deal with enough social service bureaucrats and you'd be shocked the stuff kids can find out. In large metropolitan areas filled with slums and projects, the social workers are understaffed, underpaid and overworked. I can see now why they'd become jaded.

"They aren't as careful about what's said or not said in front of a kid. Or maybe they just lose their compassion completely. Who knows?"

"I take it they didn't remove you from your mother's care until you were older."

He nodded, but realized she couldn't see him. "It wasn't until I was six that they finally pulled me away from Sara and placed me in a foster home. Why the hell they waited so long is what I could never figure out."

"How long were you in the first foster home?"

"I guess you could say I'm still there, in a sense. Leo and Susan are my parents as far as I'm concerned. They're the ones who really raised me and gave me a home. I might not carry the Mitchell name, but I'm their son. Hell, they gave me a life and I'll admit, I wasn't the greatest kid in the world, either. I had a shitload of problems they had to cope with, and no matter how much of a pain in the ass I was, they wouldn't give up on me."

"That's the way family is supposed to be," she said quietly. "I don't care how much we might want our lives to be like a sitcom where problems can be resolved in twenty-two minutes plus commercials. Life just doesn't work that way, but I learned that family sticks together and is always there for one another, no matter what."

"You don't have to convince me," he said dryly.

There was more going on here than an attempt to garner information even if he couldn't forget Pelham's threat. No matter how much he tried to maintain his focus on the assignment, the growing closeness between them wasn't a complete fabrication. He lifted their joined hands and examined them, hers slender and perfectly manicured, his rougher and darker skinned. When was the last time he'd talked so openly to a woman, hell, another human being for that matter? He couldn't remember any more than he could recall the last time he'd sat and just held someone, as he was doing now. The thought spooked him on a personal level as much as it filled his law-enforcement mentality with dread. He'd been given a week until he'd be pulled off the case, unless he came up with a new lead. Deep in his gut, he knew they'd both be shattered by the outcome.

"Is your mother still alive?" Dee asked, smoothing her thumb lightly over his knuckles.

"She was the last time I saw her."

"And you were fourteen, right?"

"Yeah."

"You said the state placed you with the Mitchells when you were six. Did you see your mother on a regular basis? At least for a while?"

"Only when she was hard up for drug money and

thought she could milk the folks for a few bucks. The
state paid my foster parents for my care and Sara thought
she should be entitled to some of it.''

"That's ridiculous."

"What's more ridiculous is that my parents would give
it to her so she'd go away until the next time she wanted
money. Right or wrong, it was their way of protecting
me from her."

"This went on for eight years?" she asked, disbelief
tingeing her voice.

"Oh, yeah. Just when I thought I'd never see her
again, she'd show up claiming she wanted me to come
live with her. She never pretended to be clean. It wasn't
me she wanted," he admitted, "but the money Leo and
Susan were being paid for my care. I was just a welfare
check to Sara, a means to keep her in needles and smack
and God knows what else."

"Why did she stop coming? I mean, she obviously
thought she had a good thing going taking money from
your foster parents, right?"

Almost against his will, Chase closed his eyes. Not in
an effort to block out the pain or even the past, but to
see it more clearly. "She stopped coming because I made
her choose. Me or her habit."

Dee moved off him and repositioned herself on the
sofa to face him. Still seated between his legs, she
crossed her own then reached for his hands, holding them
in her lap. "What happened?" she asked, her gaze intent
and filled with a concern he didn't deserve.

He couldn't bear to see the compassion in her eyes, so
he looked past her to the dancing equalizer lights on the
bookcase stereo that had a Savage Garden CD playing
softly in the background. Slowly he slipped back into the
past, right into the ugliness and pain.

"By the time I was around twelve I learned the truth about why Sara was even coming around," he said. "After every one of her visits, I'd get moody and sullen, typical abandonment issues, I guess. Susan would worry and cry, then fuss over me, trying to make me feel better. Except this time, I actually saw my dad give Sara money, and then she left. I was hurt and angry, and accused my folks of paying Sara off so she'd stay away from me."

He glanced her way again, in time to see her arched brows lift. "They were in a sense, though, weren't they?"

"Yeah, but not like I thought," he said, not looking away. "I couldn't have been more wrong. I overheard the folks talking later that night and had myself a real wake-up call. Not only did I discover Sara's real reason for showing up, but what really hit me hard was that I heard my mom crying as if her heart was broken. I did that to her because I was being such a little bastard and taking my anger out on her."

"Chase, that's not unusual. Children vent, but unlike adults, they don't know how to channel their anger in a healthy way. They take it out on the person closest to them. I'm sure all you did was act out, which was normal. Surely your mom understood."

He shifted his gaze back to the safety of the lights on the equalizer. "Yeah, well, she did, but I was too wrapped up in my own misery to see it. All I knew was that she was hurting and it was my fault. She was worried about me because I'd be so moody. It'd only last a few days and then I'd usually snap out of it and everything would go back to normal. At least until the next time Sara showed up unannounced, and the whole damned cycle would start all over again.

"Except this time it'd been different because I didn't

understand what was really going on until I overheard them talking. That's when I found out that Sara had a nifty little blackmail scheme going, threatening to report my folks to social services with some wild story about them making her an offer to purchase me. They knew it was all bullshit, but Mom was terrified Sara would actually do it if they didn't give her the money. Until the authorities investigated, I'd be shuffled off to some other home, and my mom was afraid they'd lose me for good.

"This went on for a couple more years," he explained, "but I was real careful about what I said or did after one of Sara's blackmailing visits because I couldn't stand to see my mom so upset. Then I came up with a plan."

Dee continued to hold his hands tightly within her own, quietly offering him her support and comfort. The feeling that someone other than his folks cared about him was too new and untried to leave him with anything but a strange sense of awe as he delved into the darkest memories of his past. A past he'd never forget, no matter how hard he tried.

"By fourteen I was a freshman in high school. I caught on quick that just about anything was available...for a price. I mowed lawns, cleaned out rain gutters, dug out flower beds for old ladies in the neighborhood, just about anything for an extra buck. When I had enough cash, I bought a dime of heroin."

She sucked in a sharp breath. "Oh my God, Chase. No. You didn't."

He shook his head. "No," he said, giving her fingers a reassuring squeeze. "I hid it in my room and waited until the next time Sara showed up, sniffing around for more cash. It didn't take her too long, and when she did, I gave her a choice...her son or the drugs."

Dee briefly closed her eyes, but not before he caught

a glimpse of his own pain echoed within the gold highlights of her irises. "She chose the drugs, didn't she?"

"She did me a favor that day," he admitted. "I didn't see it then, but I know it now. Somewhere. Most of the time. I still have doubts, but who isn't scarred by something in their past?"

"I can't imagine what it must've been like for you. My parents were a little strange and had their own ideas about parenting, but I don't think we ever doubted their love was anything but genuine. To have your own mother... God, that must've been so hard for you."

Chase shrugged carelessly, but the bitterness and resentment still ran deep through his scarred soul. "Truthfully? Only when I'm reminded of where I came from does it really bother me now."

He expected, and dreaded, pity from her. Instead he saw compassion and something else that added to his already overloaded conscience. Caring.

"She was only your birth mother, Chase. I hope you realize that. We can argue nature versus nurture if you want, but I've seen enough to harbor the belief that we're a product of our environment. Genetics do come into play to some extent. Take any great athlete. They might have the genetic makeup to be a superstar basketball player, but if they'd removed Michael Jordan from his environment, who knows if he would've realized his ability. All I'm trying to say is that even though your mother was a heroin addict, it doesn't mean you're predisposed to repeat her mistakes."

He slipped his hand from hers and cupped her cheek. "I do know that. Even if it did take me a while to figure it out for myself. But she did have an addiction, which made her weak. You said yourself, genetics do play a role."

She turned her face toward his palm and lightly placed a kiss against his hand before lacing her fingers around his once again. "You're anything but weak, Chase Bracken," she said.

The smile curving her lips was so sweet he ached to kiss her, to lose himself in oblivion for a while and just forget about everything. Forget duty, the past and an empty, lonely future.

She let out a contented little sigh of pleasure when he pulled her back against him. Shifting to her hip, she used his chest as a pillow and looped her arm loosely around his waist.

Close.

Intimate.

A lie.

"So did you settle down, or were you still a hell-raiser?" she asked, snuggling closer.

"My mom's hair isn't gray because she colors it that way," he said with a forced laugh. "At least that's what she likes to tell me."

He heard her failed attempt to stifle a yawn. "I have a question. What finally prompted social services to do their job and get you into a foster home?" she asked sleepily.

Resentment reared up inside him again, instantly re-filling the emotional well with the sharp tang of bitterness. "They knew Sara was trading food stamps and cashing the welfare checks for drugs, but they never did anything about it until after we got evicted from another apartment and went to live with her drug-dealing pimp boyfriend."

He must've tensed because she tipped her head back to look up at him, concern highlighting her eyes. The deep breath he took did nothing to relax him as more memories crowded in and demanded to be unleashed.

"He was a mean son of a bitch," he admitted. "He'd beat the crap out of me for whatever reason he decided was a good one. The few times Sara actually showed a shred of maternal instinct and tried to stop him, he'd turn on her. After a couple of beatings bad enough to send her to the hospital, she learned to keep her mouth shut and look the other way."

"Oh, Chase," she said, her voice strained.

He looked down at her. The tears welling in her eyes tore through him and settled around his heart, freezing him from the inside out.

He urged her away and swung his legs to the floor. "Don't," he said abruptly and stood. He snatched his mug off the end table and crossed the living room to the kitchen. Willing the memories away was a useless battle he often lost. He set the mug in the sink and braced his hands on the counter, waiting for the ugly pictures, and finally the anger and resentment, to pass.

She came up behind him and slipped her arms around his middle.

He tensed. "I don't want your pity, Dee."

"I'd never pity you. You're a survivor. I know what that's like. My heart breaks for the little boy you were, because your childhood must've been a nightmare. You had a rotten start, but look at you now. It would've been easier to end up like your mother, but you didn't. You said you gave her a choice, but I think you really were ready to face the truth and see for yourself the value your mother held for you. That took a great deal of courage, Chase. For that reason, I think you're someone to be admired, not pitied."

He dropped his head and shook it, making a self-deprecating sound that resembled a short burst of abrupt laughter. Admire him? That wouldn't last for long. Not once she found out what he was really doing in Cole Harbor. "You don't know me."

She rested her cheek against his back and held him tighter. "I suppose you're right about that," she said. He felt her lips brush against his back. "But isn't that something we can change?"

Slowly he turned to face her. With his hands clasped firmly around her upper arms, he searched her face...and tripped over his conscience at the tenderness lighting her gaze.

"What are you saying?" he asked. From an investigative standpoint, Dee was playing right into his hands. He should be thrilled with the direction they were headed. Instead he felt like a fraud.

She reached up and smoothed a lock of hair off his forehead. "I'm saying *yes.*"

# *11*

NOW THAT SHE'D MADE UP HER mind and vocalized her decision, Dee had no intention of turning back. Having an affair, even a temporary one with Chase was a risky proposition. Other than her one slip when she'd first started practicing medicine in Cole Harbor, she'd managed to keep her heart tucked safely away from intruders. She'd been witness to the darker side of humanity since her first shift as an intern and had learned quickly to keep her heart out of her work. Compassion and understanding was one thing, but anything more was emotional suicide for an M.D. So long as she viewed her affair with Chase in the same light, she'd have nothing to fear.

Perhaps she might actually have believed it, if Chase hadn't managed to touch her, deeper and farther inside her soul than anyone had in a very long time. He'd slipped into that place she'd never allowed anyone other than her family to take up residence. Whether he was consciously aware of the intrusion or not, he'd staked a claim on her heart that gave her serious doubts about ever being able to fully reclaim it as her own.

What she felt for Chase could hardly be described as simple affection or even basic lust. There was a connection, an emotional one that defied every self-sufficiency lecture by her parents. No matter what happened once she left South Carolina, he would always hold a special place in her heart. Her first true love? She didn't think so, but that didn't mean the possibility failed to exist for something more entangling than a short-term, mutually gratifying sexual relationship.

"You said all I had to do was say yes," she told him, taking the first step toward no return. She drew her fingers along his freshly shaven cheek, the skin smooth and warm to the touch. "I'm saying yes."

He pulled in a ragged breath. "Dee—"

She moved closer, wreathing her arms around his neck and aligning her body with his. "Don't tell me you've changed your mind already?"

A half smile tipped his mouth. "I wouldn't exactly say that." He settled his hands on her hips and turned, lifting her onto the ledge of the counter.

With the heels of her bare feet, she wrapped her legs around his hips and urged him forward. The instant pressure against the juncture of her thighs was nothing short of electric. Whatever it was about Chase that had her insides jumping with excitement, she couldn't exactly be sure, but the pulling sensation deep in her tummy, the warmth spreading through her limbs and the moist heat dampening her panties in sweet anticipation of his touch were more than decadent, they were perfectly erotic.

With her arms looped around his neck, she slipped her hands into his thick, wavy black-as-midnight hair and guided his mouth toward hers. "What *would* you say?" she asked him, her voice a breathless whisper.

He hesitated, his mouth mere millimeters away, as if making his own decision. Finally he brushed his lips over hers in a kiss so feathery and light she thought she'd imagined it.

"I'd say, what took you so long?"

Before she could respond, his mouth slanted over hers in a searing, toe-curling kiss. His tongue slid across hers in gentle exploration, causing electrifying sensations to spark and fuse with the emotions ricocheting through her heart and mind. This was it, she thought. This was as real as it got…at least on a temporary basis.

She forgot all the reasons why getting involved with Chase was a foolhardy mission when his large callused hands pressed against her bottom and urged her even closer. His erection wedged against the growing dampness between her thighs, heightening her instinctive need to mate. A soft moan escaped at the delicious contact as she rocked her hips forward, rubbing against the hard length straining the fly of his faded jeans. She wanted, needed to feel him deep inside her.

He tore his mouth from hers to look into her eyes. The deep hue of violet mirrored the need pulsing through her, but darker and more intense. "You know," he said, a slow, wicked smile curving his oh-so-sexy mouth. "That muffin was hardly satisfying."

"I'm all for satisfaction, so long as it's mutual." She moved against him, the rough denim scraping against her navy cotton shorts. At his sharp intake of breath followed by a low groan, satisfaction of the feminine kind reared up inside her. "If it's a meal you're interested in, then it's a good thing we're in the kitchen."

He chuckled, then dipped his head, skimming his lips along her skin, using his teeth and tongue to heighten pleasure. He zeroed in on the sensitive spot at the base of her throat, leaving her little choice but to toss her head back and arch toward him and the delicious sensation.

"I want to feast on you," he murmured against her skin.

"Hmm. Sounds…intense."

He made a low rumble of sound. "Do you like it…intense?"

"I like it hot," she said, sifting her fingers through his hair.

His fingers worked the buttons of her pin-striped summer blouse. "Just hot?" he asked, pushing the placket open. His fingers traced a slow trail along her skin, over her rib cage and upward to cup her breasts. After she'd knocked three times on the ceiling, she'd taken a quick shower, foregoing a bra in favor of comfort. The instant he palmed her flesh, her nipples puckered and rasped against his work-roughened hands.

"The hotter, the better," she murmured after a low moan of pleasure, glad she'd decided to opt for comfort rather than practicality. "And steamy."

He drew his thumbs over her tightened nipples, while his mouth worked magic over her exposed collarbone and down toward her breasts.

"Steamy, huh?"

His tongue circled her nipple and she trembled.

"Steamy," she whispered. "Wet and steamy."

"Are you wet now?"

Oh God, she couldn't take much more of this. His hands, his mouth, the sexy rumble of his voice against her skin had all the makings of an erotic fantasy come to life. The wicked visions slipping into her mind didn't help matters, either, and were almost too much to bear.

Almost.

And not nearly enough.

"How wet?" he asked, grazing her nipple with his teeth, then applying the moist heat of his tongue. He pulled her nipple into his mouth, sending flames shooting through her.

The tugging sensations in the pit of her stomach increased. She ached. She needed. "Very," she managed to say in a strained voice. "Hot and wet and..." She cried out, overcome by the pure pleasure cascading over her as he suckled harder.

His hands left her breasts to skim over her stomach, stopping at the button of her walking shorts. Lifting his head, he held her gaze. Her breath came in short, hard pants as she looked into his eyes.

Heat matched heat, desire equaled desire. Raw need crashed into her.

If she kept this up, she'd be in need of CPR when they made love. And there was no doubt that's exactly where all this foreplay was leading. Straight into the bedroom.

His adept fingers flicked the button of her shorts and worked the zipper down. The rasp of the slide echoed in her ears, dimmed only by the deafening blood pounding there, as well.

"Lift," he ordered softly.

She let go of his shoulders and braced her hands on the counter as he lifted her bottom. He tugged her shorts and panties over her hips and down her legs to land in a pile by his feet. Acute awareness filled her as she cataloged every scent, from the musky scent of sex to the tangy spice of Chase's aftershave. Each breath, every whisper and gentle, soft moan was magnified. Sensations overloaded her senses, from the hard surface of the countertop as she lowered her bottom onto it, to the cool air from the air-conditioning unit brushing enticingly over her skin. Yet none of the scents, sounds or textures prepared her for the sight of Chase dropping to his knees in front of her.

Her mouth went dry and her breath left her in a whoosh, only to be sucked in again sharply when his big hands blazed a trail of heat up the inside her thighs, pressing them open. He smoothed his hands down the outside of her legs. Gripping her heels, he gently set them on his shoulders, leaving her open and vulnerable, and not just physically.

His hands trailed lightly along the underside of her legs, moving slowly, methodically toward the center of her, already swollen and aching for him. She nearly whimpered at the reverence of his touch. Her hips jerked toward the pure pleasure of his thumbs sliding slowly along her feminine folds. His gaze caught hers, darker, even more intense and filled with heated desire. Desire for her.

He eased the length of his finger inside her, only to withdraw it and spread the moist heat over her. She moaned as he continued the sensuous teasing, applying just enough pressure to make her writhe her hips, but not nearly enough to send her over the edge into the sweet oblivion of orgasm.

"I don't think wet is going to be a problem," he murmured, his tone reminding her of thick rich chocolate, smooth and decadent. He placed a kiss on her inner thigh while his fingers worked magic, drawing the tension tighter and higher, but expertly withholding release just out of her reach. He showed her the brink, but kept her from crashing over the side.

Oh, how she wanted to crash. Hard. Fast. Wild. And right now!

"Please," she whispered around the ragged dryness in her throat.

"Soon, baby," he said, then finally, kissed her there with infinite tenderness.

She felt like a live wire blown down and left to dance dangerously over the pavement in a wicked storm, sparking and threatening to explode.

He wove the most erotic, sensual spell over her, using his lips, his teeth and his tongue while his hands alternately massaged her inner thigh or continued his delightfully tortuous exploration. He licked, he laved, he probed deeply, tasting the core of her until she trembled from the tension coiled inside her, until she finally came in a rush, hard and fast, and so beautifully perfect she nearly wept.

Before she could catch her breath, he stood. "Condoms?" he rasped, his breathing as heavy as her own.

"Medical bag."

With trembling fingers, he gently massaged her thighs. "Where?"

"Dresser."

He pulled her close, crushing her breasts against the soft cotton of his red T-shirt. His mouth slanted over hers in a kiss so hot, so wet and deep she nearly came all over again.

"Hold that thought," he said with a wink, then disappeared into the bedroom. He returned in about three seconds flat, his hands full of the condom supply she kept in her bag to hand out to the few teenage boys she happened to encounter during the occasional house call. She'd always been glad to have them handy, and liked to think she was maybe partly responsible for preventing at least one or two teenage pregnancies in the area. Being *personally* glad of the supply was the last thing she'd ever expected.

He ripped open the foil packet with his teeth, while she worked the button fly of his jeans. His hands continued to shake so she took the condom from him, easily slipping it over the tip of his penis. Her fingers lingered as their gazes caught and held, holding them both mesmerized.

"I treated a former prostitute with AIDS when I lived in L.A.," she told him in a husky voice she barely recognized. "When I asked her if she'd contracted the disease from unprotected sex, she told me that applying a condom can be the most erotic form of foreplay."

To illustrate, she wrapped her fingers around his impossibly hard length and slowly eased the condom down a fraction of an inch, using her other hand to gently massage his sac.

"Did you know a talented woman can use her mouth to apply a condom?" She didn't wait for him to respond, but slipped off the counter and settled to her knees in front of him.

Chase's breath stilled and his stomach bottomed out. Dee was never more beautiful, and never less a subject. Right now, she was the woman he wanted with every inch of his body.

He gripped the counter for support when her warm breath fanned his erection, dead certain he was close to suffering heart failure. If she had any of the little tools she'd used the night he'd slept in her apartment handy, he had little doubt she'd be calling his physical reaction to her a medical emergency.

"It's all in the lips, tongue and just the right amount of suction," she murmured softly.

The heat of her mouth covered him and he nearly came out of his skin as she began to ease the protective coating down his shaft, illustrating the most incredibly erotic technique he'd ever had the pleasure of enduring.

His knees nearly buckled as she continued to use her lips and tongue, arousing him to the point of pain. He made a drastic error in judgment by watching her, the sight of her mouth surrounding him was very nearly his undoing.

Unable to bear another moment of the exquisite pleasure, he reached for her, hauling her up against him. His breath came in such hard short pants, like he was gasping for air and would never be able to pull enough into his oxygen-deprived lungs. "Please tell me that is *not* what you show to the senior class."

She laughed softly. "I reserve that little technique for private showings only."

"I don't think I can handle any more of your techniques." He lifted her onto the counter again. "At least not without cheating us both."

She pulled him close by wrapping her arms around his neck. Using her teeth, she nipped playfully at his bottom lip. "There's no shame in premature ejaculation," she said. "It's not—"

"Not going to happen." He moved between her thighs.

Her soft laughter washed over him, making him forget all about cases and leads, forcing him instead to concentrate on the sensual, erotic woman driving him insane with her mouth, her body and her gentle, sexy teasing voice.

"I can make you come without even touching your penis," she said, a sassy glint making her gaze sparkle enticingly.

He moved closer, rubbing the tip of his penis against the hot wet valley to her soul. "Wanna bet?"

She laughed again. "You think you've got yourself a sure thing, don't you? Be prepared to lose."

"I doubt that." He teased her by pressing against her, but not penetrating as deep as they both wanted, both needed more desperately than their next breath.

She rocked her hips forward, and he pulled slightly back. The delicate lift of one arched brow spelled out her skepticism loud and clear. "Name your price, Coach," she said, her voice filled with enough confidence for both of them.

He pushed his tip inside her, her body instantly clenching around him. "Dinner," he rasped, struggling to maintain his control.

She settled her heels high on his hips, letting her legs fall open, then rocked forward. He grit his teeth.

"That's too easy," she said, placing her palms flat on the counter behind her. She rocked forward again and a groan ripped from his chest. "Winner gets to tie up the loser and have their way with them."

"When?" he asked with a great deal of effort.

She tightened around him and he struggled for breath.

"Now," she said, lifting herself and pressing forward to glide over his length. She closed her eyes and moaned, a soft purring sound deep in her throat when he retreated with equal slowness.

"Right this second?" She couldn't want to stop the sweet pleasure they were both enjoying to play some game, could she? Or was that part of her plan?

"Hmm," she said, rocking forward then lifting her bottom off the counter.

He gripped her hips and held her, moving against her.

"Later," she said, matching the increased tempo. "Right…now…I—I…Chase," she cried out as another orgasm gripped her.

Her head fell back, her long sable hair brushing his fingers. Her back bowed as a series of sexy little moans bubbled in her throat. He moved his hand to her bottom, then splayed his fingers over her throat, easing them down over her breasts and down her flat stomach to her moist curls. Using his thumb, he applied the slightest bit of pressure to her swollen flesh before the wave of pleasure passed.

A series of moans coalesced on his name as her body clenched him even tighter. Unable to bear the sweet torture another minute, he followed her over the edge into his own mind-blowing orgasm. He thrust into her over and over again as her body milked his, pulling him down into the oblivious whirlpool with her.

Slowly his sense of their surroundings returned. The gentle hum of the air-conditioning unit filled the quiet kitchen, the only other sound their own labored breathing.

He slipped his hands into her hair, cupping her silky smooth face in his palms. Slowly he dipped his head, for a kiss more sweet and tender than any he'd ever experienced.

He lifted his head to look at her. Her eyes were more gold than green, something he was certain was caused by their lovemaking. His golden-eyed...subject?

A slow, sexy smile spread across her face. "How long do you need?"

He frowned. "What?"

She laughed, the sound all husky. "What's your downtime?"

He was lost. "Downtime?"

She shifted on the counter and tugged her blouse around her, hiding her glorious body from his inquisitive gaze. "How long does it usually take you to recover after making love?"

He took care of the condom, then scooped up the lacy panties and cotton shorts he'd tossed on the floor earlier to hand to her. The look in her eyes made him downright nervous. "Why? What'd you have in mind?" he asked, planting a quick, hard kiss on her lips.

She didn't bother to put her clothes on, but slid off the counter and covered the two feet separating them. "About thirty minutes?" she asked, a wicked gleam in her gold-hued expressive green eyes.

He shrugged. "About that. Maybe sooner," he said looking down at her.

The grin canting her slightly swollen lips was getting him spooked. What was she up to this time?

"That's what I figured." She reached up, kissed him, then strolled to the refrigerator. She opened the freezer and fished around for something, then chuckled low when she found whatever she was looking for.

She pushed the freezer door closed and turned to face him. "Ready to lose that bet?" she asked.

Words failed him, so he nodded. He was lucky he could still walk when she crooked her finger. He followed, keeping his eyes locked on the bright cherry-red Popsicle in her hand.

# 12

"YOU DON'T PLAY FAIR."

Dee grinned. No, she really hadn't, but all was fair in the name of love and war. No, not love, she thought. Sex. Pleasure. Intense pleasure, that's all it could ever be. Nothing more involved than a sexual romp, even if they were destined for one of erotic proportions. No love. None. Not allowed. Or was that just a convenient method of keeping her emotions locked up tight?

She looped the ends of the blue silk scarf securing Chase's right hand around the upper post of the bed. "I told you I could make you come without touching you."

"I didn't think you meant by crooking your finger at me," he complained good-naturedly. "Your Popsicle is going to melt."

"Don't you worry about that," she said, flashing him a grin before tugging the knot of the animal-print scarf holding his left hand to test its strength. "I guarantee, you're going to love this. There. How's that?"

He arched his neck to get a better look at her handi-work, then tugged on the scarves. "I can't believe I let you talk me into this," he said, shooting her a worried look when the silk ties refused to give. "And for the record, Doc, I'd rather I be the one doing the tying."

"Maybe next time." She slipped off the bed and walked around to the foot, plucking the last two scarves from the dresser lying in a silken heap next to her still opened medical bag. "Besides, a bet's a bet, and you lost."

"You were intentionally misleading," he argued, tugging unsuccessfully on the scarves again.

She laughed while quickly securing his feet to the bottom posts before he changed his mind.

He tried to lift his foot, only to discover she'd allowed him a mere four inches of leeway. "Where'd you learn to tie knots like that?"

*My brother* nearly spilled from her lips, but she caught herself. "I was a bit of a tomboy when I was a kid," she said instead.

At least that much was the truth. More often than not, Jared was her only playmate. He'd always hated her ideas of fun, unless she dragged out her dolls, and then his G.I. Joes had done despicable things to Barbie. For the most part, her summer days had been spent as a sea captain captured by the evil pirate, or a prisoner of war to Jared's soldier of fortune, her role usually ending with her tied up and tortured. Of course her brother's idea of torture consisted of eating his ice-cream bar in front of her, as well as polishing off half of hers. Innocuous by real evil-villain guidelines, but for an eight-year-old girl, the loss of even a quarter of her ice-cream bar had been incredibly traumatic.

She waited until Chase was looking at her before letting her blouse fall to the floor in a puddle of pin-striped cotton at her feet. Slowly she peeled the paper off the frozen cherry pop while keeping her eyes locked with his.

Chase's narrowed gaze filled with an enticing combination of apprehension and intrigue banked heavily in desire. "I'm afraid to ask, but what exactly do you have planned?"

She rested one knee on the mattress between his feet. "Just a little touching," she said, smoothing her hand over his thigh as she climbed higher onto the bed, loving the texture of his skin beneath her fingertips.

"Touching," he repeated, his voice rough and deep. "Touching is good."

"Maybe some kissing," she added, slowly moving higher.

"I like kissing."

"Some sucking."

She slipped the Popsicle into her mouth.

His eyes blazed.

She pulled the Popsicle out slowly, absorbing the slightly melted, sugary liquid.

Chase groaned.

She straddled his thighs, moving slowly toward his already swollen penis until the tip brushed against her still-tender and sensitive feminine folds.

"Definitely some licking," she whispered, sliding her tongue along the frozen length of the pop and rocking her hips forward just enough to tease.

Chase grit his teeth and groaned again. Heaven couldn't possibly be better than watching Dee's tongue glide over the Popsicle. Hell couldn't possibly be worse than not being able to touch her.

She slipped the pop into her mouth then pulled it out again with agonizing slowness. The indentation of her cheeks as she sucked on the frozen treat, combined with the slight rocking movement of her hips in a tortuous rhythm, drove him close to the edge of sanity. Each whisper of intimacy reached clear down to his undeserving soul.

Damn, he couldn't remember when he'd been so hot.

And she was right. She really hadn't even touched him. Yet. If she did, he might just explode.

"Do you like cherries?" she asked.

He swallowed. Hard. "Yeah," he rasped. "I like cherries."

"Hmm. That's good to know."

He didn't know which was worse for his already straining body—the heated ignition of passion building in her eyes again, or the feel of her body when she slid with deliberate slowness over him. He felt each rasp of skin, each glide of silk. He drew in a myriad of scents, the musky hint of sex, her light floral fragrance and sugar.

She was pure fantasy, and he'd walked right into the middle of one hell of a whopper that even he would've had a hard time imagining. Until now, his fantasies were tame in comparison, consisting mostly of the physical act of intercourse, of making love until they were both too exhausted to do anything but hold each other, followed by more sensual exploration and lovemaking, over and over. The last thing he'd bargained for had been Dee and a cherry-red Popsicle.

Now that he'd tasted reality, fantasies would never be enough.

She stopped and leaned over him, close, but too far for him to touch, to taste, to make her his in an elemental way. He wanted to touch her, taste her, lose himself inside her and carry them both into sweet oblivion.

Dee had entirely something else in mind, which gave him serious doubts about his ability to survive whatever erotic fantasies she'd been busy imagining.

"How much do you like cherries?" she asked, her voice a velvety purr of sound.

"A lot," he said around the dryness in his throat.

She held the Popsicle just above his lips, the look in her eyes pure sin. "Would you like a taste?"

All he could manage was a brief nod.

The smile curving her lips was nothing short of wicked. Using one hand to support herself, she continued to lean over him, then pulled the Popsicle away from his mouth to smooth the tip over her nipple. The mauve-colored flesh puckered at the contact. A shiver chased through her and she trembled against him.

He nearly came.

An invitation didn't get much more engraved than this, he thought as she leaned forward and offered him her breast. He pulled her into his mouth, tasting her chilled sugary skin, knowing he'd never taste anything so sweet again. After this, if he looked at another Popsicle without getting a raging hard-on, it would be a miracle.

She rubbed the pop across her other breast, then shifted her position, offering him another tantalizing treat. He used his teeth to graze her nipple, then pulled her deep into his mouth. She moaned softly, an enticing little sound in the back of her throat. Her hips moved, rubbing her moist heat against his chest.

He tugged on the silken bonds preventing him from having what he wanted...Dee. He wanted to touch her, *needed* to touch her, to feel her skin, to love her with his mouth until she came again in another fierce rush.

"Untie me," he rasped.

She leaned back, her breathing as hard as his own. "Not yet," she said, her voice husky and tinged with sex.

She slid the Popsicle back into her mouth, but instead of taking it out with that same agonizing slowness, she pulled it back and forth. In. Out. In. Out. Her body rocked against him in an easy matching rhythm that tested the limits of his blood pressure.

He bit the inside of his lip in an effort to distract himself, hoping the ploy would work in maintaining desperately needed control.

She rose up on her knees, her silky smooth thighs gliding against his skin as she moved backward to settle onto the mattress between his tied and spread legs. With the Popsicle still clamped between her bright cherry-covered lips, she slipped her hand around him and held him, her fingers dancing teasingly over his fully aroused flesh.

The Popsicle slid from her mouth. She eased her lips over him. Cool. Moist. Hotter than anything he'd ever felt in his life. Pleasurable pain ripped through him when she pulled away then eased her lips around him again, this time with the last piece of Popsicle in her mouth.

His hips bucked and he grit his teeth as she pumped his flesh with her incredible mouth. The pulsing started almost immediately.

"Dee," he said in a strangled whisper as his body tightened, then exploded. Too late, waves of ecstasy tossed him over the edge. It didn't stop her, and she used her lips and throat to milk him, taking all of him until he had nothing left to give.

He struggled for breath, but she didn't give him a minute to regain his strength. She tossed the empty Popsicle stick on the end table, then kissed her way up his body, stopping to whorl her tongue around his belly button. He trembled like a damned timid virgin.

"Untie me," he demanded again. He had to touch, taste, love her.

"Hmm," she murmured against his skin. "Too soon."

He strained against the silken ties. "Do you want me to beg?" he asked when her teeth grazed his nipple. She cupped his sex in her hand and gently massaged, pulled and worked magic with her fingers.

"No begging," she said. She moved, straddling him like she had before and reached over to untie his right hand. With the blue silk still wrapped around his wrist, he cupped her bottom as she reached for the animal-print tie. The second he felt it give, he guided her forward, lifting her so he could taste her musky sweetness again.

She cried out, the sound an erotic mixture of pleasure and pain as his tongue flicked against her folds. He held her still when she tried to move away, driving his tongue deep inside her body, using his teeth to tenderly tease her. His name fell from her lips in a strangled cry of pleasure. Her back bowed and her hands landed behind her on his thighs. He supported her, gently kneading her bottom while easing his fingers closer to her core, drinking his fill as her moist heat spilled onto his tongue.

Nothing else existed. Only Dee and the intense orgasm racking her body and her soft whimpers of pleasure as he unrelentingly pushed her over the edge into yet another crashing spasm of pleasure.

Slowly he returned her to earth. But he was far from finished. Rock-hard and ready to make her his again, he carefully rolled her to her back. He tried to roll with her, but the scarves securing his ankles kept him from his goal. After a mild curse and two quick pulls on the silken bonds, he shifted, pulling her beneath him.

Her eyes. Her eyes were a brilliant shade of gold, sparkling and filled with a deep simmering passion. Passion he'd put there and would do so again before the day was over if he had any say in the matter.

Her lids fluttered almost sleepily. The tight clamp of her thighs gripping his hips belied the relaxed expression on her beautiful serene face. She lifted her bottom to meet him, seeking that link that would make them one.

He slid into her hot, swollen flesh gripping him in a fiercely erotic hold. He was gone. Lost in the intensity of swirling sensations.

Heat. Passion. Ecstasy he'd never felt completely until this moment. Until Dee.

Sounds. Music. Gentle soft moans of pleasure coalesced with his name, driving him, driving them closer to fulfillment. They both came apart as sensation after erotic sensation crashed over them, pushing them both to the top of the whirlpool, into the magic and upward to heaven.

Heaven, he thought, using his mouth to capture the last of her cries of ecstasy. A place foreign to him. A place he'd never been allowed. Definitely a place that would refuse entrance to the man who made love to the one woman he'd somehow managed to let close enough to steal his heart. All in the name of justice.

FOR THE SECOND TIME IN HIS life, Chase couldn't be more sorry that he'd been right about something. The first time had been when his mother had taken the heroin and left him alone for good. This time the effects would be much more devastating, not just to him, but to Dee.

He'd gotten close all right. That had been his goal. Well screw his goal, he thought. Because of his single-minded determination to always win, to solve each case no matter who got hurt, neither one of them would ever be the same again.

As soon as he told her the truth.

He gently tugged the peach-floral sheet over Dee's bare shoulder, then left her sleeping soundly while he quietly headed into the bathroom for a hot shower. The kinks in his body had nothing to do with the mishap on the practice field three days ago, but a much more fulfilling kind of exertion.

Sex. Hot. Erotic.

Mind-blowing sex with a woman who had somehow managed to work her way under his skin and steal into his heart when he was busy trying to find a lead to her brother's whereabouts. He was the last man on earth he'd ever call a romantic. He didn't wear his emotions on his sleeve nor believe in happy endings. Most of the endings he'd witnessed ended bloody or with families ripped apart by tragedy. As he flipped the tap and stepped beneath the stinging spray, he knew nothing would ever be the same again.

Too bad the romance he and Dee were headed for had tragic ending written all over it.

He braced his hands on the tiles and tipped his head forward, letting the steamy water sluice down his back. Why couldn't there be a way for him to solve the case and keep the girl? No matter how many different scenarios he ran through his mind, one answer always stood head and shoulders above the rest. The one that had Dee calling him everything but a human being and walking out of his life forever.

So if that was the case, then why wasn't he going balls to the wall to find Romine? Why wasn't he probing and prodding Dee with questions that would lead him to his prey? Why in the hell was he tiptoeing around her?

He clenched his hands into fists against the tiles. Because he'd known the minute he'd stared at the surveillance photos of her she wasn't a typical subject. Because deep in his gut he'd suspected all along she really didn't know dick about where her brother had been hiding the past three years.

He lifted his face to the stinging spray, silently cursing his stupidity. Bend-the-Rules Bracken had made a rookie's mistake and he had no one to blame but himself. He'd gotten involved.

He finished showering, trying to figure out where that left him, and the case. "Unemployed and unresolved, that's where," he grumbled, snagging a plush peach towel from the bar.

He dried off and tied the towel around his waist before heading back into the bedroom. He stopped in the doorway. Disappointment mingled with relief when he found her still sleeping soundly.

He had two immediate decisions to make. What exactly did he say to Dee now that they'd charged across every boundary he'd ever established for himself and every barrier she'd placed around her?

The answer left him with a tight knot in his stomach.

The other question was more complicated no matter how he looked at it. Exactly how much further was he willing to go to gain the information he needed to secure his future with the Bureau?

The answer left his heart stone-cold.

DEE GRINNED HER THANKS to the waitress and tried to ignore Lucille's probing gaze. Unfortunately her ploy wasn't working. Dinner with her friend had been a response to what she'd thought was just another one of Lucille's spontaneous invitations. Dee figured if she'd been paying closer attention, she wouldn't have fallen into the older woman's perfectly spun, blatant attempt to pry into her love life.

"I've seen that look before," Lucille said, picking the diced tomatoes from her dinner salad. "Just can't say I've ever seen it on you."

Dee sprinkled a hefty amount of pepper over her light ranch dressing and croutons. "I'm afraid to ask what look you're referring to," she said, then took a bite of salad, knowing *exactly* what Lucille meant.

"That *I'm in love* look. As old as I am, you can bet I've seen it before. You've had *dingbat* written all over you all day long."

Dee's mouth fell open, then she snapped it closed. "I have not," she argued without a hint of conviction.

"Sugar," Lucille drawled, her soft blue eyes filled with humor, "you made Netta look like a qualified candidate for one of those millionaire shows today. Now that's just plain shameful, if you ask me."

Dee frowned at her friend, then plucked a cherry tomato from her salad. "Who's asking?"

Dee's problem was that she couldn't completely deny Lucille's very astute summation of her behavior. The truth of her friend's statement bothered a perfectionist like Dee. She *had* been distracted today, and had been caught staring off into space by just about everyone at the clinic. To her frustration, cranky old Claymore was included in that very short list.

She had no one to blame but herself. And Chase.

A half smile tugged her lips.

Lucille set her fork on the edge of her salad plate. "See, there you go again. What is going on with you today? Or should I ask *who?*"

Dee looked away from the knowing smile on Lucille's gently lined face.

"Does this have anything to do with a certain new neighbor?"

Dee opened her mouth again, and promptly closed it— again. What was the point when she couldn't deny it anyway?

"I knew it," Lucille said, slapping her hand on the table. "You're banging Coach Bracken, aren't you?"

Dee looked frantically around the crowded diner, grinning helplessly at the quartet of elderly women craning their necks in her direction. "Would you keep your voice down. I am not *banging* Chase."

Lucille shrugged. "Big deal. So you jumped his bones, danced the horizontal mambo, charmed the snake. Who cares so long as it was worth your time?"

Dee stared at her fifty-something-year-old friend for a full five seconds, stunned. Then, she laughed. She couldn't help herself. And a good hearty laugh, too, that felt wonderfully liberating even if it was too rusty and foreign. "Where do you get this stuff?"

"Four teenage grandsons who listen to too much rap music if you ask my daughter."

"And I'll bet you hated your daughter's choice in music, too. Your folks probably thought Elvis was the devil incarnate. And for the record, my parents also disliked my musical preferences. It's one of those sneaky viruses that creeps into delivery rooms when no one is looking and infects the new parents. *I will hate my child's choice of music, reading and television.*"

"Okay," Lucille laughed, brushing a wisp of peppered hair away from her face. "I get your point, sugar. But I won't change my mind about that makeup- and leather-wearing guy with the obscene tongue. There's something wrong with a man who can do what he does with that thing. Honestly."

Unbidden images drifted into her mind. No, she wouldn't go there! She really wouldn't.

The stern lecture did nothing to banish the gloriously erotic thoughts of Chase and the things he could do with *his* tongue, or how he'd made her lose total and complete control, and especially how he had her practically screaming with pleasure as he'd brought her to orgasm after orgasm during the night.

Maybe this temporary affair thing wouldn't be such a bad deal after all.

Chase was way too addicting. She seriously doubted a twelve-step program existed to assist her in eliminating the habit he was quickly becoming.

Lucille narrowed her all too knowing gaze. "And now you're changing the subject, Miss Destiny."

Dee just flashed her friend a wicked grin. Lucille only called her Miss Destiny when she was pulling the mother hen routine, like now. Next she'd be getting a lecture on the practices of safe sex.

The thought instantly sobered her. It was a lecture she obviously needed to hear since they'd gotten so lost in the passion yesterday morning, they'd stupidly made love without protection during her little Popsicle show. They'd used protection later, but the subject of what happened was something they'd carefully avoided all afternoon and into the night. They both knew better, and there was no excuse for their reckless behavior. The cold, hard reality that they had both gotten completely lost in the act of loving did nothing to alleviate the gravity of what they'd done and the risks they'd both taken.

Lucille gave her head a gentle shake. "There you go again," she said, pushing that stray lock of salt-and-pepper hair away from her forehead again. "Sugar, this is serious."

Dee waited for the waitress to pick up their salad plates before answering. "I don't know," she finally told Lucille. "It wasn't supposed to be. It was supposed be…"

"Just sex?" At Dee's nod, Lucille asked, "Can it really ever be just about sex?"

Dee was quiet for a moment before answering. "I don't know. Maybe it can't. Maybe there is no such thing as an affair without emotional involvement. But it can't be anything else."

"Who says it can't?"

"Lucille, I'm moving in about eight weeks."

The other woman shrugged her slender shoulders. "So who says you *have* to leave?"

"The government does. My contract expires soon and then I'm off to New York."

"So you finally decided, huh?"

She nodded, not exactly thrilled with her decision, and afraid to pinpoint exactly when her enthusiasm had waned. But she knew. It'd been the minute she opened her door three weeks ago and found Chase on her doorstep.

Nor could she say exactly what had been the final deciding factor, but at some point between the time she'd left the hospital Sunday morning and right this second, she decided she might as well settle in New York. With the salary Presbyterian was offering her, she wouldn't have to worry about looking for a roommate, either, and might even get lucky enough to find a nice rent-controlled apartment to sublet in Manhattan.

Lucille sat back as the waitress set a platter of sizzling fajitas for two between them. "You know," the older woman said, "just because your contract is expiring doesn't mean you have to leave us."

Dee scooped a serving of toppings onto her plate, then took the flour tortilla Lucille handed her from the warmer. "What are you suggesting? That I stay here and put up with Claymore the rest of my life?"

"He can be an obstinate SOB, but he's not all bad."

Dee sighed. "I know. He's good with the patients he

still sees, or Netta, for reasons I'm not sure I want to know about. Even if I wanted to stay, the clinic couldn't afford to pay me."

"So you supplement like you do at the hospital every other weekend."

"It's been more like every weekend lately. And I'm supposed to have a life, when? After I get as old and crabby as Claymore?"

Lucille laughed softly. "Make an offer to buy him out. The clinic turns a good profit, you know."

It was Dee's turn to laugh, but the sound lacked humor. "Buy him out? With what? My good looks?"

Lucille's expression sobered. "If you've got your heart set on living life in the fast lane, then you go for it, sugar. I know you'll make us all proud. But if you want this old woman's advice, it's just my opinion mind you, but I think you're making a big mistake. Cole Harbor needs a doctor since Thaddius won't be able to practice much longer. The people here adore you. You're no-nonsense and compassionate without the bull or the arrogance a lot of big-time quacks from those fancy medical schools have." She shrugged. "You won't like hearing it, but you're a lot like Thaddius when he first came back to Cole Harbor."

"Oh, that's reassuring," Dee quipped before biting into the warmed tortilla.

"Just something else you should consider before you make your final decision."

Something caught Dee's attention and it wasn't Lucille's opinion about life in the fast lane. She set her fork down and pushed the plate aside. "What do you mean he *won't* be able to practice much longer?"

"Forget I said anything."

Dee wasn't buying Lucille's sudden interest in the red and green bell peppers on her plate. "Lucille?"

The older woman sighed heavily. "If he knows I told you…you can't let him know I told you."

"What's wrong with Claymore?"

Lucille leaned forward. "He's been diagnosed with cancer," she said in a hushed tone.

Dee closed her eyes. As much as she and Claymore argued, she really did like the old man. It was part of the reason she worked so hard to earn his respect. Well, at least she did when he wasn't being so damned sanctimonious or condescending. "How do you know this?"

"He found out Friday. He's been having some problems and suspected something could really be wrong." Lucille laid her hand over Dee's. "Sugar, he doesn't want anyone to know, so he's seeing an oncologist over in Charleston. That's where I went Thursday night. I took him down and stayed with him."

Dee slumped back in the booth and wrapped her arms around her middle. She couldn't believe she was hearing this. Thaddius Claymore might be a thorn in her professional backside, but she couldn't deny she hadn't learned more than a few tricks of the trade from his down-home, sage and simple medical wisdom. Two years ago she never would've advised a young mother to give her child lukewarm cola to cure a bellyache, or wrap thick cobwebs around a cut finger to staunch the flow of blood until they could get into the clinic. Sure, there were certain issues she hadn't hesitated to fight him on when it came to patient care, but in all honesty, she'd witnessed Claymore's use of old-fashioned medical techniques too many times to argue medical science versus home remedy when something simple worked just as effectively.

Cole Harbor would miss him. Hell, she'd even miss the old curmudgeon.

She lifted her gaze to Lucille's saddened one. "What did they say?"

"Six months. Maybe a year or two if he undergoes treatment."

"Let me guess. He's going to be his usual stubborn self about this, right?"

Lucille nodded her head. "You know how he is, Dee. The fact that he even went to see an oncologist was surprising enough, let alone asking someone to go with him."

"Damn him," she whispered vehemently. "Doesn't he know how much he's needed around this town?"

"You know as well as he does that cancer—"

"Isn't always a death sentence," she interrupted. "Unless…" she let her voice trail off and looked at Lucille expectantly. The older woman shifted her gaze elsewhere and Dee muttered a few more harshly whispered curses.

"How bad?" she finally asked, but already knew the answer.

"It's in the lymph nodes," Lucille said quietly.

She blinked back the moisture burning her eyes. Dammit! Where were her emotional barriers when she needed them. She didn't want to care. She didn't want to worry about Claymore or watch the once robust, cantankerous man wither away in extreme pain. She didn't want the concern filling her heart for the man who'd made her life a living hell or wonder what the residents of Cole Harbor would do without a physician they knew or trusted to turn to in their times of need.

She didn't want or need any of this, but here she was, smack in the middle of feeling things she'd been trained from an early age not to feel…emotional attachment. Personally, and now professionally, what was once a safe harbor had turned into an emotional roller coaster.

Just her luck, the attendant had failed to secure the safety latch.

# 13

CHASE PULLED DEE CLOSER to his side before tucking
the sheet around them. "It was hell. Pure living hell."

Her sweet laughter drifted up to him. "You're over-
reacting. It really couldn't have been all that bad."

His first day posing as a teacher hadn't been all bad.
At least until the bell had sounded, which signaled the
end of fifth period classes...and the beginning of his journey straight into teacher hell. "Believe me, Senior Health
Issues might be a worthwhile subject, but there's just
something intimidating about talking sex with twenty-
four seventeen- and eighteen-year-olds who probably already know more about the subject than I do."

"I doubt that," she quipped, smoothing her hand over
his belly. His body stirred in reaction.

Senior Sex wasn't his only problem, and he'd been
doing a stellar job of avoiding the truth. He was in trouble, and in way over his head. As an agent, he was close
to blowing the case that would just about guarantee his
continued employment with the Bureau. As a man, he
was in danger of blowing the best thing that had ever
happened to him, because no matter which way he looked
at the situation, when he told Dee the truth, their relationship would come to a screeching halt.

And therein lay his problem. He wanted that relationship with her. He'd come home from practice and hadn't
even bothered to go upstairs to his apartment, but had

gone straight to Dee's place instead. Damn if it hadn't been the most natural course of action for him to take, either. He'd showered and changed at her place, then she'd cuddled up next to him on the sofa so they could watch the evening news together. Two hours later, they were still wide-awake, although a lot more relaxed, and couldn't seem to get enough of each other's company.

All that would change when he told her, something he'd spent a lot of time thinking about the past twenty-four hours. He just had to find the right time to do it, and that wouldn't be until after he did a little more investigating. There was something about the case that had been bothering him. Not from the moment the first box had been carted into his Manhattan apartment for him to study, but during his heated conversation with Pelham. He didn't have a clue yet what it was, but there was always something somewhere in every case that had been overlooked, that one vital clue that would have all the pieces fitting together and falling perfectly into place. He'd find it. He always did. And when he had the piece in place, then he could tell her who he was and why he'd really been in Cole Harbor all these weeks.

All he could do in the meantime was pray she'd be able to forgive him.

"How did it really go today?" she asked him, her fingers teasing the line of hair that arrowed down his torso.

"The gym classes were pretty normal, and the junior level introduction to Criminal Justice and a senior elective Sociology course on law and society wasn't half bad. I started them out with serial killers and the guys really seemed to get into the discussion."

"But?"

He chuckled. "Guess you don't want to hear about the study hall I'm monitoring, either, huh?"

"No. I want to know how your health class went."

During the few quiet moments he'd had throughout the day, when Dee hadn't interrupted his thoughts, he'd actually considered teaching as a possible secondary career. Or maybe it was because of her he'd allowed his thoughts to travel in that direction, he couldn't be sure. One thing he did know for certain, however, was that any inkling toward a teaching career fell out the second-story classroom window by the end of his last, and dreaded class of the day.

"For the most part, the kids are pretty great. I don't know what I expected, maybe boredom."

"In Senior Sex?" she laughed. "Hardly."

"Yeah, well, I was hoping, okay? It wasn't too bad. If I didn't know most of the guys in the class from the team, I'd have sworn they were all mute. Other than a few immature snickers at first, no one made a sound for the first twenty minutes. It looked like a junior high-school dance in there. Boys on one side, girls on the other. Except for two Cougar football groupies, Natalie Jardine and Heather Nash, who sat with the cluster of guys."

She snuggled closer. "Ah, yes. I know them both well."

"Handing out condoms?"

"Sorry, doctor-patient privilege," she said in a suddenly quiet tone.

Had she been struck by the same thought as he? he wondered. That they'd made love without protection the day before? The damage was already done, but he'd been prepared tonight and had greatly enjoyed the benefits of her erotic condom application a second time. The last thing he needed was to knock up the town doctor, especially since he'd been assigned the Senior Sex class. Not that he'd ever get to see any kid they might have created, he thought around the heavy weight that landed on his chest suddenly. Once Dee found out the truth, he had no illusions about their future.

"How's your schedule Friday?" he asked, shifting their positions so they were facing each other. "Ready to tackle that cucumber?"

A slight grin tugged her lips. "Let me check and get back to you tomorrow. I should be free since it's my usual weekend at county and I always leave the clinic around noon."

Lying next to her, close and intimate, his heart squeezed. He liked this coming home and playing house routine. Yet, despite Susan and Leo Mitchell's influence in his life, he still had a hard time believing in happy endings. For once in his life, he sincerely wished the mythical happily-ever-after wasn't just a fairy tale.

Something had gone wrong. Bend-the-Rules Bracken actually felt happy for once in his life, and he knew without an ounce of doubt Dee was the cause. Too bad their time together was no more based in reality than a fairy tale because a reality-based relationship with Dee was exactly what he wanted, and the last thing the lady doctor would ever order.

AFTER TWO DAYS OF COMBING the Romine files again, Chase still hadn't found anything new that would help him solve the case. He needed a clue, something everyone had missed, a tiny detail that failed to make sense or fit the crime. Chase flipped open the evidence file to the first page for the third time in as many hours. He knew whatever he was looking for had to be in these files.

Some small detail he, and all the others before him, had missed. He could feel it.

Or maybe he just *wanted* it to be there.

With Dee in a neighboring town for the night on what she called her backwater rounds, Chase spent Wednesday evening alone in his apartment with the case files. He'd graded his first set of papers from his Law and Society class, and with his intentionally unremarkable surveillance reports out of the way, he'd decided to search the files again, certain the answers he was looking for would be there. Of course finding answers would be a whole lot easier if he knew the questions.

He pulled out a yellow pad and drew two lines down the page, separating the sheet into thirds. He wrote evidence and motive/means in the first and second columns, and in the third, a big question mark.

He jotted down the evidence pointing at Romine. There was little doubt about Romine's guilt, at least on paper. Ballistics reports, prints, hell, they even had DNA from a hair sample collected at the scene. Still, as he read through each detail of the case again, he couldn't shake the feeling that the evidence against Dee's brother might just be a little too airtight.

*Maybe too pat?*

Chase shook his head and scanned the background information on Romine. Forty minutes later, according to everything he'd covered again, the only real motive Chase could find for Jared having committed the crime totaled close to a couple of million bucks.

He wrote the figure down. Okay, so two million dollars was a pretty strong incentive for murder, especially for a guy who'd had to scrimp and save to put himself through college in order to join the Bureau.

Still, the theft made no sense, Chase reasoned, since

Romine had spent four years in Naval Intelligence while gaining one of those fast-track degrees that only required occasional physical attendance. Dee had made it through college and med school on partial scholarships, loans and by supporting herself with part-time jobs. The only exception was the small monthly check her brother sent to her.

Frowning, he pulled out the file with Romine's financial records and spread the documents over the worktable in the spare room. A monthly check had been directly deposited into Dee's checking account during her time in school, but the amount was hardly enough to cover the most basic living expenses. No out-of-the-ordinary withdrawals or deposits, no outrageous living expenses to raise a red flag. There wasn't so much as a bounced check or an unpaid parking ticket in Romine's background.

He double-checked the dates of the deposits made to Dee. As he suspected, once Jared had gone underground, the payments stopped. Either he was smart and hiding the cash, or he didn't have a dime of the money Senator Phipps reported stolen from his office.

Chase leaned back in the chair, folded his hands over his chest and formed a steeple with his index fingers. What was the senator doing with nearly two million in cash in an unlocked drawer anyway? he wondered, tapping his fingers together. Payoff money? Bribes?

He let out a sigh and straightened. In the column with the question mark, he jotted "money drawer."

He flipped open the file with the crime-scene photos, then rifled through another file for the M.E. reports on the victims. No chalk lines in these shots, he thought, dispassionately studying the images of Special Agent Brad Dysert and the senator's right-hand man, Roland Santiago. Dysert lay facedown on the senator's bloodstained cream carpeting, a bullet to the back of his head. Santiago lay about six feet away, face up with a bullet straight to the heart.

The M.E. report indicated bruising on the back of Dysert's skull, not associated with the gunshot wound. Why did Romine strike Dysert before shooting him? Santiago's death was listed as a cardiac arrest with the gunshot a suspected contributing factor. It was all bull in Chase's opinion. Santiago might have had a heart attack, but the gunshot wound killed him.

Chase made another notation on the column with the question mark.

Maybe Dysert and Santiago had surprised Romine when he was helping himself to the senator's money drawer. That could be true of Santiago and could explain the heart attack, but the photos of Dysert indicated otherwise. The body was facedown, and in his experience, when a victim surprised a robbery in progress, more often than not the force of the bullet knocked the victim halfway across the room. A bullet to the back of the skull was planned, not a spontaneous response to an interrupted theft.

So why would Romine wipe out his own partner and a senatorial aide if it wasn't for the money? A deep-cover agent, such as Romine, collected contacts like Wall Street execs collected business cards at a cocktail party. Money laundering was a distinct possibility, but Chase had his doubts, just as he doubted Romine had passed the greenbacks to Dee. She lived like a pauper, even below her means, in his opinion. She drove a ten-year-old tin can she called a car, and had a savings account with a balance close to eight grand. There were no high-interest bearing certificates of deposit, money market accounts, or T-bills. About the only item of any financial significance was a relatively small stock portfolio made up of nothing more exciting than a few mutual funds.

So where was the money? He'd bet his badge Romine didn't have it, or even knew of its existence.

He slipped Jared's personnel file out of the box near his feet and settled back to read through the contents yet again. Professional background, personal history, known associates, even his vaccination record from elementary school were tabbed. None of the documents had changed since the last time he'd reviewed the file.

He let out a frustrated sigh and tossed the papers on the desk. Leaning back in the chair, he rubbed his eyes with the heels of his hands. There had to be something, somewhere that would give him a hint as to Romine's whereabouts.

*A fool's errand if one ever existed.*

He picked up the file again and flipped to the page of known associates. Dee, of course was listed, as well as a couple of guys Romine had served with in Intelligence. Margin notes indicated one had been killed on assignment, the other had retired in Hawaii and now ran a charter-boat service. Once a sailor, always a sailor, he thought.

Deeper into the file, he read the handwritten note by one of his predecessors.

*Peyton Douglas, attorney with Justice Department. Last contact two days prior to suspect's disappearance. No follow-up required.*

A small mark near the top of the sheet caught his attention, so small, he nearly missed it since it was all but covered by the clips holding the documents in place. He opened the fasteners and slid the other documents from the file.

"Well, I'll be damned," he muttered and grinned. The

mark, a heart split into two ragged pieces, was written in the same hand as the note. "Looks like ol' Romine had himself a girl."

He searched deeper into the file, but could find no other reference to Peyton Douglas. Odd, he mused. No initial contact form, no dictated report of the interview, nothing. Very strange for the government agency that practically invented the term "in triplicate."

He shrugged. What the file couldn't tell him, the FBI's computer system would, but he still found it damned strange that the lead hadn't been pursued more thoroughly. A lead was a lead, and you followed it until you hit a dead end.

He went through a series of doors in the Bureau's security system then waited for the cyberguard to wave him past the locked gate of the most extensive computer database the government operated. After nearly a minute, he received the prompt to continue and typed Peyton Douglas's name.

Seconds later, the black screen flashed with bright red letters, warning him security clearance was required to continue.

Security clearance? "What the…" He *had* clearance. He tried again only to receive the same flashing red letters on the screen.

The escape button brought him back to the central security menu. He tried one last time. Nothing changed. He entered Dee's name. The screen immediately shifted to her South Carolina driver's license photo and statistical data. A few more clicks of the mouse button and he accessed her financial records, personal history, voter registration, even her college transcripts.

He clicked back to the central security menu and entered Peyton Douglas again.

Just as he expected, the screen flashed with those irritating words in red. *Security Clearance Required.*

The files on Peyton Douglas were blocked. There was no other explanation. Blocked by someone high up in the chain of command, too, he'd bet. It wasn't uncommon for government employees to want to keep data private, but the only way anyone in Justice could access files in the security system was through official Bureau channels.

He exited the system and hit the white page listing along northern eastern seaboard on the Internet. Nearly a couple dozen listings for P. Douglas loaded onto the screen, but only nine of them were near the D.C. area. He scrolled down the page and found three additional listings under the name Peyton Douglas, in Arlington, Baltimore, and the other in some town in Maine he didn't recognize.

He printed the page, then checked the yellow page listings for courier services and criminal defense attorneys in the area. Five minutes later, he started at the top of the list and dialed the first number.

"Hello?" A woman's gentle voice came over the phone lines.

"Is Ms. Douglas available?" he asked, forcing a harried note into his voice.

"This is she," the woman said.

"This is Cameron Burns from A-1 Delivery Service. I'm trying to deliver the motions Mr. Lexington had promised you'd have today."

"I think you have the wrong Douglas."

"You're not Peyton Douglas?"

The woman's laughter was as gentle as her voice. "Sorry. Pauline Douglas. Good luck," she said and hung up the phone.

None of the other four contacts he made were as nice

as Pauline Douglas had been. Two of the calls were to the answering machines of Peter Douglas and Prudence Douglas. By the tenth call, he realized he should've started with the Peytons on the list. The P. Douglases weren't getting him anywhere.

A woman answered on the third ring. "Hello?"

"P. Douglas please," he said.

"This is Peyton Douglas. Can I help you?"

This one sounded young, somewhere around Dee's age, he guessed. And a lot more friendly than the others he'd called.

"This is Cameron Burns from A-1 Delivery Service," he repeated the line again. "I'm trying to deliver the motions Mr. Lexington at Sterling, Keating & Mills promised you'd have today."

"There must be some mistake," she said. "I don't have a case with Mr. Lexington's office at this time."

A lawyer. So far so good.

He rustled the papers on the desk. "Says right here on the envelope to deliver at home to P. Douglas, Justice Department."

She laughed, a light, gentle sound. "Oh, they must be for *Paul* Douglas. We're always getting each other's mail." She paused for a moment. "Can you give me the name of the service again? I'll get in touch with him and have him call your office."

*Bingo!*

He had his Peyton Douglas. Any other time, he would've appreciated her caution. He rustled more papers. "That's okay. I'll get the number from Mr. Lexington. Thanks for your time, Ms. Douglas." He hung up before she could question him further.

He shifted his attention back to the computer and checked the Web site for the Department of Justice. A few wrong turns and he finally hit pay dirt with a list of counsel.

Douglas, Paul.

Douglas, Peyton.

She was the one all right. No doubt about it.

He rolled the mouse over her name and clicked. A professional head-and-shoulders shot of a lovely woman with sleek blond hair and luminous periwinkle eyes loaded onto the screen along with her professional résumé. It might not be the security file on Peyton Douglas, but any information at this point was better than flashing red letters on his monitor.

He hit the print button while reading the information on the screen. Nothing out of the ordinary as far as lawyers were concerned. Law review, Ivy League, law clerk for a Supreme Court Justice, nothing he hadn't expected for a D.C. mouthpiece born with a silver spoon in her mouth.

He scrolled farther down the page. Again, nothing unusual amid the listing of her memberships in the typical professional organizations and Bar associations. She even held a seat on the board of directors and stood as fundraising chair for a scholarship foundation for underprivileged children. Nothing to send up a single warning flag.

Except foundations and charities needed money. Somewhere, two million bucks was collecting dust. On a hunch, he exited the program and headed back into the Bureau's database to enter the foundation name. More flashing red letters.

He let out a rough sigh, and tried a second time. He had a connection. He could feel it, but without something solid, he was no closer than when he'd been handed the case.

A check of the white pages on the Web garnered an

800 number. He called, but considering the hour, hadn't expected anything more than the recorded message he'd received.

Someone was hiding something. He knew just the person to help him find out what, and maybe even who, was behind the two blocked files.

He exited the computer and fished his little black book out of his hip pocket. What he needed was a way into the locked files of the Bureau's database, and there was only one person he knew who had the talent to break into any system, no matter how secure. He could send a request through the proper channels, yet something kept him from contacting Pelham. He had a feeling he'd be better off making use of those contacts all good deep-cover agents collected.

He dialed the number and waited.

"Yeah?"

"It's Special Agent Bracken."

"I'm clean," Brian Morrison ground out with a hefty dose of anger.

Chase sighed. He needed Morrison's expertise, but couldn't blame him for being angry. Managing a lawn and garden shop under a new identity in Decatur, Georgia, was a far cry from a Wall Street computer programmer and analyst. Morrison had been the key witness in a case of bank fraud. Key witness translating to he'd received immunity for his crimes in exchange for turning over evidence that led to the arrest and conviction of half a dozen top banking officials around the country.

"That's good to hear," he said smoothly. "You wouldn't want to end up on the wrong side of the bars, now would you, Brian?"

Morrison let out a stream of breath. Chase could imagine his ratlike eyes narrowing to near slits.

"What do you want, Bracken?"

"A favor."

"Piss off. After what you did to me, you want me to help you? You nearly got me killed, you son of a bitch."

"How's your little brother doing?" he asked in that same smooth voice with just enough threat to be convincing. "I hear Attica can be a real dangerous place if a guy isn't careful."

Bend-the-Rules Bracken was back.

*Long time no see, buddy.*

"You really are a son of a bitch," Brian spat into the phone.

"So you've said."

"Is this going to take long? I'm busy."

"Bulb season?" Chase taunted.

"What do you want, Bracken?"

"Information. You up for a challenge?"

"You're not giving much choice here."

"I knew you'd see it my way," he said, and quickly calculated the miles. "I'll be there in about three hours."

Brian let out a long-suffering sigh. "See you then," he said, and disconnected the call.

Chase hung up the phone. He was operating on a hunch that could lead him nowhere. But it was more than he'd had since he'd started on the Romine case. And if he was right, the information could very well bring him closer to Jared Romine. And the truth.

He had a chance to salvage his career, but was it worth the cost of a relationship with one very special woman?

Get his man. Lose the girl.

He weighed the options.

Solve the case. Say goodbye to Dee.

"Some option," he muttered, scooping his keys off the worktable.

He'd bent rules before. Maybe this time around he could manage to bend them so no one got hurt. No one being the beautiful lady doctor who'd stolen his heart.

# 14

ONCE THE LAST PATIENT of the day left the clinic, Dee quietly stepped into Dr. Claymore's office and closed the door behind her. Thank goodness Lucille was a forgiving woman because Dee knew this was one promise she'd never be able to keep. Thaddius Claymore might be a difficult man to work with ninety-five percent of the time, but he was someone she respected. Because she respected him, she wanted to make sure he was doing all he could to extend the quality of his life for the duration of his illness, and maybe if he'd let her, help him in some small way until she left for New York.

"What are you sneaking in here for, girlie?" he said, not bothering to look up from the thick medical journal he was studying. "Trying to hospitalize another one of my patients for a little bump on the head?"

She let out a sigh. Couldn't he for once in his life address her as Dr. Romine? Was it really too much to ask?

"He was *my* patient," she reminded him gently, propping her hands behind her bottom to lean against the door. "With an injury like Chase's, a night in the hospital was in his best interest. And he would have gone, too, if you hadn't intervened."

Claymore grunted and looked at her over the rim of his bifocals. "How's *your* patient now?"

Heat scorched her cheeks. Her patient was perfectly fine, in every sense of the word.

"So that's the way of it, huh?" Claymore chuckled and slipped off his reading glasses. "The whispers about you and *your* patient have merit, do they?"

She opened her mouth to protest, but Claymore lifted his salt-and-pepper eyebrows, silently daring her to out-and-out lie to him. She nodded slowly instead.

"You could do worse," he said gruffly.

Was that his backhanded method of telling her he approved of her relationship with Chase? Funny, but the thought of his approval almost made her smile. She'd depended on no one but herself for so long, she'd almost forgotten the warm fuzzies of someone caring about *her* for a change.

"I didn't come in here to talk about me, Dr. Claymore."

It was his turn to let out a sigh. "Lucille's got a big mouth," he complained. "I knew I shouldn't have trusted that cantankerous old busybody with a secret."

Despite the gravity of their impending discussion, Dee laughed. "That's a little like calling the kettle black, isn't it?"

He turned his stock ferocious frown on her. "You calling me cantankerous?"

"If the attitude fits," she said, pushing off the wall. She crossed the faded and worn Oriental rug to the over-stuffed burgundy-velvet chair and sat.

He shut the book in his lap and set it on the desk. "Well, I'm no busybody. I say live and let live."

"Really? Since when?"

Something that could actually be considered a tease of a smile tipped his mouth. "You watch your tongue," he said, shaking his finger at her. "Last time I looked, I was still the boss around this place."

She sobered and leaned forward, wrapping her arms around her middle before looking up at him. He didn't look terminally ill. In fact, he appeared just as ornery and robust as ever. Unfortunately, in a matter of weeks, that would all change and Thaddius Claymore, M.D., would be a shadow of his former self. "Tell me what the oncologist said."

"Damn highway robbery, that's what he told me. This staying alive business is going to be expensive."

"Then you're going through with the treatment? What did he recommend?"

Claymore shifted his gaze to the window. Dust motes floated and danced in the rays of sunshine streaming through the slats of the miniblinds. The mechanism of the anniversary clock on the edge of his rich mahogany desk twisted and turned silently beneath the glass dome, slowly ticking off a full minute before he looked back at her.

"I haven't decided," he said quietly, his usual deep, gruff voice, uncharacteristically soft and gentle.

She closed her eyes and pulled in a slow breath. Pain circled her heart. For someone who'd been taught to maintain emotional indifference, she sure was doing a rotten job of it lately.

"Why?" she asked him. "Why are you being so selfish? There are so many people in this town who depend on you. They need you, Thaddius. Just like you need them."

He grunted again, no doubt in disagreement. "They'll do just fine."

She shook her head. "That's not true and you know it. Or did you forget how long it took the people around here to accept me? There are still a handful of patients who insist on seeing you. My contract's up soon and I'm off to New York. How are you going to have time to ease another physician into the clinic? Or are you going to be even more selfish and let the clinic close? Then what's going to happen to the people of Cole Harbor?''

Claymore stood and glared down at her, his thick brows pulled in a deep frown over eyes filling with agitation. "Don't you dare lecture me, missy. I'm not the one jumping at the gate like a damned nervous racehorse after the first bell. New York City," he scoffed. "A city like that will eat a little girl like you alive."

"This isn't about me, Thaddius," she said quietly. "It's about you."

He turned away and crossed the room to the rich wood mantel, where dozens of photographs in a variety of frames graced the top. He shoved his hands into the pockets of his white coat and stared at the pictures for a moment before he spoke. "I'm not afraid to die," he said, his voice solemn. "I'm an old man now. I've outlived my family. My son wanted nothing to do with medicine. Darn near broke my heart when he told me he wanted to become a marine biologist, but nothing hurt worse than when we lost him."

Thanks to Lucille, Dee knew quite a bit about Claymore's life. He'd married an only child from Louisiana and had brought her back to Cole Harbor with him when he joined his father at the clinic. He'd had one son, Trey, who at seventeen, had drowned in the Atlantic when his sailboat capsized during an unexpected storm. Thaddius's wife had followed her son within a year. He'd never remarried, although Dee had her suspicions about a long-term, occasional relationship with Lucille, but that was one area Lucille had remained unusually silent.

"It's time for me to step down and turn the clinic over to someone young, someone who cares about the patients," he said, turning to face her. "You interested?"

Nothing could have surprised her, or intrigued her, more. From the way Claymore always talked down to her, how he constantly questioned her ability, overrode her orders and undermined her authority with Netta, she was the last person she'd ever expected him to offer to take over for him.

She pulled in a deep breath and let it out slow. "I can't."

"Mind telling me why not?"

"I'm not a family practitioner. My specialty is emergency medicine."

"Not exciting enough for you?"

She shook her head. "It's not that. It's..."

"I'll tell you what it is," he said, propping his hip on the large desk. "You don't want to get hurt."

"That's ridiculous," she retorted.

He crossed his arms over his chest. "You play it tough, but you're a marshmallow under that chip on your shoulder."

"What chip?" Could this conversation have gotten any more ridiculous? "I don't have a chip on my shoulder."

The look he gave her was stern, but filled with a trace of affection she was certain she imagined. "The one I've been trying to knock off ever since you waltzed into town with your big-city doctoring ideas. These are down-home people. They didn't need some fancy medical degree flashed under their noses. They needed someone to care about them."

She stood. "I don't have to listen to this." So much for her imagining affection in his crusty old gaze.

"Sit your butt down," he ordered, the gruff voice booming with authority. "You're a good doctor. You'll make a damn fine one someday, too, if you get off that high horse and put yourself on the same level as your patients."

"I do no such thing," she argued.

"That's crap and you know it," he said, lowering his voice. "You're too afraid to get close to the patients. You're too busy hiding behind the illness to see them."

"No," she said, shaking her head vehemently. "You're wrong." He *had* to be wrong. She'd never treat an illness over the patient. The patients were always her first priority.

"Am I? Isn't that why you're so hot to trot off to New York and that big city emergency room?"

"Emergency medicine is my specialty," she said again, this time more heated.

"Gunshots. Stabbing. Suicide attempts. Twelve vehicle pileups on the freeways. Drug overdoses." He ticked them off on his fingers. "And not a one of them will be anything more to you than a goddamned chart to be filled out and filed away before you're on to the next gunshot victim, drug overdose or MVA."

"That's part of emergency medicine," she countered. "It's who you treat. The E.R. is never the same thing twice. You might set three broken arms in one night, but each one is different. The learning never stops."

"Each patient is different, too," he countered.

She sat in the chair suddenly, hit with the memory of her conversation with Chase the day they'd gone to Myrtle Beach. He'd questioned her choices, too. The thought made her pause.

"We've all got something we're afraid of, Dee," Claymore said. "If it makes you feel any better, even I've got a fear or two in my closet."

"You?" She laughed, but the sound held little humor. "What could you possibly be afraid of?" she asked with more than a hint of skepticism. Claymore was afraid of nothing, death included by his own admission.

"Pain," he said resolutely. "I'm terrified at the thought of suffering with this damned disease. You and I both know there's only so much morphine can do for a cancer patient. I'll face it because I have to. I'm not about to turn into a pansy-ass at this stage of my life, terminal illness or no terminal illness."

The hours she'd spent with one of her first patients in Cole Harbor came back to haunt her. She'd been able to take a slight edge off of his incredible pain for a while, but otherwise, she'd been completely helpless. And she'd hated every second of it. Watching Claymore go through the same end wasn't something she wanted to face.

She looked back at him. "I can't afford to stay in Cole Harbor," she told him, actively sidestepping the emotions threatening to choke her. She tried to feel nothing more than a minuscule twinge of regret, but deep in her heart she knew the horrible sinking feeling in the pit of her stomach hadn't so much to do with leaving Cole Harbor as it had to do with Chase. She'd miss Cole Harbor and the people who had become a part of her life the past two years, no doubt about it. But Chase? Her feelings for him were much more complicated than she wanted to admit.

Avoidance wasn't as simple as it once was when it came to those other, deeper emotions she'd been telling herself for days were nothing more than lust. There was a lot more to her relationship with Chase than sex. But was it enough for her to seriously contemplate remaining in Cole Harbor? The answer to that question alone made her as nervous as the racehorse Claymore compared her to.

She was being ridiculous. Since when did she base her decisions on another human being?

The answer was crystal clear. First Jared, and now Chase. If she stayed, she might never see her brother again, although she had zilch by way of guarantees if she moved to New York. If she left, her affair with Chase was over and she'd never know if what they had was the real thing. Long-distance relationships never lasted and she wasn't about to put either one of them through the stress of such a vain attempt.

She pulled in a deep breath, relief washing over her. Her reasons for leaving despite Claymore's attempt to convince her to stay had nothing to do with anyone but herself and her future. But what if...

She mentally shook herself. No what-ifs. Period.

"My agreement with the government forgives a lot of my student debt," she told Thaddius, "but not all of it. You're facing a great deal of medical expenses and couldn't afford to pay me what I need to make a living wage." There. Now that was an argument she could live with—almost.

"Who said anything about paying you? I'm offering to sell you the clinic. Everything down to the last rectal thermometer."

She stared at Claymore, momentarily stunned beyond speech. "I can't afford that," she finally said when she found her voice. "My loan payments alone make buying the clinic a financial pipe dream."

"How do you know?" he scoffed, waving away her argument. "We haven't even talked turkey yet."

"An established practice isn't cheap. You've spent

time away from Cole Harbor. You know what it takes to buy into an existing practice, and that's with partners. A sole practitioner has got to be ten times that amount.''

He stood and wandered back to the mantel, his gaze sweeping the photographs once again. "Do you know who these people are?" he asked, lifting a rough wood frame in his hand. He carried it with him and handed it to her.

She looked down into the smiling face of a young woman with wide brown eyes. She couldn't have been more than twenty-five, although the photograph was probably older. Her shining, near-white blond hair hung straight with a center part, the long strands secured with a leather headband. She wore a leather vest of the same chocolate color over an orange tie-dyed peasant blouse and a dozen or more colored beads hung around her slender neck.

Dee shrugged and handed the frame back to him, not having an inkling of his intent by showing a photograph over thirty years old.

He took the picture from her. "They're all patients of mine. Each one special for a different reason, but this one, she's…she's one I won't ever forget.''

He looked at the girl in the photograph with a kindness she'd seen only when he was with his patients. There, that look, was the reason she admired and respected him, even if he refused to grant *her* the professional courtesy she deserved.

"It was about five years after my wife passed away. We were having the mother of all summer storms that night,'' he said, his voice changing to quiet and thoughtful. "It wasn't a full-blown hurricane, but one of the most temperamental tropical storms Mother Nature had tossed at Cole Harbor in fifty years. There was an accident out on one of the county roads. A group of kids were coming home from a rock concert. The roads were so bad they probably couldn't see squat and ran headlong into another car coming in the opposite direction.

"The storm claimed half a dozen young lives that night. This little girl was the only survivor on the scene. We couldn't get the ambulance out to her because most of the roads were washed out, but by the sheer grace of God, the sheriff found a way to get through and brought her to me."

He traced his thumb over the edge of the frame, his gaze riveted on the picture. "Lora Murdoch was her name. There wasn't much left of her by the time the sheriff got her to me, but I did everything I knew how to save her. In the end, not a lick of my training made a damn bit of difference. All I could do for her was try to patch her up a little and make her as comfortable as possible.

"I didn't leave her side all night. Just her and me, alone, right here in this clinic. We couldn't even get in touch with her parents because the phone lines were down and the roads were shot. The times Lora was lucid enough to talk, she'd tell me her dreams that I knew she'd never see. She even apologized to me, telling me she didn't really mean all those awful things she said when I'd order her vaccinations when she was no taller than a weed."

A half smile filled with reminiscence, softened his weathered face. "It took over seven hours for her to die."

"Why are you telling me this?" Dee asked when he slipped into silence.

He lifted his pain-filled gaze to hers. "After Trey and my wife died, I shut down. I wasn't going to let anyone hurt me again. When I was working on Lora that night, trying to save her, the only thing I felt was the rush of adrenaline that takes over in a trauma situation. I sat beside her as she was dying, listening to her tell me that she planned to go to San Francisco and be a folk singer just as soon as she got well. I listened, but dispassionately."

Dee shrugged. "What does that have to do with me?"

He closed his eyes momentarily, as if the pain of remembering was suddenly too heavy a weight to bear. When he looked at her again, regret replaced pain. "A few minutes before she finally died, she grabbed my hand. For someone as torn up as she was, she had one hell of a grip. And then she died, holding on to me like that. I must've sat there, with Lora's cold, lifeless hand in mine for a good hour or more. And I lost it. I bawled like a pansy-ass."

"There's nothing wrong with feeling compassion for your patients. It makes us real."

"It wasn't compassion, it was self-pity. This poor girl needed someone to hold her, to listen, really listen to her last words, to offer her more than medical comfort, and I was so used to keeping a lid on my feelings, I didn't know how to give her the last thing she needed to feel while she was still on the face of the earth," he said passionately. He stood and crossed the small space separating them to reach down and place a hand on her shoulder.

"Don't make the same mistake I did for too many years," he said, his voice sounding oddly choked. "You're a damn good doctor, Dee. You can be a great one if you stop closing yourself off and let your patients mean something to you other than a procedure or another lesson in some new medical technique."

She looked away, uncomfortable with the truth—that

he could be absolutely right? Had she become so adept at closing herself off, her patients were suffering because of it? So if she feared letting anyone too close, why had she chosen a profession where she would face loss continually? She'd always believed keeping her cool and not letting her emotions get in the way would make her a better doctor. Now, she just didn't know anymore.

"Death and loss hurt," she admitted, shifting her gaze back to Claymore's. "They hurt like hell. My parents' deaths had been devastating to me, I kept it together for…for my brother's sake."

Claymore returned to his seat on the edge of the desk. "I didn't know you had a brother."

"I…" *I don't* would have been her stock answer, but if he was serious about her taking over the clinic, then he had a right to know exactly who he was selling to, didn't he? "I do. I haven't seen him in three years."

"Service?" he asked when she looked away.

She shook her head.

"Is he in some kind of trouble?"

She looked back at Claymore. She'd never told another living soul about Jared. If she was about to break her vow of silence, then it should be to Chase. After she told him she was staying in Cole Harbor. "I'll tell you about him another time," she said, and he nodded, probably understanding that after keeping the doors closed for so long, swinging them open would be a slow and careful process.

"So," Claymore said, rubbing his hands together as he moved behind his desk. "You ready to admit I'm right, girlie, and you belong here in Cole Harbor where the real medicine is?"

She pulled in a deep breath. There would be no turning

back, but she couldn't walk away from the chance to be completely self-sufficient.

"I still don't know how I can afford it," she admitted, and for the first time in a very long time, felt a twinge of hope for the future. Maybe even a future for her and Chase.

Claymore's grin widened and he pointed to the chair across from his desk. "Have a seat, Dr. Romine. Let's talk turkey."

# *15*

INSTEAD OF HEADING STRAIGHT to Dee's place as he'd done all week following the Cougar's practice, Chase climbed the stairs to his apartment. There would be no cuddling on the sofa during the late-news show tonight. There would be no pulling at each other's clothes as they made their way into the bedroom, desperate for each other. There'd be no falling on top of her fluffy peach comforter as they made love and lost themselves in the pleasure and ecstasy.

There would be nothing but honesty and betrayal from tonight onward. Maybe even hatred.

He expected to be gone from Cole Harbor by morning.

He let himself inside, showered and changed, then unlocked the surveillance room. The manila envelope with the information he'd gleaned on his trip into Decatur last night sat on the edge of the worktable. He stared at it, knowing the minute he picked it up, everything would change. Dee would hate him, but it could be no other way. She deserved to know that her brother could very well be innocent. He might not have solid proof to proclaim the case closed and Jared Romine an innocent man, but he certainly had garnered more than a few interesting details that confirmed the evidence against Romine was just a little too airtight.

He moved closer to the worktable, his feet leaden. Before he could change his mind and put off the inevitable, he scooped up the envelope, locked the door to the surveillance room and descended the wooden stairs that would lead him to Dee's unit. Dread weighed heavily on his shoulders. He tried to shrug it off, and failed. Nothing could alleviate the weight, nor douse the ball of fire burning his gut. He hated himself for what he was going to do to Dee. He'd destroy whatever trust she'd given him, a trust that hadn't come easily for her thanks to the parade of agents constantly dogging her every move.

Every insecurity he'd ever felt came clamoring back to haunt him as he opened the screen and rapped his knuckles on the door in two short bursts.

"It's open," she called out from the other side.

He sucked in a deep breath and twisted the knob. The door opened slowly, and he stepped through the threshold and came to an abrupt halt.

The room was alive with scented candles, fresh flowers and soft jazz playing on the CD player. The burning in his gut intensified. He'd come to rip out her heart, not lose himself in the sweet seduction scene she had going. He would've closed his eyes and prayed for the strength to tell her the truth, except they landed on Dee posed seductively in the archway leading to the bedroom. Soft light from the bedroom flickered behind her, more candles he guessed, the soft light illuminating her slender curves. She was a heavenly vision dressed in the sheerest nightie he'd ever seen and a smile seductive enough to drive him to his knees.

"You're late," she said, the gold highlights in her green eyes sparkling in the candlelight. She'd swept her thick sable hair up into a soft romantic style, but the silky strands refused to be tamed completely, leaving a few tendrils to cling to her throat and frame her pretty face.

"Practice ran over," he said, surprised his vocal cords responded.

"Hmm," she murmured. She moved suddenly, her body fluid, her face serene. "I want to kiss you, Chase. I want to kiss you everywhere." She turned and glided like a sensual apparition into the bedroom.

The envelope nearly slipped from his fingers. He tightened his grip, the thick paper crinkling. The truth threatened to intrude into the fantasy she'd created. He should douse the candles and turn on the lights. He should hit the power button on the CD player and force her to sit down and listen to every word he had to say. He nearly gave in to the demand for nothing but truth and honesty from this moment forward.

He couldn't. Not yet. For now, the tempting promise of sweet oblivion and the chance to forget the real reason for his coming downstairs beckoned to him like a siren song. He was helpless to stop his body's answering call, or his heart's need for Dee and the closeness that would be theirs for one last time. For one more sensual interlude to carry with him, because that's all of Destiny Romine that would be his again.

Fantasy. The promise of home on her lips.

Pleasure. The promise of her body pressed intimately against him.

Reality. The knowledge that it would never be this way for them again. With a muffled curse, he tossed reality onto the closest chair and followed her into the bedroom to lose himself in the pleasure and the fantasy of forever.

He stopped short in the threshold, suddenly unable to breathe. She stood with her back resting against one of the bedposts, her head tipped slightly to the side. He followed the trail of her fingers tracing lightly over the low scooped neckline of the sheer chemise. The look in her eyes was pure sin. Just looking at her had him impossibly hard in seconds.

"Stand over there," she said, pointing to the double-sliding mirrored doors of the closet. "Turn around and face the mirror."

He hesitated for all of two seconds, then moved to the mirrored doors. Candlelight flickered in the reflection, casting the room in a soft, seductive light. He refused to look at himself in the mirror, but he couldn't have stopped himself from watching her move toward him to save his sorry life. She stepped behind him and disappeared from view, until her hands smoothed over his sides and around to his stomach.

She tugged the shirt from his jeans, then smoothed her hands over his skin before urging him to pull off the T-shirt.

"Take off your shoes," she ordered, then worked the fastening of his jeans while he toed off his sneakers.

The rasp of the zipper drowned out the sharp breath he sucked in as her fingers dipped into the sides and eased his jeans and briefs down, pushing them over his hips. She kissed his back, then teased his spine with blazing heat as she traced the line with her tongue. She eased lower, pushing his jeans farther down his legs, gently nipping his hip, tasting his thigh, tonguing the back of his knees until they threatened to buckle.

"Put your hands on the mirror," she said, while she pulled away his jeans, briefs and effectively removed his socks before easing around in front of him. "And keep them there, no matter what."

Her hands slid over his body and she pressed against him, lifting her lips to his for a kiss. He didn't consider hesitating or disobeying her gentle commands. Their lips touched tentatively, but he needed her, desperately. He needed the oblivion and the heat, so he captured her mouth beneath his for a tongue-tangling kiss meant to seduce and inflame her desire.

Her hands were everywhere, sliding over his chest, down his sides, cupping his buttocks and rocking his hips so his erection pressed and rubbed against her. She moaned softly, followed by a whimper full of emotion when he thrust forward with a demand of his own.

She pulled her mouth from his, kissing his neck, his chest, working her way down his body, before finally settling to her knees in front of him. "I want you to watch in the mirror," she said. "I want you to watch me take you inside my mouth."

His body throbbed and his heart thundered behind his ribs. She slid her lips over his hardness, taking him inside her warm, sweet mouth, gently urging his arousal deeper.

He grit his teeth and groaned as pure pleasure crashed over him. His breath came in short hard pants as her lips and tongue pulled and promised, as her fingers teased and tantalized, as he watched her reflection in the mirror, her own hips gently rocked, her own pleasure building as she loved him in the most intimate way a woman could love a man.

*Love.* A word he hadn't thought himself capable of using. An emotion he'd never believed himself capable of feeling. It crept inside him and squeezed his heart with an iron band. He'd never be the same again.

He could feel his penis touch the back of her throat, and he was helplessly lost, unable to maintain control. He came in a powerful rush of heat, her name ripping from his chest on a wild groan of pleasure so intense he was powerless to do anything except surrender to her and ride out the blissful storm on wave after wave of passion, tossing him around helplessly in an erotic sea of ecstasy.

She touched him everywhere, kissed every inch of his body, and then she was gone. "Don't move," she said, her voice a husky whisper.

He kept his hands braced on the mirror and found her reflection. She climbed onto the bed and turned to sit facing him. With her feet on the edge of the mattress, she opened her legs and graced him with a wickedly seductive smile that had his breath stilling. Her core glistened with moisture in the candlelight. He fisted his hands against the glass.

"Tell me what you want to do to me," she said. "Tell me what you think about when we're not together."

His mouth went dry, and he briefly closed his eyes. She wasn't only incredibly sexy, but a fantasy come to life. "First, I kiss you, and hold your breasts."

She used one hand for support behind her and palmed her breast with the other. "Like this?" she murmured, rubbing her thumb over her hardened peak.

"Like that," he rasped. "Then I'd kiss them."

Keeping her gaze locked with his in the mirror, she lifted her breast in her hand beneath the whisper-thin chemise, and bent her head, tracing her tongue over the tightened rose-colored flesh through the material. Her eyes were dark green, sparkling brightly with gold. He'd never seen anything so beautiful in his life.

Heat rushed south, stirring him again. He tightened his fists against the mirror, willing himself to remain standing.

"Then I touch you," he said, without waiting for her to ask. His gaze dipped to her glistening core. "There."

Her gaze locked with his, and she smoothed her hand over her flat stomach beneath the gossamer-thin chemise. She hesitated. "How do you touch me?" she asked, her voice a silky purr.

He swallowed. "With my index finger, I slip inside you and you're wet and hot. Then I bring it out to taste."

She did, and his knees nearly buckled.

"I use two fingers now," he rasped. "I tease you. In and out. Slow. Up and down and back inside."

He stared in fascination as she did as he instructed. Her head fell back and her hips rocked in a tantalizing rhythm. He couldn't take any more. He had to have her. All of her.

"Can you feel how wet I am for you?" she asked in a breathy whisper. "How much I need you inside me, loving me?"

"You're hot," he said, the words strained and tight. "I make you hotter when I taste you. I'll taste you deeply, until you come on my tongue again and again."

"Chase," she whispered on a soft moan of pleasure.

Whether she was lost in her own pleasure or calling him to her to fulfill his erotic promise, he didn't care. He was at her side instantly, touching her, kissing her, giving her the pleasure with his mouth he promised until she cried his name, calling him over and over again as the intense orgasm consumed her.

He didn't stop.

He couldn't stop.

He loved her with his mouth, using his fingers to help push her over the edge until she came again, and then again, each time harder and more intense than the last. When neither one of them could stand another second of the erotic torture, he rose up and slipped inside her to the hilt, their bodies joined with fierce need and demand for fulfillment.

Together, they climbed higher and higher, until they came together one last time in a rush of intense emotion and exquisite pleasure.

"Are you sure you wouldn't rather have a Popsicle," she teased. "I bought a big supply of cherry."

Chase lifted his eyebrows skeptically. "You're dangerous with those things," he said, and took the bowl of chocolate chip cookie-dough ice cream she offered.

He held hers as she climbed into the bed beside him. The thin nightgown he'd practically torn from her body was a thing of the past. The seductive siren had given way to the girl next door dressed in a pair of bright purple socks to warm her feet and his white T-shirt. Her hair was mussed and her lips were slightly swollen from his kisses. She had the look of a woman well-loved. She smelled of sex, and flowers, and ice cream.

"I have something to tell you," she said, after adjusting the mound of pillows behind her to lean against the headboard. She took back her bowl of ice cream.

He had something to say, too. Only his news wouldn't be well-received. A perfectly planned bite of ice cream kept him from saying a word.

"I've decided to stay in Cole Harbor."

Her news hit his gut like a sinking anchor. If he was just the high-school teacher and football coach for Cole Harbor High School, he'd have been thrilled with her news. If she was just the town doctor, he'd have responded by asking her if she planned to make an honest man out of him. But he was Special Agent Chase Bracken. She was Jared Romine's little sister. The two did not equate to selecting china patterns and sending out embossed invitations to their family and friends to join in their happiness at the local church on a Saturday afternoon.

He kept his attention on the bowl of ice cream. He couldn't bear to see the hopefulness in her eyes. Hopefulness that they really did have a future together.

"What changed your mind?" he asked, hoping he conveyed a casualness he was far from feeling.

"This needs to stay between us," she said, before taking a bite of ice cream. "Dr. Claymore has terminal cancer. He asked me if I wanted to take over the clinic and I agreed."

That dragged his attention away from the most fascinating bowl of ice cream in his life to look at her. Her face was impassive, as if she hadn't made a monumental decision and was waiting for his reaction. A happy reaction he'd never be capable of giving her.

"I thought you said family practice wasn't your thing?" he questioned her.

She sighed and set her bowl on the nightstand. "It's an excellent opportunity," she said, facing him. "I'll still work in the E.R. at County two weekends a month. But Cole Harbor is going to need a physician. The residents here know me, and other than a few holdouts Claymore still sees, most of them trust my ability."

She looked at him, curiosity mingled with a hefty dose of apprehension and something else he could only define as a trace of fear. "There's something else you need to know," she said resting her hand over his thigh beneath the sheet. "I wasn't completely honest with you about something."

He felt her touch as if they were skin to skin. He felt her words clear to the bottom of his lying soul.

"Remember when you asked me about my family?"

Oh God, could this get any more complicated? Was there any way he could manage to dig a hole any deeper for himself? He knew what this was about. She was going to tell him about her brother, and he had to stop her.

"Dee," he said, shaking his head.

"No, this is important. I lied to you, Chase. And I'm

sorry about that, but it was something I had to do at the time and I hope you'll understand after I tell you everything.''

"Sweetheart, please let me—''

"No. Let me finish,'' she interrupted him. "My parents really are dead. I didn't lie about that, but I have a—''

The ringing of the telephone stilled her words.

"I better get that,'' she said climbing out of bed. "I'm the only one on call now that Claymore's ill.''

He slipped from bed and pulled on his jeans, stopping in the living room to pick up the envelope he'd tossed on the chair before following her into the kitchen. She answered on the third ring.

The second she hung up, he was telling her the truth. If she had to leave to take care of a patient, then he was going with her until she listened to every last word, every apology, every truth about the last month they'd spent together.

Then he'd tell her he loved her and get the hell out of her life as he knew she'd order him to do.

"Dr. Romine,'' she said into the receiver, glancing in his direction, an adorable smile curving her lips when he walked into the kitchen, envelope in hand.

She frowned. "Hello,'' she said hesitantly after a moment.

Her eyes widened suddenly and her hands started to tremble. "Jared? Oh my God,'' she cried out in what had to be a gut reaction. "It's too soon. Jared? Are you all right. What's happening?''

She closed her eyes, but not before he saw them well with tears. "Yes,'' she said, her voice a strangled, tear-filled whisper. "It's been so long.''

Chase didn't stop to think about what he was doing or

how his actions would affect Dee. He reached for the phone. "Let me talk to him."

Her eyes snapped open and she stared at him as if unable to move or react. He took the phone before she came to her senses and hung up.

"Romine," he said. "I know you're being framed. If you let me, I can help."

Silence.

"I have proof," he continued, praying Jared wouldn't sever the call. "It's scant, but it just might be enough for you to get what you need to prove your innocence."

"Who are you?" the other agent finally asked.

"Special Agent Chase Bracken," he said, carefully avoiding Dee's gaze. "Federal Bureau of Investigation. You didn't kill Santiago and Dysert, did you?"

Silence again.

"Dammit, Romine," he shot at the agent. "Don't hang up. Tell me when and where to meet you. I swear, I can help you."

"Is this line secure?" Jared asked.

"No. I'm recording it. But I can take care of that. This conversation never took place."

"How do I know this isn't a setup?"

"You're just gonna have to trust me," he said, lifting his eyes to Dee's. His heart constricted at the pain and betrayal consuming her entire body. *She'd* trusted him, and what had it gotten her? "Romine? Peyton Douglas could be in danger. My guess is it's a ploy to get to you and bring you out in the open."

Jared swore ripely. "I'll be in touch at this number within the hour," he said, and disconnected the call.

Chase hung up the phone then turned back to face Dee. The look in her eyes ripped at his heart. The accusations and betrayal squeezed it even tighter. The hatred made his chest feel like he was on fire.

"Just who the hell are you?" she spat at him.

Only one answer came to him. The first completely honest thing he'd ever say to her. "I'm the guy that fell in love with you."

# 16

CHASE WINCED AT THE deliberate coldness of Dee's laughter. There were a million other ways he could've handled her learning his identity, but he doubted any of them would have lessened the degree of anger or pain blazing in her eyes.

"You expect me to believe you? Get the hell out," she shot at him, then spun away.

He reached for her, but she was too quick. "Don't touch me."

The bitterness in her voice clawed at his conscience. She was pulling even farther away from him, not just physically, but emotionally, as well, and he was helpless in finding a way to lessen the distance. "Dee, you have to listen to me."

"Why? So you can tell me more lies?" She stalked into the bedroom, her back stiff, her head held proud and high.

Left with no other choice, he followed her. He didn't believe he'd ever be able to make her understand what he'd done. How could he when even he had a hard time trying to understand exactly why he'd let things get so far out of control. She was hurt, and he hated himself for being the one responsible. Somehow, he had to find a way to convince her he was dead serious about his feelings for her. That much, at least, was the cold hard truth. Even though his pleas would never change the fact that he'd lied to her, used her and, God help him, hurt her. "Look, I know you're angry—"

She glared at him before tugging his T-shirt off and throwing it on the bed. "Anger doesn't even begin to describe what I'm feeling right now." Wearing only the bright purple socks, she crossed the room to the dresser and tugged open the top drawer. "Didn't I tell you to get out of here?" she snapped, stepping into a pair of sensible cotton panties.

"I'm not leaving until you hear me out."

A pair of loose fitting pink-and-gray plaid pajama bottoms followed, along with a matching pink crop-top. "Who do I need to call to get the FBI out of my apartment? The CIA?"

"Your brother is calling back soon," he said, ignoring her sarcasm. "I can help him."

"Oh, you'll help him, all right. Right into a pair of handcuffs." She brushed passed him and stormed back into the kitchen. He heard a drawer open and slam closed followed by her angry footsteps as she headed back in his direction. She made a right at the hallway and walked into the bathroom.

"It isn't like that," he said, filling up the doorway to block her escape. "I did some poking around. He's been set up."

She opened the medicine chest and lifted his toothbrush from the holder, tossing it into the plastic bag in her hands. "I could have told you that much." She picked up his razor and pointed it at him. "That's what I was about to tell you when the phone rang. God, I can't believe I felt guilty for keeping Jared a secret from you. Could I be any more blind?" The razor followed the toothbrush.

"Or stupid," she continued to rail. "I've gotten so

used to you bastards hounding me, I could have picked you guys out of a crowd at a hundred yards. I must've gotten lax in the last nine months. Not one of you so much as tapped my phone or sifted through my mail.''

She looked up at him after tossing his ceramic shaving mug into the bag to land with a sharp crack against the razor. ''Was that your plan? Leave me alone. Let me think you guys finally figured it out and realized I had nothing to tell you, then send in the secret weapon? Did your assignment include sleeping with the enemy, Chase? Or was that just one of the perks of the job?''

Chase sighed. He deserved every word she threw at him. Her sarcasm, her anger, even her contempt.

''You were good, I'll give you that much,'' she said, continuing her search for any other items he'd left in her medicine chest. ''I didn't even see you coming.''

''Dee, listen—''

She snapped the mirrored cabinet closed and turned, zeroing in on him with her heat-filled gaze. ''You've said all I care to listen to, *Special Agent* Bracken.''

She scooped his bottle of Old Spice off the counter and took aim toward the bag. He snagged her wrist before she sent it crashing against the ceramic mug. ''Stop, dammit, and listen to me.''

She let out a pent-up breath that did little to lessen the tension stringing her body tight. ''What? Why? What are you going to tell me now? That you were really here all along to prove my brother's innocence in this mess? Sell it somewhere else, G-man. My bullshit quota has already been met.''

He closed his eyes, and she issued a fresh string of curses.

''I'm sorry,'' he said, looking down at her. ''I never meant for any of this to happen.''

She tugged her hand, and he let her go. The bottle of aftershave went into the bag with less force than the other items. "Neither did I," she said before pushing him out of her way.

Chase let out a sigh and followed her into the bedroom. He understood her anger. Plain and simple, he *had* used her hoping to gain information. Somewhere along the way, everything had changed. He may have started out with nothing short of single-minded determination to salvage his sagging career by solving what he now believed to be an unsolvable case—until they'd made love. The time he'd spent with Dee hadn't all been about the job even though he'd foolishly tried to tell himself otherwise. It was a night for truths, he realized, only he hadn't a clue how to explain it to her so she'd believe his feelings for her had nothing to do with the case and everything to do with her.

"You have to understand, I didn't plan for this to happen."

She dropped the bag on the bed and looked at him as if he'd lost his mind. Maybe he had.

He shook his head and tried again. "When I first came here, I didn't think it, we, would come to this."

"Wouldn't come to what, Chase? Do you mean it wouldn't come to me finding out that you're a lying son of a bitch with the morals of a cockroach?" She snapped her fingers as if an idea came to her. "Maybe you mean that it really wasn't your intention all along to make me trust you and fall for you so that I'd tell you where my brother has been hiding out the past three years."

He closed the distance between them, stopping when he came up beside her. The need to touch her, to pull her into his arms and hold on for dear life was strong. "I'm sorry I did this to you," he said, picking up the T-shirt she'd discarded and slipping it over his head. "I never wanted to hurt you."

She pulled in a shaky breath. "You've been wasting your time," she said quietly, keeping her gaze focused on the rumpled sheets. "I haven't known from the beginning where Jared has been, and I still don't. He's never told me and as much as I hated not knowing where he was or if he was even alive, I finally understand why. Now more than ever."

She lifted her eyes to his. The anger had waned to a small degree, but the pain banked in her gold-green depths gripped his heart with viselike strength, making breathing difficult.

"If you'd taken the time to read any of the miles of paperwork you Bureau boys have on my brother," she continued, "you might have read that I've told the same thing to every single one of your precious agents that have come crawling around looking for information I didn't have."

He opened his mouth to say something, but she poked his chest with her index finger. "I. Don't. Know!" Her voice rose with each word.

He snagged her wrist before she drilled a hole in his chest. "I know you don't," he admitted. "I realized that when I saw the calendars."

Dee's eyes widened as she stared at Chase in disbelief. Realization dawned as the memory of him standing beside her bed with the drawer from her nightstand clutched in his hand, the contents spilling onto the floor. She'd played right into his hands every step of the way. Her anger peaked along with the searing pain tearing through her chest.

She tugged her hand from his grasp and stepped away from him. Violence had never been a part of her life, but right this second she wanted nothing more than to flay him alive for what he'd done to her—for what he'd done to them. The anger bubbling inside her felt foreign. Hurt, and more disappointment than she wanted to face, collided with the heat of her anger, throwing her into an emotional storm she wasn't prepared to handle.

"You bastard," she said in a low, dangerous voice. "Everything. All of it was just…"

Unable to face the agony etching Chase's features, she turned away and sat on the edge of the bed. She held on with a death grip, wrapping her fingers around the edge of the mattress and squeezing tight.

"I think you should leave now," she said with as little emotion as possible. She kept her eyes locked on the hardwood floor. Every time she looked at Chase she was reminded of what a fool she'd been.

"I'm not leaving," he said. "Not until we settle this."

That got her attention and had her looking up at him anyway. "What's to settle? You're a lying bastard who used me to try to find my brother. There's nothing to be settled because I was never more important to you than a link to Jared."

He dropped down in front of her, balancing himself on the balls of his feet. His hand settled on her knee and she closed her eyes. No matter how badly she hurt, it didn't stop her body's reaction to his gentle touch.

*Damn him.*

"That might have been true in the beginning, but it's the furthest thing from the truth now."

She made a sound that could have been a caustic laugh, but humor was one emotion absent from her repertoire at the moment. "Oh, I see. I was so good in bed that you're giving up the search now, huh? If I'd known it was that easy to get you creeps off my brother's back,

I'd have screwed the first agent that came knocking on my door three years ago and saved myself a whole lot of trouble.''

He swore, then sprung to his feet and walked toward the door. Good. Maybe now he'd leave her alone so she could crawl onto the bed, pull herself in a tight ball and just not feel anything.

He turned and came back. She needed distance, especially the emotional kind, and she couldn't get that with Chase pacing her hardwood floor.

He stopped in front of her. ''What do I have to do, Dee? What do I have to say to get you to let me explain?''

She bit back a snippy taunt and let out a slow breath instead. Nothing he could say would change her mind. She knew that clear down to the last tattered shred of her heart. Talk meant nothing when his actions had spoken clearer than any words he would use in an attempt to placate her. He'd used her. He'd slept with her to further his investigation. There was no explanation as far as she was concerned.

''Look,'' he said, but quieted when she sprang off the bed.

''Not here,'' she said and walked into the living room. She couldn't stand being in the room where she'd given every inch of herself to Chase. Chase, the one man on the face of earth she never should have fallen for, but she had. Hard. For reasons she was too strung out to understand, somehow he'd been the one to reach past her barriers to the heart she'd kept locked safely away from harm.

She turned on the lamp and lowered herself onto the sofa. Pulling her knees up to her chest, she wrapped her arms around her legs and rested her head on her knees.

Her head throbbed. Her heart ached. Her entire body was tight with tension. All she wanted was for blissful numbness to take over so she could forget. Forget Chase. Forget Jared. Forget the entire mess.

She lifted her head and glanced at Chase. He sat on the chair closest to the sofa, leaning forward with his elbows braced on his knees. He looked as miserable as she felt, but the thought offered her little by way of comfort.

"Tonight was the first time I'd heard his voice in almost three years," she said evenly. "Do you know what it's like to want to talk to someone you love so much it hurts and you can't?"

"Yeah, I do," he said, giving her a level stare.

She knew he was referring to the mother who had forsaken her son for her next fix. While the circumstances of her separation from Jared were far different, Jared's disappearance and silence had been to protect her from guys like Chase. Fat lot of good it had done her, she thought, and looked away.

"So is this where you interrogate me?" she asked him.

He sighed. "No. Dee, I want you to understand when I first came to Cole Harbor, I had no idea we'd get involved to the extent we have. Granted, I was sent to make contact, to find a way to get close enough without you learning I was with the Bureau so I could bring back information that might lead us to your brother, but I never thought it would go as far as it has."

"So you admit to sleeping with me to get what you wanted."

"No. But I believed I could if I had to. That's the kind of agent I've always been. I never gave a rip about anything or anyone so long as I solved the case. It's gotten me into more trouble than you can imagine lately."

"If this is supposed to make me feel better, you're failing."

A wry grin twisted his lips. "The minute our relationship changed course, I couldn't do it anymore. Whenever I wasn't at the high school or here with you, I was upstairs poring over those miles of paperwork trying to find something, *anything,* that would give you back your brother."

She frowned. "You lost me."

He let out a long breath and stood. "I guess I figured if I could give you back your brother," he said, edging his way around the coffee table to the chair near the door, "by finding information that would lead me to believe his innocence, then maybe you'd be able to forgive me for not telling you the truth once we'd made love."

He held up his hand before she could issue a reply. "I don't know if what I have is going to be enough, but I have a feeling Jared will know where to look once I give him the details of what I found last night."

He scooped a manila envelope off the chair and tossed it on the coffee table. The package slid across the cheap laminated-pine surface. She caught it before it hit the floor.

She was confused and hurt, and didn't know whom or what to believe any longer. How could she trust him to tell her the truth now when she couldn't even trust her own instincts? She thought she knew Chase, but the man who turned her inside out with need was nothing more than a fabrication, a cover, a lie. Chase Bracken, high-school teacher and football coach, was the man she'd fallen in love with, not an agent with the FBI intent on seeing her brother prosecuted for crimes he couldn't have committed.

Was he really telling her the truth now? And if so,

why? For the reasons he'd stated, or was this just another facet of his investigation that would bring him closer to bringing in her brother on bogus murder charges.

He remained standing, looking down at her, his handsome face impassive. If she didn't know him better, she might have believed he didn't care whether she believed him or not. Only she did know him better. The man, not the agent. And the man's beautiful violet eyes that had once looked at her with such heat, such desire and affection, now mirrored the same pain that had been clutching her heart since he took the phone out of her hands less than an hour ago.

He moved, finally, and walked toward the door. "Give that to Jared when you see him," he said, his hand gripping the knob.

She dropped her feet to the floor. "Where are you going?" she asked him.

He looked over his shoulder at her. "Back to New York."

"But…what about Jared?"

"I'm marking the case unresolved. He'll call soon. Tell him I've left. There's a way for him to reach me in that envelope. Give it to him and tell him I'll do whatever I can to help."

He turned to go. Panic raced through her. Ten minutes ago she wanted nothing more than for him to leave and never come back, but now, faced with him walking out of her life for good, she couldn't stop the horrendous fear camping out right in her heart. "Wait!"

He stopped and bent his head, his fingers clasped around the silver-plated knob. "This is hard enough, Dee. Don't make it worse. Please."

The tears that had been mysteriously absent from the

moment she heard Chase identify himself to Jared, burned her eyes and blurred her vision.

*I don't want to say goodbye. Not yet.*

As ridiculous as it sounded, it was true. She didn't know if she'd ever be capable of fully getting past his deception. Deep down, as much as it pained her, she knew there could never be anything more between them than a past darkened by heartache. Even so, there was a nagging part of her conscience that couldn't stop her from wondering if Chase Bracken was somewhere inside the same man she'd fallen in love with, no matter what he did for a living.

"What about Jared?" she asked him. "You know things about what's really going on here that I can't answer."

She watched him closely. He didn't move so much as an inch.

"You need to be here when he calls," she told him.

Maybe her decision had something to do with Chase being so willing to leave before Jared called that she believed he really did have proof of her brother's innocence. Maybe his willingness to no longer be a part of the deception had her thinking that perhaps she really did need to find it within herself to trust him one last time. Obviously Jared trusted Chase when he hadn't even trusted her to know his whereabouts.

Or maybe, she thought, it was something deeper that her tattered emotions and aching heart were too tangled and raw to decipher. Either way, as much as she wanted to see her brother again, to have him safe and be able to reclaim his life, she needed Chase with her when she met with Jared. For reasons she couldn't begin to comprehend, Chase was the one person Jared obviously trusted with his life, and hers.

"For some reason," she said and stood, "you're the only person my brother has spoken to that I'm aware of in the past three years. I don't understand why, but Jared trusts you."

He turned and looked at her, an intensity in his gaze that gave a whole new meaning to his do-or-die agent mentality. "It's because of you."

She frowned. "Me? How?"

"I'm guessing it's because I was in your apartment after midnight."

She shrugged. "So?"

That wry grin was back to twist his lips again. "How many men have you had in your apartment after midnight in the past three years?"

Her face heated as realization dawned, along with memories of exactly what they'd been doing past midnight. "That's the only reason?"

"The only one I can come up with that makes any sense."

"You need to be here, Chase," she told him, stepping around the coffee table. "*He* trusts you." She didn't need to add that she didn't believe she ever could trust him again, but for now, for Jared's sake, she had to summon at least a little faith in Chase. "He needs the information you have to finally reclaim his life."

"I don't know if it will or not, but I'd bet my badge he's been set up. The evidence against him has been airtight from the beginning. Not a shred of evidence out of place or questionable. Solid. A little too solid."

She set the envelope on the coffee table. "But you've known that all along. What made you change your mind? What made you look closer?"

The answer hovering on his lips died the instant the telephone started ringing.

## 17

"ARE YOU SURE WE'RE IN the right place?"

Chase clasped Dee's hand tightly in his, keeping her behind him as he moved slowly along the side of the building. "According to Jared's directions, yeah, we're in the right place," he said, keeping his voice low.

The "right place" was the back end of a strip mall located just outside of Charleston along the coast. The imitation antebellum entrance with its overstated foliage was a poor attempt to mask the here today, gone tomorrow shops. As Jared had instructed, instead of sitting and waiting in the triple-acreage blacktopped parking lot, Chase had parked beneath the dim yellow fog lamps on the side of the mall. In the thirty minutes they'd been there, he hadn't spotted so much as a rent-a-cop patrolling the area. The only sound to break the heavy silence had been a couple of cats arguing over territory around a trash bin outside the Chinese restaurant on the western edge of the mall.

Dee's foot scraped against an empty aluminum can, sending it rolling across the pavement. He instinctively hauled her closer and drew his weapon.

Dee let out a sigh and tried to tug her hand from his. "What are you going to do, shoot the can?" she whispered harshly.

He held on tighter. "I like to think of it as being cautious." Instead of slipping the 9 mm back into the leather shoulder holster beneath his lightweight jacket, he tightened his fingers around the grip and kept the barrel pointed upward. He'd have felt a whole lot better leaving her behind for her own safety, but he knew without issuing the argument she'd insist on coming along, even if it meant spending nothing more than five minutes with her brother.

"I thought Jared said this place was safe?"

"Nothing is ever safe," he answered, continuing toward the rear of the building. "Romine picked this location, I didn't."

She inched closer behind him. "I don't care what you guys think Jared might have done, he would never put me in danger."

Chase let out a rough sigh and stopped. He agreed with her to a certain extent, that Romine would not intentionally put his sister in danger. Whether or not Romine's silence had been to protect his own backside or Dee's, Chase wouldn't know until he saw the renegade agent. Until then, he was taking no chances with her life.

Turning so his back was parallel with the building, he surveyed the area. Seeing nothing out of the ordinary, he glanced down at her. "Sweetheart, you're in danger now just because your name is Romine."

She frowned. "That's ridiculous," she said, but her voice held just enough insecurity to make him tighten his hold on her hand in what he hoped she'd accept as a gesture of reassurance. Nothing would happen to her, he vowed. At least not as long as he was alive to prevent it.

He continued to scan the area and wait. Once Romine assured himself they were alone, he'd signal. Until then, there was nothing left to do but watch and wait. Again.

"A few weeks ago I would have said the same thing," he told her in a low tone. "But not after last night."

She inched closer. Under any other circumstances, he might have accepted her actions as a hopeful indicator that perhaps the end of their relationship hadn't just come crashing in on them a few hours ago. Nor did it change the truth that surviving the Romine case had indeed become the toughest he'd ever faced. And it had nothing whatsoever to do with the man he'd been sent to locate, but with the woman who had somehow stolen his heart faster than a computer hacker could clear out the checking accounts of unsuspecting depositors.

Despite the tension between them, the strong need to hold her in his arms, to promise her forever if she'd let him, hadn't dissipated one iota. Since Jared's call, conversation of a personal nature halted.

"What happened last night?" she asked in a hushed tone.

He inclined his head toward the envelope in her free hand. "That happened," was all he said.

As much as he hated to bring back the reminder of the emotional bomb he'd dropped on her, there was still something he needed to know. Intentionally keeping his gaze away from Dee's, he asked, "When Jared called the first time tonight, what did he say to you before I took the phone?"

She was so silent, he wondered if she'd even heard him. He dragged his gaze away from the safety of the darkness to glance down at her. Tears welled in her eyes, but she blinked them back and fought for a facade of stoicism.

"'I'm coming home soon.' That was it."

Chase frowned. How could Romine come out of hiding without the information he'd unearthed in Decatur last night? He'd find out soon enough, he thought as the flare of a match beneath a broken light across the street shined like a beacon for no more than a split second. If another match flared, then he and Dee would move behind the strip mall until they came to an open metal door and slip inside, no doubt to wait again until Romine declared it safe for him to follow them inside.

"Get ready," he said when the second match flared and was extinguished just as quickly. He inched closer to the edge of the building, then made sure it was clear before turning down the alley. The fourth metal door they came to stood ajar. "I'm going inside."

"Not without me you're not."

"I'm going inside and you're waiting here until I know it's safe. You hear anything, you run to the truck and drive."

"I don't think so."

"Dammit, Dee," he whispered harshly. "Let me do my job."

"Jared had to know I was coming with you," she argued. "Do you really think my own brother would put me in a dangerous situation if he didn't have complete control?"

"There's no such thing as controlling a situation like this." Even under the pale light of the half moon he could see the stubborn tilt of her chin, combined with an equally obstinate glint in her eyes. He was wasting his breath. "Take hold of the back of my jacket. I don't care what we find inside, if you let go before I tell you to, I'll shoot you myself."

He wouldn't and they both knew it. He could tell by her little huff of exasperated breath. But she did as he'd ordered, and he'd have to find solace in that for now.

She gripped his jacket. "Ready."

He moved then, closer to the edge of the doorway, then stood to the side and waited. Hearing nothing but the pounding of his own heart, he toed the door, pushing it wide. Not a single noise came from inside the building. They moved in and kept their backs against the wall.

Waiting for his eyes to adjust to the darkness, he had to give Dee credit. She hadn't uttered a sound when he was dead certain she was near to bursting with wanting to see the brother who had abandoned her for nearly three years as he ran. Not from justice as Chase and all the others sent to bring down a man accused of murder had believed, but for his life. He'd bet his badge on it, and to an extent, he probably already had.

Shadowed shapes began taking form. With the assistance of the pale light of the moon filtering through the opened door, he realized they were in a storage area for one of the shops. Metal shelving filled with marked boxes he couldn't make out were arranged in librarian rows. He and Dee were to move to the last row on the right and wait.

With increased vision once his eyes adjusted to the light, he carefully guided them toward the right side of the storage area, keeping close to the wall while checking each aisle for any sign of movement. They reached the end and turned down the last aisle.

Just as Romine had told him, Chase made out a small worktable in the far corner. With the same amount of precaution he'd used to get them this far, he neared the table, located the banker's lamp resting on top and tugged the chain.

Dee gasped. Chase stared in shocked disbelief at Jared Romine leaning casually against the wall. He'd known the other agent was one of the best. That's what had made tracking him such a challenge, but he'd never expected to find him waiting for them.

"Jared," she whispered, and took a tentative step forward then halted. He felt the tug of her fingers on his jacket.

With his weapon still clutched in his hand, he used his left to block Dee's path. "Not yet," he told her.

Romine shot him a sharp look, the first indication that he wasn't as relaxed as he appeared. "She's safe here."

"You're not safe here. What makes you think she'll be?"

Jared lifted a sable brow. "Why wouldn't I be?"

"You tell me."

The other agent resumed his casual pose and shrugged. "Maybe because someone knows what you have," he said.

"Anything's possible," Chase agreed, not quite willing to let Romine know he and Brian Morrison were the only ones with the information that could give him back his life.

"You weren't followed," Romine said, pushing off the wall. He glanced at the wall clock above the worktable. "We don't have a lot of time. This place starts buzzing with workers as early as four-thirty."

Chase nodded, then glanced down at Dee. "Make it quick," he told her, then reached for the envelope in her hands. "I won't be far."

She offered him a grateful smile. Before he could turn and make himself as scarce as he dared to give brother and sister a few minutes alone, she flew across the space into her brother's arms. He heard her gentle sobs followed by whispered words of comfort from the only family she knew. Chase took solace in knowing that he'd been the one to give her at least one happy memory to treasure from their time together, a brief reunion with her brother.

He moved along the exterior wall toward the door,

using the time to check and recheck the area. Their being followed was a thin bet, but he wasn't about to take any chances with Dee's safety.

A good ten minutes passed before he finally heard Dee's sweet, quiet laughter. As much as he hated to break up the family reunion, they didn't have much time.

By the time he headed back the way he'd come, turning at the last aisle, Dee's laughter had faded. She sat on the edge of the table, a deep frown creasing her brow. Low heated words he couldn't make out halted the second Romine looked in his direction.

"We're almost out of time," Chase told them.

Dee slipped off the table as he tossed the envelope he'd taken from her onto the surface. "There it is, Romine. A down payment on your innocence."

Jared pulled out a metal folding chair from against the wall for Dee, before reaching for the envelope. He opened the package and slipped the documents onto the table before glancing at Chase with eyes a shade or two darker than his sister's. "How'd you figure out I wasn't the one who killed my partner or Phipps's right-hand man?" Romine asked him.

Chase propped his hip against the table. "I looked at it from a different point of view," he said, shifting his gaze to Dee then back to Jared. "And once I did, I realized the evidence against you was just a little too perfect. But now it gets complicated. Someone questioned Peyton Douglas early on in the investigation. I found a handwritten note in the file, but no contact report. It was the one piece that hadn't made sense. I'd seen it probably a hundred times and never put it together until the other night that someone must have *ordered* no follow-up with Douglas." He inclined his head toward the documents spread on the table. "So, I checked it out and ended up with what I think is the reason you've been framed."

Dee peered over the edge of the worktable at the documents Jared had spread over the surface. A different point of view, she mused. Did that mean he'd stopped looking at her brother from an agent's perspective? From what he'd told her about himself tonight, she found it difficult to believe, although not unreasonable. So long as he was willing to help Jared and give him the information he needed to clear his name, she didn't care if he looked at it from a dog's point of view. Because none of what she'd heard changed the fact that he'd lied to her, used her and had broken her heart. During their brief conversation, Jared had told her she should trust Chase. She already had, and look what it'd gotten her.

She shifted her attention back to the documents and as far away from her own miserable thoughts as possible. There were financial records for two separate nonprofit charity organizations, what appeared to be corporate portfolios on several health-maintenance organizations, some of which she'd even dealt with in the past as a physician, various newspaper clippings and three dossiers complete with ink-jet reproductions of photographs of the individuals.

She picked up the first one with a printout of a beautiful young woman. A gentle smile curved her mouth. The severe navy-blue business suit she wore, combined with honey-blond hair swept up into a sophisticated style failed to detract from the hint of mischief sparkling in her wide blue eyes. Her name was Peyton Douglas, an attorney with the Justice Department. Dee didn't know much about her, except when Chase had told Jared this woman was in danger, it had prompted her brother to agree to meet with him. Obviously she was important to

Jared and she couldn't help wondering about the young lawyer.

The second reproduction was instantly recognizable. The sharp angular features of popular Texas senator, Martin Phipps. The last was of a middle-age man of Spanish decent, with black hair grayed at the temples and intense dark eyes. She recognized the name, Roland Santiago. The man Jared was accused of murdering in cold blood.

Jared braced his hands on the table to look over the documents Chase had provided. "That note's probably been in the file for years. Why now? Why you?" he asked.

"When I went into the Bureau's security system, I was locked out of any files related to Douglas. It made me nervous."

Jared looked at Chase. "But why her? To draw me out?"

Chase nodded. "I'm sure that's part of it, but my gut tells me it's to further implicate you in Santiago's and Dysert's murders." He reached across the table for the newspaper clipping of an anonymous donation to a scholarship foundation for underprivileged children. "Douglas has a seat on the board of The Elaine Chandler Foundation. They fund college scholarships, primarily to underprivileged young women in and around Maine. It's the same foundation that gave Douglas a free ride to Georgetown where she earned another full academic scholarship to law school. I don't think it's a coincidence that the same foundation received a million-dollar *anonymous* donation two months after you went under.

"This," he added, pulling a bank statement from the pile, "shows a separate account in Douglas's name receiving period deposits in the amount of one hundred thousand dollars, around every six months for the past three years. The first payment was made two days after the foundation received their anonymous donation. The real interesting part is, within a few days of receiving the deposit, fifty grand goes to the Biddeford Home, every six months, just like clockwork.''

Jared's gaze was sharp when he looked at Chase. ''That's the orphanage where Peyton was raised. You saying she's involved in this mess?''

''Oh, she's involved all right,'' Chase said, crossing his arms over his chest. ''But considering this account isn't linked to any of her other accounts, which are *all* linked, I'd bet the lady hasn't got a clue she's worth a quarter-million bucks. The statements go to an attorney on Capitol Hill, who just happens to be an old frat buddy of Steven Radcliffe, the aide who replaced Santiago. That might look like her signature on the card, but you know as well as I do that documents and signatures can be forged.''

''That doesn't make sense,'' Dee said, taking the bank statement from Chase. ''Wouldn't the IRS catch on eventually? The interest earned on this account is huge. Surely that would set off one of their red flags.''

Jared shook his head. ''Not if you've got someone on the inside with access to the most detailed files the government has at its disposal. The burning questions are *who* and *why*.''

''I think I figured out the why,'' Chase said. ''This is where it gets really strange.'' He tapped another set of newspaper clippings with his finger. ''And if I'm right, a whole lot bigger than I think anyone imagined. Two Supreme Court justices have announced they'll be retiring from the bench next year. From what I can tell, there's already buzz around the Hill of about half a dozen candidates who've made the shortlist. One of those candidates is the same circuit court justice that Douglas clerked for when she was a law student. Another is on the Texas Supreme Court. Phipps is backing both of them and his lobbyists are working overtime to see these two seated.''

"You lost me," Dee said, lifting the newspaper articles from the table. "What does this have to do with Jared? It's too recent a development.''

Chase looked down at her. "It's no secret Phipps is a big backer of HMOs and rallies hard against anything that limits their power in the health-care industry. Last year the Supreme Court ruled in favor of HMOs to continue paying their physician owners bonuses for keeping down health-care costs. There's another case in the Federal Appellate Courts now that challenges that decision. If it makes it to the Supreme Court, it could cause a reversal.''

"Meaning if I became a physician partner in an HMO, I'd no longer receive a bonus for finding alternative, less-expensive treatment for my patients," she said, trying to understand where Chase was going with all this information.

"Exactly," Jared confirmed. "As it stands now, the court wouldn't even hear the case because it's already been decided. But, with a new bench, the case could be heard and then a lot of people stand to lose a lot of money. If Phipps gets his two guys on the bench, the appeal comes before the court, it still gets denied. And our dirty little senator continues to receive kickbacks from the physician owners of half a dozen or more HMOs around the country.''

"You know that for a fact?" Chase asked.

"I know that's why Dysert and Santiago were killed.

Dysert and I went undercover and were supposed to get in on the scam. Someone tipped off Santiago. He killed Dysert. I have no idea who killed Santiago, but I know it wasn't Phipps since I was tailing him that night.''

"Then it had to be someone who knew every move you and Dysert were making," Chase said.

Jared nodded. "The only people that knew about what we were doing were the higher-ups in the Bureau. Someone has something to hide and is using me to cover it up."

Dee looked from her brother to Chase. She couldn't believe what she was hearing. The same bastards that had hounded her for so long were the ones behind the allegations against Jared. No wonder they'd been so persistent, she thought. They didn't want to bring her brother down in the name of justice, but to hang him for their own crimes.

"Like an association with Senator Phipps," Chase said, drawing her attention.

Jared straightened. "So where do we go from here?"

Dee held her breath. This was it, she thought, even though the logical part of her brain knew he wouldn't have given Jared all the information he had if he'd planned to arrest him.

"I go back to New York, tell Pelham I found nothing new and the case is still unresolved, and collect one hell of a severance package. I suggest you hightail it to D.C., find Douglas and keep her safe until you can determine who's behind all this."

"Severance?" Dee asked, surprised. While the truth of Chase's identity was still raw, she hadn't expected him to lose his job. "You mean they'll fire you?"

"Oh, yeah," he said with a laugh that held no humor.

"Solve the case or else. I think those were Pelham's words."

"But you did solve it," she argued, her mind still whirling with the information that Chase was really letting Jared go, just as he'd promised.

His lilac eyes filled with that same intensity that always made her heart beat just a little faster. "They won't know that," he said quietly. "Not if you want your brother to stay alive."

He shifted his gaze back to Jared. "You told Dee you were coming home soon. You know something, don't you?"

Jared grinned, and Dee shivered at the cold lifeless look in his once warm emerald eyes. "It's in everyone's best interest if you don't know...for now. When this mess is behind me, we'll split a bottle of scotch and a few fish tales."

Jared extended his hand to Chase and he shook it.

"What about that note you found in the file?" Jared asked, scooping up the documents and slipping them back inside the envelope. "It led you this far, which means the next agent they put on the case could pick up the scent."

A chilling smile curved Chase's lips as he crossed his arms over his chest. "What note?"

# 18

CHASE PARKED BENEATH THE magnolia tree in front of
the triplex just as the sun began to clear the horizon. He
killed the engine, but neither he nor Dee made any move
to exit the vehicle. It had been a long night, a long emotional night for both of them, but especially for Dee. The
morning didn't look a speck brighter, either, in his opinion.

Romine was on his way to D.C. to find Peyton Douglas, telling Dee before he left if she should hear a report
of a kidnapping charge that would be her signal that he'd
found Peyton and had managed to spirit her away somewhere safe. She'd understood, but that hadn't stopped the
tears from cascading down her cheeks when her brother
slipped away in the darkness as quietly and efficiently as
he'd first appeared.

Chase had desperately wanted to reassure her Jared
would be safe, but he refused to make her false promises.
At least now she truly understood the kind of danger her
brother faced. Her faith in him would see her through the
uncertainties that lay ahead, just as they had the past three
years.

"It's been a long night," he said, breaking the heavy
silence.

"Yes," she answered quietly. "Too long."

He reached for the snap on the seat belt. "I'll walk
you to the door."

"No. Chase..." She pulled in a deep breath and turned to face him. She needed sleep, as evidenced by the dark circles underscoring her tired gaze. Even as worn-out as she looked, it didn't detract from her beauty, nor did it lessen the viselike grip around his heart.

"I wanted to thank you for what you did tonight. For Jared. You didn't have to let him go," she said. "You could've arrested him and saved your job. I just hope you didn't do it for the wrong reasons."

He let out a stream of breath through his teeth and shoved his fingers through his hair. "What reasons would that be?" he snapped irritably. He was tired. He was frustrated, and his goddamn heart was breaking because he'd been stupid enough to fall in love with her. "You think I let Romine go to score a few brownie points with his sister?"

"I don't know why you did it."

He gripped the steering wheel with both hands and stared straight ahead. "Your brother's innocent. Someone high up in the Bureau is using Jared to cover his own ass. I might do things my way, and bend the rules to suit my needs when it comes to getting a break in a case, but I'm sure as hell not going to hand over an innocent man on a friggin' platter so they can strap him down and stick a needle filled with blue juice in his arm.

"This wasn't some grand gesture," he said, finally looking at her. "Justice, Doc. No more. No less. You can read into it all you want, but that's all it was. Justice."

She nodded. "I was just afraid you'd done something illegal, hoping there could be a chance for us."

He tightened his grip on the steering wheel, knowing what she'd say before she said it—*Goodbye, G-man.* "Why can't there be?" he asked before he could stop himself.

She unbuckled her seat belt and reached for the handle. He heard the click of the door as it opened, but could do nothing but watch her slip from his truck and out of his life.

With her hand still holding the door open, she turned to face him. "Because you're not the man I fell in love with," she said, her face a mask of serenity he wasn't buying. She had to be as torn up inside as he was, he knew it as well as he knew he'd be without a job before the end of the day.

"The man I fell in love with," she continued, "is a football coach for the local high school. He teaches Criminal Justice and is terrified of teaching sex education to a bunch of seniors. He's stubborn, sexy and he makes me laugh." She paused and pulled in a shaky breath. "He makes me feel alive. And he's the only one who makes me feel…who makes me feel like I'm really the woman I see reflected in his eyes."

"None of that has changed," he said. "Only the job title."

"You're wrong, Chase. It's all changed *because* of the job title."

She closed the door and headed up the walkway to her apartment. He didn't know how long he stayed in the truck, staring at nothing and remembering everything.

All his life he'd walked around with a chip on his shoulder, feeling as if he was never good enough and working twice as hard as the competition in some vain attempt to make up for his background. He'd always had to be the best, and what had it gotten him? At the end of the day, nothing. The woman he loved wanted nothing to do with him. In a matter of hours, he'd be unemployed. He was who he was, and nothing could change that fact.

It *didn't* matter how he'd started his life, but what he did with the life he'd been given.

He had choices to make that would affect the rest of his life. Whatever course of action he decided would have to be for himself. Not for the Bureau, not for Dee, but for Chase Bracken. Regardless of the decisions he made about his future, he knew in his gut they weren't over. Not by a long shot.

DEE SET HER MUG OF TEA on the white wicker table she'd set up in the corner of the wide front porch of her apartment. A pair of sparrows hopped across the wood floor, pecking at the small bits of dried toast she brought out every Saturday morning while she opened the Friday edition of *Chicago Sun Times* to the national news section. It had been three weeks since she'd seen or heard from Jared. Having been privy to the facts Chase had discovered surrounding her brother, now more than ever she worried about his safety. Instead of using music from the CD player to fill up the background, she constantly flipped the remote from CNN to the network news shows. Instead of reading through the Cole Harbor *Sea Breeze* each morning with her bagel and tea, she now subscribed to newspapers from New York, Washington, Los Angeles, Chicago as well as three smaller newspapers from Maine. So far, nothing. Until now, she'd always operated under the assumption that no news is good news. No longer was that her mantra when it came to Jared.

As was true with most small towns, word had spread quickly about her breakup with Chase. Lucille and Thaddius were the only two people in Cole Harbor to know the truth, all of it. Every Thursday night since she'd agreed to take over the clinic, the three of them had dinner together in Lucille's cozy kitchen, and every Thursday night they both told her she was a fool to let Chase go without a fight.

Thaddius was still as robust and cantankerous as ever, but he'd already started cutting back on the time he'd spent at the clinic. And so had Lucille, confirming Dee's suspicion of a longtime affair between doctor and nurse, although they both denied her gentle teasing vehemently. A little too vehemently, in her opinion.

Already she'd hired a new part-time nurse to pick up the slack from Lucille's cutting her hours to spend more time with Thaddius, and she planned on hiring a physician's assistant sometime in the next year if the balance sheets allowed it. Netta surprisingly had remained on staff and hadn't scoffed when Dee had assigned her additional duties.

She scanned the paper and found nothing to alert her to Jared's whereabouts or safety. As usual, thoughts of Chase filled her mind. Some days, she wondered if perhaps Thaddius and Lucille were right. Maybe she should've fought it out with Chase, but at the time, she hadn't had the emotional energy. Besides, she told herself, she was far too busy at the clinic to build a relationship. She was too busy making her apartment feel like the first home she'd really known since her parents' death. Already she'd replaced the uncomfortable rental furniture with a small muted-floral sofa and matching chair. Since her apartment was tiny, she'd decided on white-washed oak accent tables and entertainment center. Imitation antique brass lamps and framed reproduction prints of Monet's garden collection added perfectly to the now cozy living room, along with a large soft-peach area rug that covered most of the hardwood floor. Next she planned to replace the rummage sale bedroom furniture with real antique pieces, but first she needed the money and the time to scour antique shops and tag sales.

Those were only diversions to fill up her days, she realized suddenly. The truth was, she missed Chase. The nights were the worst. No matter how hard she worked during the day, hoping to fall into an exhausted sleep at night, she still tossed and turned and ached for him. Her body ached for his touch. Her heart just ached.

No matter how much she did miss him, she didn't know if she'd ever be able to get completely past his betrayal. She'd meant it when she'd told him she'd fallen in love with him, but her argument that the man she'd fallen for wasn't a federal agent was slowly beginning to lose steam. When Jared had questioned her about her association with Chase the night they'd gone to meet him, she'd told her brother she hadn't known Chase was FBI. If she had, they never would have gotten involved, but what bothered her now was that even though she knew, it hadn't stopped the ache surrounding her heart from intensifying whenever she thought of him. It hadn't stopped her body from craving his touch. And it hadn't stopped her brother from telling her Chase Bracken was a good man, no matter what he did for a living, even if his methods sometimes couldn't be found in any of the Bureau's procedure manuals.

None of it mattered. They were over. She'd already accepted that fact when he'd cleared out his upstairs apartment and been gone by the time she'd returned from the clinic the following day.

She folded up the newspapers and was about to head back into the house when a large blue-and-white moving van pulled up in front of her apartment. When she'd dropped off her rent check a couple of days ago, Mrs. England hadn't mentioned anyone moving into the building. Aside from missing Chase in her life, she'd almost enjoyed the solitude of having the place to herself.

With little else to occupy her time this morning, she decided to feed her mild curiosity. Leaning back in the wicker love seat, she picked up her half-empty mug of tea and sipped.

Two burly movers exited the truck. The taller of the two checked his watch, said something to the other guy who shrugged, then opened the rear of the truck. Before long, the two men started hauling furniture out of the van and carrying it along the walkway, halting at the foot of the stairs to the vacant upstairs apartment. The shorter man took the stairs two at a time and banged on the door. After a moment he returned, said something to the other fellow and the duo continued to unload furniture only to leave it near the foot of the stairs.

She watched them as they carried a long black leather sofa across the walkway, leave it on the lawn, then head back to the van just as a black truck she instantly recognized pulled up behind them.

Her heart started pounding the second she spied Chase's dark, wavy hair, his broad shoulders and lean hips. He glanced in her direction, but his eyes were hidden beneath a pair of dark sunglasses. After he handed something to the movers, they headed off in the direction of town.

She wanted to get up, dart into her apartment and lock the door. Instead she stayed in the wicker love seat as if she were glued to it, watching helplessly, hopefully, as Chase came purposely up the walk and bounded up the stairs two at a time.

"What are you doing here?" she asked, surprised her vocal cords cooperated.

He grinned.

Her heart hammered even faster.

"That's a hell of a greeting for your new neighbor," he said, propping his backside against the railing. He braced his hands along the ledge, looking as if he *belonged*. "Whatever happened to all that southern hospitality that's so popular down here?"

She crossed her arms to hide the fact that her hands were trembling. Surely he didn't expect to just walk back into her life as if nothing had happened. "Maybe because we're not too partial to Yankees," she said, wishing her voice had sounded stronger. "Especially ones that lie about who they really are to the people they claim to care about."

He nodded slowly, as if mulling over her words. "I can see why you'd have an aversion to those kind."

She didn't want to play mouse to his cat. She wanted to know what he was doing here, moving in of all things. "Why are you here?" she demanded.

He glanced casually behind him, at the stark furnishings cluttering up the lawn before turning back to face her with a wide sexy grin canting his mouth. The very same mouth she'd dreamed of kissing again since she'd left him sitting in his truck three weeks ago.

"I live here," he said, and finally removed his sunglasses.

She avoided his gaze and laughed, but the sound lacked humor. "You live in New York, remember?"

"Correction. I did live in New York. I live here now. Right upstairs. Nice place. Have you seen it?"

She frowned and looked at those lethal violet eyes anyway. Despite the casual, teasing tone of his voice, his eyes were filled with caution and hope. The caution she understood. The hope scared the life out of her.

"Actually, no," she said. "The guy that lived there

wouldn't let anyone into his apartment. I guess it was because he had something to hide. Like surveillance equipment and FBI files.''

He nodded slowly again. "I'd say the guy was a jerk."

"You won't hear any argument from me."

"Ouch," he said, covering his heart with his hand. "Good thing there's a doctor in the house. With barbs like that, a guy could easily get cut to ribbons."

She was getting irritated with his playful attitude. She wanted answers. Despite everything, she wanted him! "Ribbons are the last of your problems, G-man. Stop playing games. Why are you here?"

"I told you, I live here." He shrugged. "Besides, it's one long commute from New York to Cole Harbor High every day."

She didn't want to feel the well of hope. She didn't want to feel the sparks arcing between them when there was still so much hurt. "What are you talking about?" she asked cautiously.

His smile faded as he folded his arms over his chest. "I didn't give Pelham a chance to fire me. I quit."

"But I thought—"

"I lived for my job?" He chuckled. "Yeah, I thought so at one time, too, but I figured out there are more important things than tracking down criminals, even innocent ones."

He wasn't making sense. Or he was and her emotions were going haywire and she was having trouble processing the information. "But you're not a teacher. You're not even credentialed. How can you have a job at the high school?"

"That wasn't as easy as I'd hoped, or I'd have been back sooner. I do have friends in high places, and called in a few favors," he said his grin widening again. "There is such a thing as an emergency credential that a lot of inner-city schools are using. I have two years to make it legit.''

He pushed off the railing suddenly, closing the distance between them. She wanted to run, but couldn't have moved if a bomb were under her chair. Mesmerized, she watched him crouch in front of her. He rested his hand on her knee and she trembled, her body already humming from his gentle touch. ''I came back, because I want to make this our home. Provided I can win over the town doctor I can't stop thinking about and to make up for every last thing I did to hurt her.''

She blinked back a rush of tears. As much as her woman's heart loved hearing those words, she was terrified of what could happen if she let herself fall victim to his incredible brand of charm once again.

''You said you fell in love with me,'' he pushed. ''That hasn't changed, Dee. I can see it in your eyes. *I'm* that same football coach you fell in love with. I'm the same teacher who's terrified to talk sex to a bunch of high-school seniors. The Bureau's a thing of the past. Can't we put the pain in the past, too? Say we can move beyond it and build a future together.''

''I'm afraid,'' she whispered. So very afraid. Afraid to love him. Afraid to lose him again.

''You don't have to be. I love you, Dee. I think I fell in love with you the minute you opened your door looking all sleepy and sexy in that old blue robe.''

She pulled in a shaky breath and let it out slowly. ''The people you love always hurt you. It hurts when they leave, when they disappear without a trace, when they die. I don't want to hurt anymore, Chase. I can't do it again.''

''You of all people know life doesn't come with guarantees. Not that kind. I won't ever intentionally hurt you again. It's the only thing I can promise you, other than to love you for the rest of my life.''

How could she deny it when he was absolutely right? Life didn't come with guarantees and she could either live hers in constant fear of being hurt, or she could trust her heart and take a chance. The alternative, a life without love, without Chase, left her feeling cold inside. And that, she decided, was far worse than the fear of being hurt.

She unfolded her arms and cupped his cheek in her hand. ''We'd have to take it slow,'' she told him.

''I'll go as slow or as fast as you want,'' he said, turning to place an achingly tender kiss against her palm. ''You set the pace and I'll follow.''

She gave him a wicked grin. ''Well,'' she said, not the least bit shocked by the husky tone of her voice. ''I don't always want to be the one to set the pace. And slow is nice, but sometimes fast can be *very* good.''

He chuckled and stood, pulling her into his arms. ''Now we're getting into some interesting territory, Doc. I might need a little instruction in that area. It's been a while.''

She laughed, and pulled his head down for a tongue-tangling kiss filled with love and trust. By the time he lifted his head, they were both out of breath.

''You know, it's getting awfully warm out here,'' she said, taking his hand and leading him toward the door to her apartment and back into her life where the only guarantee that existed would be their love for each other. ''What would you say to a cherry Popsicle?''

His wicked answering smile, filled with all the love evident in his luscious lilac eyes was all the answer she needed.

\* \* \* \* \*

*Jamie turns up the heat
with Jared Romine's story in*

SEDUCED BY THE ENEMY.

*Determined to clear his name, he needs the help of
sexy lawyer
Peyton Douglas. What he doesn't anticipate is
needing her as a woman, too!
On sale Spring 2002*

*Available at your favorite retail outlet.*

*"Jamie Denton creates excellent characters and
an intricate conflict."—Romantic Times*

*"Ms. Denton sure knows how to light the fire
between her characters."—Rendezvous*

*"(Jamie Denton) is well on her way to carving out
a niche for herself in the world of hot and sassy
romances!"—Heart Rate Reviews*